All the Beautiful Lies

All the Beautiful Lies

A Novel

Peter Swanson

HARPER LUXE

An Imprint of HarperCollinsPublishers

HarperCollins books may be purchased for educational, business, or sales promotional use. For information please e-mail the Special Markets Department at SPsales@harpercollins.com.

FIRST HARPERLUXE EDITION

ISBN: 978-0-06-279150-4

HarperLuxe™ is a trademark of HarperCollins Publishers.

Library of Congress Cataloging-in-Publication Data is available upon request.

18 19 20 21 22 ID/LSC 10 9 8 7 6 5 4 3 2 1

For Nat Sobel

A treacherous smiler
With teeth white as milk,
A savage beguiler
In sheathings of silk,

The sea creeps to pillage,
She leaps on her prey;
A child of the village
Was murdered today.

—ELINOR WYLIE,
   "Sea Lullaby"

All the Beautiful Lies

PART 1
Grey Lady

Chapter 1

Now

Harry was briefly blinded—the bright May sun hitting just the right spot on his windshield—as he turned onto the crushed-shell driveway of the house in Kennewick Village. He pulled his Civic next to the orange Volvo station wagon—a car his father had loved—and covered his face with his hands and almost cried.

Alice, his father's second wife, had called Harry early the previous morning to tell him that his father, Bill, was dead.

"What? How?" Harry asked. He was on his cell phone, walking across the tree-lined quad toward his dormitory. He'd been thinking about graduation, less than a week away, worrying about what he was going to do for the rest of his life.

"He slipped and fell." Alice was speaking with gaps between the words. Harry realized she was crying, and trying not to show it, trying to sound calm and reasonable.

"Where?" Harry asked. His whole body was cold and his legs had turned to rubber. He stopped walking, and the girl behind him, also on her cell phone, grazed against his backpack as she moved around him on the brick walkway.

"Out on the cliff path, where he liked to walk." Alice was now audibly crying, the words sounding like they were coming through a wet towel.

"Who found him?"

"They were tourists. I don't know. They didn't know him, Harry."

It took a second phone call later that day to get all the details. Alice had gone out in the afternoon to do errands. She'd stopped by the store to see Bill, and he'd told her that he planned on going for a walk before it got dark and that he'd be home for dinner. She'd told him to be careful, as she always did, and that she was making shepherd's pie for dinner, the way he liked it, with the cubed lamb instead of ground hamburger.

The food was ready by six, the time they normally ate dinner, but there was no sign of Bill. And he wasn't answering his phone. She called John, the only other employee at the bookstore, and he said that all he knew was what Alice knew. Bill had left a little before five to go for a walk. It was dark now, and Alice called the police station, where she was patched through to an Officer Wheatley. Just as he was explaining to Alice that there was nothing they could do if he'd only been missing a little over an hour, she heard another voice interrupt him in the background. The officer told Alice to hang on for a moment, and that was when she knew. When he came back on the line, his voice had altered, and he told her he'd be transferring her to a Detective Dixon. A body had just been found near Kennewick Harbor, and would Alice be available to make an identification.

"How did he die?" Harry asked.

"They won't rule anything out, but they seemed to think he slipped and fell and hit his head."

"He did that walk every day."

"I know. I told them that. We'll find out more, Harry."

"I just don't understand." He felt as though he'd thought those words a hundred times that day. It was Thursday, and his graduation ceremony was scheduled for Sunday afternoon. His father and Alice had been planning on coming down to New Chester in Connecticut on Saturday night, staying through till Monday, and helping Harry pack up his things for his temporary return to Maine.

Instead, Harry packed everything himself, staying up half the night. Among his textbooks and notebooks, Harry found the paperback edition of Hillary Waugh's *Last Seen Wearing . . .* that his father had given him at the beginning of the school year.

"It's a crime novel set at a university," his father had said. "I know you like Ed McBain, so I thought you might like this one, as well. It's a very early procedural. If you find time to read it, of course."

Harry hadn't, but he opened the book now. Inside was a slip of paper in his father's handwriting. One of his father's favorite activities had been making lists, almost always related to books. This one read:

Five Best Campus Crime Novels
Gaudy Night by Dorothy Sayers
The Case of the Gilded Fly by Edmund Crispin
Last Seen Wearing . . . by Hillary Waugh
The Silent World of Nicholas Quinn by Colin
    Dexter
The Secret History by Donna Tartt

Harry stared at the note, trying to process what it meant that his father—the only person left in his life whom he truly loved—was gone. In the morning he wrote an e-mail to Jane Ogden, his thesis advisor, telling her he'd have to miss the history majors' dinner that night, and explaining why. Then he went onto his college's website and found an e-mail address for letting the school know that he wouldn't be attending graduation. In bold letters on the website it said that cancellations could not be made within two weeks of graduation. But what were they going to do? If his name got called, and he wasn't there, what did it possibly matter?

There was little else to do. His work and exams were all finished, all his requirements submitted. There were friends to see, of course. And there was Kim. He'd run into her the previous weekend at the St. Dun's party. They'd kissed in the billiards room, and promised to see each other one more time before graduation. But he didn't really want to see Kim now; he didn't want to see anyone. His friends would hear the news, eventually, one way or another.

Harry rubbed his eyes with the palms of his hands, shut off the engine, and stepped out into the sea-salt air, much cooler than it had been in Connecticut. He spotted Alice in a second-floor window—his father's and her bedroom window—and when she saw that

Harry had noticed her she waved briefly. She was in a white robe, her skin and hair pale as gold, and she looked almost ghostly in the arched Victorian window. After waving she disappeared from view. He breathed deeply, preparing himself to see Alice, and preparing himself to walk into the house he'd only ever known as his father's house, full of his father's things.

In the doorway, Harry hugged Alice. Her hair smelled of expensive shampoo, something with lavender in it.

"Thank you for coming back early," she said, her voice huskier than usual, strained from crying.

"Of course," Harry said.

"I made up your old room for you. Can I help you bring things in?"

"No, no," Harry said. "It's not much."

It took just three trips from the car to the second-floor bedroom. Harry's old room had never really been his room; at least he had never thought of it that way. His mother had died of lung cancer when he was fifteen years old. Back then they'd lived in a two-bedroom apartment above his father's first shop—Ackerson's Rare Books—in the West Village in New York City. Because Harry had just begun high school when his mother died, his father had decided that it would be best for them both to stay in Manhattan until Harry had graduated. Living with his father in the dark, narrow apartment, made somehow smaller by his mother's absence, was both terrible and comforting. As long as they continued to live there, they could feel Emily Ackerson's presence, and the cold fact that she was gone forever.

In summertime, Harry and his father tended to spend more time in Sanford, Maine, than they did in New York. It was Bill's hometown; his sister and her family, plus a cousin he was close to, still lived there. On those trips, Bill began to scout locations for a second rare-books store, one along the coast. They rented a cottage on Kennewick Beach so that Bill could spend more time looking at properties. That was how he'd met Alice Moss, who was working as an agent at Coast Home Realty. They became engaged during Harry's senior year of high school, and when Harry went off to college, his father had made the permanent move to Maine, marrying Alice and buying the Victorian fixer-upper that he'd named Grey Lady. His business partner, Ron Krakowski, kept the New York store running, and Bill and Alice opened a second store in Kennewick Village, walking distance to the house.

The summer after freshman year was the only full summer that Harry spent in Maine with his father and his new wife. Alice, who had never married and was childless, had been ecstatic, transforming one of the guest bedrooms into what must have been her notion of a young man's room. She'd painted the walls a dark maroon—"hunting-coat red," she called it—and bought furniture from L.L.Bean that looked like it belonged in a fishing lodge. She'd even framed an original poster of *The Great Escape*, because Harry had once told her that it was his favorite film. He'd been grateful for the room, but slightly uncomfortable in it. His father, as he'd always done, traveled the country scouting books at estate sales and flea markets. Harry was left alone with Alice, who worked hard at being a replacement for his mother, constantly making him food, cleaning his room, meticulously folding his clothes. She was thirteen years younger than his father, which made her exactly thirteen years older than Harry, although she looked young for her age. Despite living on the coast of Maine her entire life, she avoided the sun because of her pale complexion, and her skin was unlined, almost lucid. Her only exercise was swimming, either at the community pool or in the ocean when it was warm enough. She ate ravenously, drank glasses of whole milk like she was a teenager, and was neither thin nor overweight, just curvaceous, with wide hips, and a narrow waist, and long legs that tapered to childlike ankles.

It had been hot and humid that summer, and there was no central air-conditioning in the house. Alice had spent all of July and August in cutoff jeans and a pale green bikini top, unaware of the effect she was having on her teenage stepson. She was a strange kind of beautiful, her eyes set too far apart, her skin so pale that you could always make out the blue veins right near the surface. She reminded Harry of one of those hot alien races from *Star Trek*, a beautiful female who just happened to have green skin, say, or ridges on her forehead. She was otherworldly. Harry found himself in a state of constant, confused sexual turmoil, guiltily obsessing over Alice. And the way she mothered him—making sure he had enough to eat, making sure that he was comfortable—made the attraction all the more distressing.

After that first and only summer in Kennewick, Harry had arranged to spend his college breaks either staying with friends or remaining in New Chester, doing research for one of his professors. He saw his father fairly often, because of how much time he still spent in New York, meeting with Ron Krakowski, negotiating purchases and sales. New Chester was less than two hours away from the city by train.

"You should come to Maine more often," his father

had told him recently. They'd been browsing through some of the recent arrivals at the Housing Works Bookstore in Soho. "Alice would like it."

Bill rarely mentioned her name, as though doing so somehow tainted the memory of Harry's deceased mother.

"I'll come this summer," Harry said. "How is she?"

"The same," his father said. "Too young for me, probably." He paused, then added: "She's a loyal woman. I've been lucky, twice, you know."

The room—Harry's room—was nearly the same as it had been when Alice had first decorated it, three years earlier. The major difference being that the empty bookcase she'd originally provided—"You can leave some of your favorite books here, Harry"—had been filled with a number of his father's first edition crime paperbacks, and the top of the bookcase had been covered with framed photographs, probably selected by Alice. Most were of Harry and his father, but one was a picture of his parents that he'd never seen before, back when they'd first met, sometime in the early 1980s, sitting together on a balcony, each with a cigarette perched between their fingers. They were roughly the age Harry was now, and yet they looked older somehow, more sophisticated. Harry felt like he'd just barely left adolescence and knew that he looked that way as well. He was tall and very thin, with dark, thick hair that flopped over his forehead. Kim had affectionately called him "beanpole." At parties, random girls sometimes told him how much they envied his cheekbones and eyelashes.

"Harry." It was Alice, just outside the door. She had whispered his name and he jumped a little at the sound. "Sorry. I didn't know if you'd want tea or coffee so I brought both." She stepped into the room, a mug in each hand. "They each have milk and sugar. That's right, isn't it?"

"Thank you, Alice. It is." He took the coffee, not planning on drinking much, since what he really wanted to do was sleep. Being at the house had already exhausted him. "Is it okay if I take a nap? I didn't sleep much last night."

"Of course it is," Alice said, backing away. "Sleep as long as you want."

After shutting the door, he took a sip of the coffee, then removed his shoes and belt and slid under the plaid comforter, his mind filling with unwanted images of his father in his final moments. Had he died instantly without any knowledge of what was happening? Maybe he'd had a heart attack or a stroke, and that had caused him to fall?

Harry opened his eyes, giving up on the possibility

of sleep. He could not bear to think of his father any longer and thought instead of college, the immersive reality of his last four years, and how it had suddenly ended. A surreal emotion came over him, the way you sometimes feel when you return from two weeks abroad, and the trip immediately seems like a mirage, as though it barely happened. That was how he felt now, thinking back on four years of college. Those years, his small group of friends, Kim Petersen, the professors he'd bonded with, were scattered now, permanently, like an ornate vase that shatters into a thousand pieces. His father was gone as well, leaving him with no family but Alice, and cousins he loved but with whom he had very little in common.

He stood by his bed, not knowing what to do next. Alice was vacuuming; he could hear the familiar hum from somewhere in the immense house.

His phone rang. Paul Roman, his best friend from college. He'd call him back; the last thing he wanted to do right now was talk. Instead, he walked to the window, cracked it slightly to let in some air. He looked out over the tops of the bright green trees. The steeple of the congregational church was visible, as was the shingled roof of the Village Inn and, in the distance, a snippet of the Atlantic Ocean, grey beneath a hazy sky. A young woman with dark hair held back in a headband walked slowly up the street. Harry watched as she noticeably slowed while passing the Victorian, glancing up at the windows. He instinctually stepped back into the bedroom. In the small, gossipy village of Kennewick, word must have gotten out.

His phone rang again. It was Gisela, another friend from college. Clearly, word had also gotten out among his friends at school. His father's death had actually happened. He held the phone, knowing that he needed to call one of his friends back, but unable to get his fingers to move. The sounds of the vacuum were closer now. He sat down on the hardwood floor and leaned against the wall, rocking back and forth, still not crying.

Chapter 2

Then

Alice Moss was fourteen when she moved to Kennewick, Maine.

Her mother, Edith Moss, having finally received her check from the Saltonstall Mill settlement, took herself and her daughter from a one-bedroom apartment in downtown Biddeford to a single-family house in Kennewick Village. Her mother told Alice that now that they had money, and a house to call their own in a nice town, Alice would have to start acting like a little lady. Alice was just happy to be near the ocean. She claimed she had never seen it before even though Biddeford, less than twenty miles north of Kennewick, also bordered the shore.

"Of course you've seen the ocean," her mother said. "I used to take you there all the time when you were a baby."

"I don't remember it."

"Alice Moss, of course you do. You used to be afraid of the gulls."

The mention of the gulls triggered a memory. Alice pictured her mother feeding them corn chips, laughing, as hordes of the dirty birds swarmed around them. She also remembered the prickly feel of her sunburned skin and the way the sand clumped to the side of her juice box. Still, to her mother she said: "I don't remember any of that. That must have been some other baby you had."

Her mother laughed, showing her crooked teeth, stained where they overlapped. "Well, now you can go to the beach all by yourself whenever you want. Show off that body of yours." Edith darted out a hand toward her daughter's breasts, probably thinking about twisting one of them, but Alice jumped back out of her reach.

"Gross, Mom," she said, and left the kitchen. Her mom's happiness since the settlement money had come in had been kind of nauseating. The boiler explosion had nearly killed her, but when the check arrived, she'd danced around their apartment like she was a teen-ager, then gone out and bought a carton of her favor-ite cigarettes, plus a big bottle of Absolut vodka. Alice had panicked that her mom would spend all the money right away, doing something stupid like taking her girl-friends on a cruise, or getting a brand-new sports car, but after the fancy vodka and the cigarettes, she only bought a bunch of new clothes, then told Alice how they were moving out of Biddeford to a real nice town called Kennewick. Alice pretended to be dismayed, but she was okay with it, especially when she found out that the house they were renting had her own bedroom *and* bathroom in it. That made up for leaving her friends behind and having to start over at a new high school. And the house was pretty nice, with big windows and wooden floors instead of stained wall-to-wall carpeting that smelled like cigarettes.

They moved at the end of May, and Alice had the whole summer to herself. Back in Biddeford there was nowhere to go but Earl's Famous Roast Beef and the roller skating rink, but here she could walk to Kenne-wick Beach, a long, sandy stretch packed with tourists all summer. And even though she *had* privately con-ceded that she'd seen the ocean before, it still felt like the first time. When the sun was out, the clear, cold water would sparkle, almost looking like pictures she'd seen of tropical places. The first time she walked down to the water by herself was Memorial Day. The beach was crawling with people, mostly families, but lots of teenagers as well, muscular boys and skinny girls in bikinis. Underneath her high-waisted jean shorts and Ocean Pacific T-shirt, Alice was wearing a dark red one-piece that was a little too snug. She'd bought it the previous summer to swim at her friend Lauren's aboveground pool, but her mom had rarely washed it, and it had faded at the seams from all the chlorine in the pool water.

That first day at the beach, she walked along the water's edge, carrying her sandals, liking the way the wet sand felt, sucking at her toes. But she never swam. Later that week Alice bought herself two new bathing suits with her own money at a gift store on Route 1A. One was a black bikini she wasn't sure she would ever wear and one was a green one-piece, kind of boring, but with high slits up the sides. She also bought a straw bag, a towel, and a bottle of Coppertone sun oil. She began to go to the beach daily, developing a strict routine. She quickly learned that she hated getting too much sun. It made her itch, and she didn't tan; her white skin just burned, or broke out in hideous heat rashes. She swapped out the sun oil for sunblock—the highest number she could find—and each morning of the summer, after showering, she would thickly spread the sunblock over her entire body. It made her feel impervious. Then she would pack her bag with a tuna fish sandwich, a thermos of Country Time lemonade, and one of her mom's romance novels, and set out for a day at the beach. There, she would spread her large towel out, making sure to put small rocks on all the corners so that it would stay flat. She would sit and read the romance novel, occasionally taking a break to watch other beachgoers play Frisbee or dart in and out of the water. No one ever approached her, but occasionally she caught boys or even sometimes older men taking surreptitious glances in her direction. It didn't matter if she was only in her bathing suit, or if it was a cooler day and she was still wearing shorts and a T-shirt, but it did seem to happen more when she was in her black bikini.

Before lunch every day on the beach she would take one swim, forcing herself to walk straight into the bone-chilling water without hesitation. She learned that if you stayed in the water, swimming back and forth, for at least two minutes, your skin would turn numb and it would no longer feel cold. The salt in the ocean made the water so much more buoyant than the water in Lauren's pool, and if she put her arms back over her head she could float on the surface and look up at the sky.

She swam only once during each beach trip because of how long it took her to dry off, making sure that not a single grain of sand got onto her towel. Then she would eat her sandwich, drink her lemonade, and go back to her book.

Her mother came to the beach with Alice only once during the summer. It was a Saturday in late July. Edith had gotten up early, taken a shower, and put on makeup, all because she was expecting her friend Jackie from Biddeford to come visit for the day. But Jackie called and canceled. "You'd think I'd asked her to drive half-way across the state," Edith said after the call. "It's two fucking towns over. What are you doing today, Al?"

"Beach."

"Of course, the *beach*. I should go along with you just to find out if you really go. How is it you go to the beach every day and your skin is like chalk?"

"I wear sunblock."

"When I was your age I went to the beach all the time and I was practically black. Well, maybe I *will* come with you, unless you'd rather I didn't."

"You should come. I'll make another sandwich."

It took Edith forever to get ready. Half of her stuff

was still in boxes and she puttered back and forth looking for just the right bathing suit, one that turned out
to be a leopard-skin one-piece that exposed a lot of
her chest, her skin leathery and darkly freckled. The
bathing suit also exposed her left arm, puckered and
scarred from the accident at the paper mill.

"I think I'm ready, Al. Can I bring a bottle of wine
to the beach or is that a no-no?"

"I can put some in a thermos for you," Alice said, already swinging open the refrigerator where her mother
kept her bottles of Mateus rosé.

It was almost noon by the time they had settled on
the sand, each on their own towel. It was a perfect day,
the only visible clouds thin ragged wisps on the hori-
zon line. The air smelled of the ocean, but also suntan
lotion, and the occasional trace of someone's cigarette
smoke clinging to the light breeze. Alice started reading; she was halfway through *Lace* again, by Shirley
Conran. Her mother cracked her own book, but wasn't
looking at it. She was twitchy and unsettled, and she
began to drink from her thermos of wine. "Wanna
walk?" she asked after a while.

"Sure," Alice said.

They walked the length of the beach and back, Edith
keeping the shawl over her shoulders. "Look out, Al,
it's a gull," she kept saying, prodding Alice's shoulder.

"I'm not scared of gulls anymore," Alice said.

"So you *do* remember the gulls."

"No. You told me I was scared of them. I don't remember those trips, if we ever went on them."

When they got back to their beach towels, Alice was hot, the back of her neck damp with sweat. "Do you want to swim?" she asked her mother.

"God, no, it's freezing."

Alice went alone, swimming out past where the waves were breaking so that she could lie on her back and rise and fall with the swells. She closed her eyes and watched the small explosions of color behind her lids, and if she leaned far enough back, and submerged her ears, all she could hear was the blank roar of the ocean.

When she returned to her mother there was an older man standing above her, his feet spaced apart and his hands on his hips. He wore black swim trunks, cut high up on his thighs. His hair was parted on the side and greying at the temples. Even though he was in good shape, it was clear that he was standing extra rigid, pulling in his stomach a little.

"Alice, this is Jake," Edith said, squinting up into the sun.

"Hi, Alice," the man said, transferring a lit cigarette from his right hand to his left to shake her hand. He wore aviator sunglasses with reflective lenses. Alice wondered if he was looking at her body from behind them. When he released her hand, she bent and picked up the towel she used to dry herself, wrapping it around her.

"Your mother here—" Jake started.

"Jake helped me open up an account at the local bank. That's where I got the new clock radio from, the one that's in the kitchen."

"Oh," Alice said. She'd dried her hair and sat down on the edge of her towel, being careful to keep her wet feet firmly in the sand.

The man called Jake crouched down. Edith propped herself up on an elbow. She had a lit cigarette as well, perched between her fingers, the heat from its tip causing the already warm air to ripple.

"I was just telling your mother," the man said, "how I'd be happy to show you two around Kennewick. Give you the real local's point of view. Best clam roll, et cetera."

Alice must have made a face, because he laughed. "Okay, then. Best ice cream place."

"Sure," Alice said, and scooched a little farther back on her towel. The man turned his attention back to Edith. Alice lay back, and concentrated on the way the hot sun was drying the droplets of water on her face.

She could almost feel them evaporating, leaving behind tiny deposits of salt.

"Okay, then. It's a date," the man said, and Alice opened her eyes. He was standing again, blocking the sun. He wasn't actually bad looking, Alice thought. He looked like a man who should be in a Newport cigarettes commercial.

The man crouched again, his bathing suit tightening around his crotch so that Alice could see the bulge of his genitals. She looked instead at his sunglasses, a silvery blue in the bright sunshine. "Alice, so nice meeting you. If you grow up any more the opposite sex won't stand a chance."

"That's what I tell her," Edith said. "All the time. Don't grow up. It's not worth it."

The man stood, both he and her mother now laughing in that obviously fake way that older people did. He said good-bye and wandered off, still holding his body stiffly as though it might collapse if he fully let a breath out.

Edith stubbed her cigarette—the man's brand, not her own—out in the sand, and said, "What did you think of Jake?"

She said it expectantly, her voice pitched a little too high, and Alice suddenly realized that this meeting had been at least partly arranged, that the man and her mother had not simply bumped into each other at the beach, or if they had, they'd seen each other before. And not just at the bank.

"He seemed nice," Alice said.

"He's very successful," Edith replied, digging out one of her own cigarettes from the purse she'd brought.

Alice lay back down. She was worried she hadn't put enough sunblock on her face that morning, and so she draped the towel over her head. It felt nice on her face, damp and cool. She thought about the man her mother had met. He was old and a little cheesy, but not that bad. When her mother was a mill worker at a paper factory and a single mother, she had to date a building manager who wore sleeveless T-shirts and had thick moles all over his shoulders and neck. Now that she didn't have to work, and lived in a nice town like Kennewick, Edith could date men who worked in banks and cared about how they looked. It was the way the world worked. She knew that much from the books she read. Rich girls married rich boys, and their lives were better. It was simple.

She couldn't see it, but a cloud must have crossed the sun because she could feel a sudden coolness on her skin. She sat up too fast, becoming a little dizzy. She realized she must have fallen asleep. There were fewer people on the beach now, and her mom was packing up.

"Ready to go, Al?" she asked.

Chapter 3

Now

Harry couldn't sleep that afternoon. He kept thinking back to the time after his mother had finally
succumbed to cancer, and the immense anger that he,
then a moody and truculent teen, had felt.

"We have each other now," Bill had said, after the
funeral, "it's important to remember what we have,
and not what we've lost."

"Whatever you say," Harry had replied, not making
eye contact, and his father had let him get away with
it. But what his father had said had stuck with Harry
through the following years. He missed his mother
constantly, but he did feel close to his bookish, low-key

dad. It was a family of two. Not nearly enough, but it was what it was.

And now he was a family of one, Harry thought.

The vacuuming had stopped, and Harry stepped out of his room, went down the stairs, coughing purposefully when he reached the first floor so that he wouldn't startle Alice. He entered the large front living room, spotted her lying on one of the sofas, the crook of her arm across her eyes as though she had a headache. He began to turn away when she said, "Harry, come in. Talk with me."

"That's okay. Keep sleeping."

"No, no. Come here."

Harry sat on the edge of the oldest upholstered chair in the room, a transplant from the Manhattan apartment, and said, "Have the police told you anything more?"

"They haven't, but they'll be doing a full autopsy."

"It seems strange that he would fall."

"Something else might have happened. He could have had a heart attack."

"Do you think so?"

"It makes more sense to me than him suddenly slipping off the path and—"

"Had it rained?" Harry asked.

"Um, a few days ago, I think, but I don't think the

path would have been slippery. We'll learn more from the autopsy. It'll be important for you, too, Harry, in case, for instance, he had a weak heart."

"Oh, right," Harry said. The thought hadn't occurred to him, that his father's death at an early age might be a harbinger for him, as well, if it had been a natural death. He bit at the inside of his cheek, an old habit that was suddenly resurfacing, and wondered if he'd care if a doctor told him that his father had a weak heart that he'd inherited. He tried to feel something—some fear for his own future—but couldn't. What would it matter?

Alice pushed forward a little on the sofa. "Your father was really looking forward to you coming here for the summer. He talked about it a lot."

Harry, not trusting his own voice, nodded his head, and Alice immediately asked, "How was your coffee? Was it the way you like it?"

"Oh, it was fine," Harry answered, then quickly added, "Better than fine. It was really good."

"Thank you," Alice said, placing her palms on her knees as though she was about to stand, and Harry added, "Don't get up. I didn't mean to disturb you." He stood. "Maybe I'll take a walk or something."

"Okay, Harry, that sounds nice," she said. "If John's in the store, then maybe you'd drop by and say hello.

We're both hoping you can help out a little. John won't be able to . . ."

"Yeah, of course," Harry said.

Alice's gaze settled on the bay windows. "It's staying light for so long these days," she said. "Go for your walk."

Outside, Harry exited the driveway and turned left onto York Street, walking down toward the few businesses that comprised Kennewick Village. His father's store was flanked by a florist and an ice cream shop; all three shared a single-story brick building that had once been a lumber mill. Harry looked through the tinted plate-glass window stenciled with the words ACKERSON'S RARE BOOKS. It was dark inside—no John Richards, his father's elderly assistant—but there was enough light to see that the interior was cluttered with too much stock, stacks of books lining the edges of filled shelves. A flicker of movement made Harry jump. It was Lew, a Maine coon that lived in the store. Lew leapt onto the window's display case, dipping his head and rubbing his tufted ears against a first edition of *Peyton Place*. Harry hoped the cat hadn't been entirely forgotten since his father's death. He'd ask Alice about it later.

Harry walked east, passing in front of the Cumberland Farms convenience store, then took the Old

Post Road toward Kennewick Beach. He knew he was walking along the same route his father had most likely taken to get down to the cliff walk, but it was the direction he felt compelled to go, toward the ocean. He hadn't yet decided whether he wanted to walk along the footpath and see if there was any sign of where his father had fallen. For now, he just wanted to move his legs, and be away from the house.

The Old Post Road took Harry to Sohier Road. Kennewick comprised four distinct sections. There was Kennewick Center, now mainly dispersed along Route 1A; Kennewick Village, with the town's oldest buildings; Kennewick Beach, with its affordable rentals and campsite; and Kennewick Harbor, the most exclusive section of Kennewick, studded with weathered mansions and the two biggest resort hotels.

Harry stayed on Sohier Road and reached the three-quarter-mile beach, flanked by Micmac Road, metered parking along the narrow strip of sidewalk. The beach itself was half sandy and half rock strewn, expansive at low tide, but reduced to a sliver when the tide was high. He walked along the sidewalk and found the grey-shingled rental that his father and he had rented for an entire month the summer his father decided to open up another store in Maine. It looked empty now, but it was early in the season. Only some of the rentals had cars in front of them, and the beach was almost abandoned. There was one walker, a woman in a hoodie striding along the sidewalk that lined the beach, and one rock collector, idling along the tide line, occasionally crouching to pick up a find. It was a slack tide, the water as still and glassy as Harry had ever seen it. A truck rumbled by, its inhabitant glancing at Harry from underneath a sun-bleached Sea Dogs cap.

He decided he'd walk all the way up to the Buxton Point Lighthouse. He kept thinking about that summer with his father, how he'd spent so much time with Alice Moss, the Realtor showing him commercial properties in the area. Harry had liked the idea of his father opening a new store, of taking the chance to leave New York City and settle closer to where he'd grown up. And he'd liked Alice. She was low-key for a Realtor, not flashy or loud. She might have been blond and leggy, but she didn't wear too much makeup, she didn't drive a white Lexus, and her fingernails were unvarnished and cut short. These weren't necessarily attributes that Harry had noticed, but his father had, and he'd mentioned them on a number of occasions. In retrospect, it was clear that his father had already fallen hard for Alice Moss and was testing the waters with his son, nervous that Harry might not approve. It was only at the end of the summer, after they had packed up and were driving back to New York City so that Harry could start his senior year of high school, that Bill confessed his relationship with Alice had become romantic.

"I'm happy for you, Dad. I like Alice."

His father's relief was palpable. His shoulders relaxed, and he began to talk about Alice, how much they had in common, having both lost parents when they were young, and how they both felt left behind in this new, modern world.

Harry really did feel okay about his father seeing Alice, but in October, she came down to New York to visit, and her presence in their apartment, the apartment that was still filled with so many of his mother's things, unnerved him. Alice was giddy, expressing to Harry several times how much it meant to her that he had given his blessing. The first time she said it, she followed up by hugging Harry, even kissing him on his cheek, and whispering "My darling boy" in his ear. The kiss, and the feel of her breath in his ear, caused Harry to involuntarily shudder and tense, and Alice broke the hug, clearly embarrassed. Harry retreated to his bedroom, and tried to forget the awkward moment, but it wasn't easy. He could feel the softness of her waist in his hands, and the lingering sound of her voice in his ear. It had been nice but awkward at the same time. Down deep, he felt a revulsion that he was sexually attracted to a woman that his father was also attracted to. It felt unnatural, but the more he tried to push the images from his mind, the more they held strong.

Harry was suddenly out on Buxton Point, on the outskirts of the parking lot that surrounded the white lighthouse topped with red, now a historic landmark and Kennewick's only major tourist attraction. He circled, going around the keeper's house, and started back toward Kennewick Beach. He'd been walking for well over an hour, the sun now low enough in the sky that it was casting long shadows along the beach. Even so, he made the sudden decision to walk all the way to Kennewick Harbor along the cliff walk. He would have to do it sooner or later, and he needed to see if there was any sign of his father, and what had happened to him, along the path.

Harry stayed on Micmac Road, heading south. Once he'd cleared the beach, Micmac began to curve and twist, with sporadic views out over the bluff toward the ocean. The house lots were wider, the houses bigger, most of them old, but there were new mansions here and there, including one monstrosity that looked more like a hotel than a house.

He had to double back but Harry found the path through the scrubby pine that led to the northern start of the cliff walk. It seemed narrower than he remembered, rose hip and winterberry bushes scraping at his legs, and he wondered if anyone used it anymore. Maybe the path was on private land now, the owners hoping it would be forgotten. Still, it took him out to the cliff walk, with its view along the rocky shore to the half-moon beach of the harbor. This was his father's usual walk, and the one he ended his life on. Harry walked a quarter mile, slowly, scanning for any sign of where, exactly, his father had fallen. He wondered if there might be police tape at the scene, then dismissed the idea. It wasn't a crime scene. It had been an accident. He took a break and sat on one of the wooden benches along the path. There was a small metal plaque on the bench saying that it was given in memory of Blanche Audet, who had died in 1981. Harry stared out toward the ocean, and thought of how many times his father must have taken this very walk, and wondered if he'd ever sat on this bench. The view was beautiful, but there was something bleak about staring out to the ocean, as well. All that crushing, grey water that had never changed and never would. Except for the new resort hotel on the far edge of Kennewick Harbor Beach, this view must have looked the same to Blanche Audet, and whoever was here before Blanche, and whoever was here long before this path was carved out of the rock.

Harry's phone vibrated in his jeans pocket but he

ignored it. He stayed on the bench until he was cold, pulling his sweater on, then stayed awhile longer.

When he finally stood, his legs felt stiff. He was out of shape, he realized, having spent all the last semester writing his thesis, crouched over his laptop. He'd stopped swimming, and he hadn't played squash since before Christmas.

He checked his phone. Several friends from college had texted or called. He put the phone back in his pocket, feeling irrational, unfair anger at their concern. They cared for him, but Harry dreaded the inevitable conversations. He wasn't always good at talking. Words and sentences filled his brain—he felt as though he was constantly narrating his own life—but bringing those words from inside his brain and out into the world had always been difficult for him. When he was younger he'd suffered from a lateral lisp, his words often coming out with embarrassing hisses. Speech therapy had corrected it, teaching him to let the words flow from the top of his tongue, and not from its sides, but the lisp had done its damage.

He silenced his phone, and decided to finish the remainder of the cliff walk before turning back toward Grey Lady.

He scrambled up a short incline, then ducked to get under a wind-bent tree. It was the highest point of the walk, and one of the narrowest sections of the path. A sharp drop led to a cluster of black rocks, green and slick where the seawater reached during high tide. Waves slapped at the rocks, sending out fans of spray. The path was packed gravel, and slabs of shale. It wasn't slippery, but it wasn't completely flat, either. He kept walking, and almost missed the small bouquet bunched together and left leaning against the twisted root of a white pine.

He bent and picked up the bouquet; it was made from bittersweet with its familiar red berries, some still cocooned in yellow, that bloomed in the autumn. These had somehow survived through the winter, the berries shrunken and almost black. They had been bound together loosely by a long strand of grass. Harry looked at the stem ends of the bittersweet; they had been broken, not cut. Whoever had put together this bouquet had done it impulsively, without using clippers or proper string. And had it been meant for his father? Was this the place he had slipped? He'd ask Alice if she knew exactly where he'd fallen. It seemed suddenly important. He'd also ask her if she'd left the bouquet, but he doubted it. He put the bittersweet back where he'd found it, some of the wizened berries popping off the vine as he rested it against the tree.

It was fully dark when he reached the driveway

of Grey Lady. He paused, wondering if he could get away with entering the house and going straight to his bedroom. He'd brought some cheap bourbon with him from college and maybe he could drink himself into oblivion, stay that way throughout the next few days. There was a soft glow of light coming from the bay windows, the curtains now drawn.

Instead of walking directly to the front door, Harry cut diagonally across the short front yard and stood in front of the windows. There was a gap between the curtains, and he could see through the living room and into the kitchen, now fully lit, where Alice was moving around. There was a glass of wine on the island, and a cutting board loaded with vegetables, but Harry watched the way Alice was moving, twitching her hips a little as though she was listening to music. She turned and found her glass of wine and took a long sip. Her face was slightly distorted by the window glass, but she looked . . . was it happy? No, not exactly, but she did look peaceful, at ease. Harry watched for a while longer, getting colder, waiting to see if her expression changed. But it didn't—she continued to move through the kitchen, light on her feet, her lips now moving along to the music Harry couldn't hear.

Chapter 4

Then

Edith and Jake got married the following summer in the city clerk's office in Portland, Maine. Alice went, and so did one of Jake's dull friends from the bank. Afterward, they all drove back toward Kennewick, stopping in Ogunquit to eat a late lunch at a fancy restaurant made almost entirely of glass. It was built on a bluff with a view of a rocky stretch of coast. Edith and Jake pointed out houses they'd like to own if they ever won the lottery. Alice ordered the prime rib because her mom told her she could have anything she wanted.

After the wedding, Edith and Alice moved into

Jake's three-bedroom condominium at the north end of Kennewick Beach, up near the lighthouse. The building, except for its location, was not that impressive on the outside, just a three-story, grey-shingled box segmented into four equal condos, each with two parking spaces under the unit. But the condo interior *was* impressive. Jake had hired an interior decorator, and everything inside was spotless and shiny, with a kitchen full of gadgets and plants. The only thing Alice missed from their rental house was the wooden floors, the way they felt on her bare feet. Here, there was white shag carpeting, spotless because Jake had a cleaning woman who came every week. Also, Jake instituted a no-smoking-in-the-house policy. He smoked his occasional cigarette on the second-floor deck, and he insisted that Edith did as well, even when it was freezing out.

"He doesn't expect you to clean the house?" Alice asked her mother, when she learned about the cleaning lady.

"No," Edith said, as though she'd been asked if she was a cannibal. "Of course not. He makes good money, you know."

Alice wondered what her mother would do with all her spare time now that she didn't even have a house to take care of. Actually, she didn't wonder. She knew that she'd drink more. It hadn't bothered her that much when it was just the two of them, but now it worried her because there was a third person in their family. Did Jake know what his new wife was really like? Would he want a divorce and they'd all have to leave their beautiful-smelling new home?

It turned out that Alice didn't need to worry. For the first two years of the marriage, Edith spent her mornings doing aerobics in the living room; Jake had a VCR, and Edith had invested in a slew of aerobics tapes. In the afternoons she would plan that night's dinner, following intricate recipes from cookbooks with French-sounding names. When Alice came home from school, her mother was usually in the kitchen, watching an afternoon talk show on the cabinet-mounted television, preparing ingredients and drinking a red smoothie that Alice knew contained as much vodka as it did strawberries. As soon as Jake walked through the door she would make proper drinks, martinis usually, and a Shirley Temple for Alice, and the televisions would be turned off.

By dinnertime Edith was slurring her words and barely picking at her food. After dinner Alice's job was to wash the dishes, although Jake usually helped by bringing them to her. Edith took a brandy into the living room. "I just need to relax," she would always say. She'd turn the television on, and finish the brandy and then she'd be asleep. Jake never seemed to mind. He'd gently slide her down the white leather sectional, then take control of the remote, usually finding a game to watch. If Alice wasn't doing homework in her room, she'd watch television with him, and he'd sometimes let her pick what she wanted to watch.

But usually Alice stayed in her room. It wasn't that she didn't want to watch TV with Jake. She loved television. It was that she couldn't stand the sight of her mother passed out on the couch, her mouth open, emitting raspy snores. Jake didn't seem to notice, only occasionally shifting her when the snores got too loud.

One night, after Alice had finished her homework, she came out to the living room. Jake was watching hockey, and Edith was facedown on the couch, a little pool of drool next to her mouth. "Gross," Alice said before she could stop herself.

Jake laughed. "Your mother likes to drink," he said, as though that particular thought had just occurred to him.

"Does it bother you?"

"Not too much. People are who they are, don't you think?"

"I guess so."

"You finish your homework?" Jake glanced over at the empty recliner, and Alice took her usual seat, accepting the remote control from her stepfather.

"Yeah, I didn't have too much to do. Just algebra, and some reading." Alice flipped the channel to CBS. *My Sister Sam* was on.

"School going all right for you?"

Alice shrugged. "Yeah, it's fine."

"You have friends?"

"Gina."

"Oh, right, Gina."

Alice turned to look at Jake, still staring at the television, lips pressed together as though he was concentrating on what was happening on the screen. Alice assumed he must be asking these questions only because Edith had asked him to, or because they'd been discussing it together. But discussing what? The fact that Alice seemed to have only one friend at school?

The truth was that Alice hated Kennewick High School and the students who went there. The incident that sparked this hate had happened her freshman year, when she'd met a senior named Scott Morgan because their lockers were next to one another. He was a lacrosse player with a good smile and bad acne on his forehead. When Alice told him she was from Biddeford, he said that his dad owned a car dealership there, and he mentioned a pizza place that Alice knew. Whenever he saw her again at the lockers, he'd always ask, "How's Biddeford?" as though she still lived there. On the first warm day in April, he told her about a party that was happening on the beach at midnight. It had been easy for Alice to sneak away; she didn't even need to be quiet, knowing her mom could sleep through pretty much anything. She wore cutoff shorts and a big hoodie, and carried a bottle of Sprite that she'd spiked with some of her mother's vodka—not because she wanted to drink it, but because you brought alcohol to a party. When she got to the section of beach that Scott had mentioned, Scott was there alone. He handed Alice an open can of beer and said, "I lied about the party."

"How come?"

"To get you here alone."

They were on the south end of the public beach, near the playground and a picnic area shaded by pine trees. They walked to the darkest bench and began to kiss, Scott's hands instantly fumbling under Alice's hoodie, and pulling at the zipper of her shorts.

"You a virgin?" Scott asked, when he'd gotten Alice's shorts down around her ankles.

"Yes."

"My friend told me that all the girls in Biddeford do it in middle school."

"Well, I didn't."

"Do you want to do it now?"

"Sure," Alice said. It wasn't something she had

planned, but now that it was happening, it seemed like the right thing to do. Clearly, it was what they did in Kennewick, and if she let it happen now, then she wouldn't need to worry about it later. And Scott was opening up a small plastic packet that looked like a condom, so she wouldn't have to worry about getting pregnant. Alice reached down to touch him, but he bucked his hips back, saying, "I don't want to come yet." But even without being touched he only got about halfway inside of her before he shuddered, his jaw clenching, tendons tensing in his neck.

"Don't fucking tell anyone, okay?" he said, as he pulled out of her, holding on to the condom.

"Okay. I won't."

But on Monday at school, the word *WHORE* had been written in capital letters with a silver marker across the front of Alice's locker, and while she was crossing the open walkway to the science building for Period C, a girl that Alice had never noticed before started yelling at her from the smoking pit. "Stay away from Scott, you fucking slut." She was a blonde with crimped hair. One of the blonde's friends held her upper arm, restraining her from coming over. Alice kept walking, her heart jackhammering in her chest. Why had Scott told people after telling her not to tell anyone? For the rest of the day she felt like everyone in school was staring at her, and either laughing or judging. She didn't see Scott once, and assumed that he was avoiding her.

When she did finally see Scott, the following day, he didn't even look at her, just slammed something into his locker and took off. Alice watched him walk away, still wondering what had happened, when a girl—another friend of the blonde—shoved Alice hard in the shoulder and said, "Don't even look at him, Bitcheford." A group of students walking by burst into laughter. For a brief moment Alice almost went after the girl. She imagined grabbing her hair, pulling her hard to the floor, stamping on her neck. But Alice controlled herself; she showed nothing.

It was only at the very end of freshman year that Alice heard the whole story. Gina Bergeron was another freshman whose family had recently moved to Kennewick. She was tall and gangly, and spoke so rapidly that sometimes spit would bubble from her lips. They'd met in science class, where they'd been paired together to dissect a fetal pig. She had two older brothers and two younger sisters, all about a year apart. Alice and Gina became friends almost by default. They were both new to Kennewick, and both friendless, and that was where the similarities ended. Still, it was someone to eat lunch with in the cafeteria.

Gina's brothers were both athletes; the sophomore

was a tennis player, and the junior, Howie, was good at lacrosse. Gina got the story from Howie. There actually had been a party the night that Alice had sex with Scott, but not on Kennewick Beach. It had been down at the Harbor Beach. Scott had skipped out to be with Alice, but when he returned he got drunk and bragged to all his friends how he'd just fucked a freshman girl. His on-off girlfriend, Stacy Homstead, the girl with the crimped hair, heard about it, and she was the one who spread it around school the following day, the story of the slutty freshman from Biddeford who'd steal your boyfriend. The *Bitcheford*.

"Did you really have sex with him?" Gina asked. They were walking together to Alice's house, along the sidewalk that bordered the beach.

"Sort of, I guess. It didn't last very long."

Gina covered her mouth and laughed, more of a snort.

"What was it like?"

"It was like nothing," Alice said, and meant it.

"Geez," Gina said. Alice knew that despite being fascinated, Gina had judged her as well. She also knew that Gina, gawky now, with her giraffe legs and wobbly head, was going to be beautiful by senior year, and that their friendship would not last. She didn't really care. She'd already resolved to just get through high school on her own. She'd gotten through her whole childhood on her own, after all, without a father or brothers or sisters. She had her mother, who barely counted. Alice felt that she'd been counting down the days to being on her own as an adult for longer than she remembered. She didn't really need friends, even though Gina and she remained somewhat close throughout all of high school. But Alice's first prediction did come true. Between junior and senior year, Gina lost her awkwardness and turned into a runway model. It didn't make her as popular as Alice thought it would, though. The girls seemed to resent her, and the boys were frightened away.

Alice, by senior year, was almost as pretty as Gina. Despite her aloofness, boys occasionally flirted with her, sometimes asking her out, but she had no interest. She'd learned her lesson from Scott. She knew what teenage boys were like, and she'd decided that she preferred the company of men. What she really preferred was the company of Jake Richter, her stepfather. Edith's afternoon drinking had gotten worse, and, more often than not, she'd either forget to prepare dinner for her husband, or she was already passed out by the time he'd gotten home. One Friday night, Alice and Jake had arrived back at the condo at the same time, finding Edith asleep on the recliner, one of her vodka strawberry smoothies tucked between her legs. They found a chicken in the oven but the oven hadn't been turned on. Jake laughed.

"It's not funny," Alice said.

"No, it's not, Ali." He was the only one who called her that. "Tell you what. Your mother isn't going anywhere. How about you and I go out for dinner?"

"Okay."

"Good. I'll have a quick drink while you change, and then we'll go out."

Alice assumed that they'd be going to the Papa Gino's on 1A—it was where they usually went out to eat when Edith hadn't managed to get dinner ready—and she asked Jake why she needed to change.

"We're going somewhere special," he said. "Wear your nicest dress."

They drove all the way to Kennebunkport and ate at a waterfront restaurant that was attached to a hotel. Jake was still wearing his suit from work, although he'd loosened his paisley tie, and she was in a pale pink, sleeveless dress, the one she'd worn to her uncle's third wedding over the summer.

"Have you had French food before?" Jake asked, after they were seated at a corner table.

"Do French fries count?"

Jake smiled at her joke, his lips spreading wide while

his teeth remained together. "No. Not tonight. Can I order for you?"

"Sure."

Jake ordered escargot as a starter, which turned out to be snails in their shells. Alice agreed to try them and they were not bad. For dinner they each had steak with béarnaise sauce. Jake drank wine, and Alice drank sparkling water. It was clear that their waitress thought that they were father and daughter, but Alice pretended, in her mind, that they were a sophisticated couple out for a casual dinner at the end of a busy week. She tried not to think about her mother at home in the recliner, and whether she'd wake up and wonder where her husband and daughter were. Instead, she made her mother disappear into nonexistence, and shrunk the world so that it was a perfect bubble that only contained her and Jake.

"Save room for dessert," Jake said. She'd been using some of the still-warm bread to sop up all the amazing sauce that was left on her plate.

After the chocolate mousse for her and just a cappuccino for Jake, they drove back in Jake's BMW, listening to one of his Roxy Music tapes. It was early fall, but still warm enough to have the windows open, and Jake was driving along the coastal route. Alice kept pretending her mother didn't exist, imagining that they were going back to the condo they lived in together, and alone. The song was "Avalon," Alice's favorite. When they got home, Edith was there, although she was now stretched out on the couch instead of the recliner, and the television was on, the volume turned up way too high.

"Where'd you two go?" she said, as Jake turned the television down. She had propped herself halfway up on an elbow, and was pulling a strand of hair away from her mouth.

Jake said, "Out to dinner, Ed. You forgot about our reservation, and I didn't want to wake you."

"What? Where?" Her voice was thick and sleepy.

"The Brasserie. In Kennebunkport."

"Oh yeah. I'm so sorry, honey. I completely forgot."

Alice went to her own room as Jake bent and kissed Edith on the forehead. Alice shut her door, and sat on the edge of her bed, wondering if Jake and Edith really had had plans to go to the restaurant and her mom had forgotten. Or had Jake just made that up? She remembered the chicken, her mom's attempt at cooking dinner, but that didn't mean much of anything. Her mother was forgetful, and even if they'd had dinner reservations, that didn't mean she'd have remembered them. Thinking about it was starting to give Alice one of her headaches, like fingers jabbing into her temples, so she took four ibuprofen, changed into her pajamas, and got into bed. She lay there awake for a long time, staring up at the textured ceiling, so similar to the apartment ceiling from back in Biddeford, although that ceiling had had glitter in it. She took deep, regular breaths, trying to get back inside the bubble, the one in which Jake took her to French restaurants all the time, and they traveled to Europe, and her mother no longer existed. She could feel the headache start to go away, like poison seeping out into her pillow, and then her limbs got heavy, and her eyes closed, and she was asleep.

Chapter 5

Now

The funeral was Sunday afternoon, the same time as the graduation that Harry was missing. Despite Harry telling him not to, Paul Roman skipped the graduation ceremony as well, and drove up to Maine. He arrived just before noon. Harry was in his bedroom, the window open, and heard the car brake sharply on the driveway. He met Paul at the doorway. Alice was out back, cutting flowers, and Harry desperately wanted a little time alone with Paul before he had to change into his suit and attend his father's service. He took him straight to his room.

"You have any idea what happened?" Paul asked, as soon as the door was shut.

"You mean, how did he die?"

"Yeah. Did he just trip?" Harry had met Paul their freshman year, when they both had single dorm rooms on the same hall. Paul's second question to Harry, after asking his name, had been: "You sleep with boys or girls or both?"

Harry, flustered into honesty, replied, "Girls. In theory, though, not in reality. Yet."

"All right. Let's go find some. Girls for you, and boys for me."

They'd stayed best friends through four years of college, building a group around them. Well, Paul had built the group, being one of those people who attract friends as easily as a flower draws bees. Harry felt privileged to be in his company, and sometimes over-shadowed. Paul was funny and gregarious, filterless at times, but always knowing what to say and what to do. Privately, Harry pictured Paul as a fellow soldier of the social realm who would draw enemy fire in his direction so that Harry could make small incremental advances, trench by trench.

"There's going to be an autopsy," Harry said to Paul, now sitting on the edge of the bedroom's one chair. "But he probably just fell. Just a freak accident."

"You don't think anyone else was involved?"

"What do you mean? Like someone pushed him?"

"I don't know, I'm just wondering."

"I think it's more likely that maybe he had some sort of heart attack, or a stroke, and that caused him to fall off the path and hit his head. It was a pretty steep drop."

"What does Alice say?"

"I think she thinks it was a medical condition. She thought it would be good to find out. For me, that is, in case it's something that's genetic."

"Oh, right," Paul said, then added, "So what are you going to do? I mean, you going to stay here?"

"I don't know. I guess I'll stay for the summer. I can't just up and leave Alice, and she's already asked me to help out in the store. Honestly, I have no idea."

"Don't figure it out today." Paul unzipped the backpack he'd brought up from his car. "You want a drink?"

They drank gin and tonics (Paul had brought the ingredients, plus glassware, and even a ziplock bag of half-melted ice) while Harry dressed in his only dark suit, a Ludlow from J.Crew that was a little short in the sleeves. Then together they went downstairs and found Alice, who was in the kitchen, meticulously arranging the flowers she'd cut. Harry thought of the ragged bouquet on the footpath and wondered again who had left it there. He'd forgotten to ask Alice if it was her.

Paul had probably met Alice three times at most, but he hugged her as though she was related, holding on until she let out a small, sniffly sob. "Paul, are you staying? I didn't make up the guest room."

"I'm not. Just for the service, then I'm going back to Mather. I'm missing the graduation but I'm not missing the graduation party. Unless, Harry . . ." Paul turned toward Harry, a questioning look on his face.

"No, no, no. Please go back. I'll be fine."

"I'll come and visit this summer," Paul said, as Alice wiped tears from her face with an index finger. Her blond hair was swept back in a French braid that went down her back. She wore a dark grey dress, low cut in the front, but with a black shawl over her shoulders. Her face was chalky white, more startling because of the bright crimson lipstick she'd put on. Harry tried to remember if he'd ever seen her with lipstick, and decided that the last time had probably been when she had married his father, at a low-key ceremony at a hotel in Ogunquit. It seemed a long time ago, but it was less than four years.

The service was held at the First Parish Unitarian Universalist, a white wooden church with a high steeple that was on the Old Post Road. Harry, Alice, and Paul arrived early, and Harry and Alice spoke to the minister, a grey-haired woman over six feet tall, who went over what she planned on saying. Harry knew most of it already. It was going to be a short service; two hymns, a eulogy, a reading by Carl Ridley, Bill's cousin from Sanford. Alice had already met with the minister to go over some of the details of Bill's life, and the minister briefly recounted them now. Harry was glad that there was significant mention of his mother, and how devoted Bill had been to her. It was his only concern, worried that Alice had only seen Bill's life as beginning when she had come into it. But the words the minister planned on saying comprised all of Bill's life, including both his marriages, his son, his lifelong affair with books, even his infamous cooking. As Harry, Alice, and the minister talked, a few early-arriving guests filtered slowly into the church. Harry wondered how many there'd be, and how many he would know. The interior of the church was cool, but Harry's palms were sweating, and he could feel a trickle of sweat along his rib cage. He'd only ever been to two funerals in his life. His mother's, and now his father's. He'd never known his grandparents on his father's side, since they'd both died before Harry was born. His maternal grandparents were both alive, but they hadn't left their retirement community in Florida in many years.

"And how about you, Harry?" The minister was speaking to him, and he wasn't sure what she was asking.

"I'm sorry," he said, aware he was blinking his eyes rapidly.

"Did you want the opportunity to say a few words?"

"Oh . . . Oh, no. Alice already asked me. Thank you, though."

"Why don't you two take a seat, up here in front."

It was a relief to sit, to hear the murmur of people behind him, and know that he didn't have to acknowledge them, at least not yet. He felt guilty that he wasn't saying anything at his father's funeral, but he couldn't bring himself to do it. He didn't trust himself to speak in public, worried that he'd be overtaken by either anger or grief, or a combination of both. He even still worried about his lisp, long eradicated except in his mind, where he often heard the echoes of how he used to speak. There'd be a receiving line after the service, and he'd have to speak then, of course, but just to people one-on-one. Still, the thought of it made his skin feel prickly, and his breathing shallow.

Before the service began, his aunt Anne and her three silent, muscle-bound sons, all in high school now, sat in the pew directly behind Harry. He leaned back to kiss her, and she said: "I still don't believe it, Harry," genuine grief in her voice.

"I know," he said, "I don't, either."

"I meant to call you, Harry, but I didn't have your phone number. I spoke with Alice and she said you'd be coming home soon, but I want you to visit us as soon as you feel able to leave her alone."

Harry said he would.

She was telling him again how she was still in shock when the service began. Harry turned back as the minister adjusted the microphone at the pulpit. He took a deep breath to prepare himself, but the service was relatively painless. The minister, except for the opening and closing prayers, kept the religion to a minimum, aware that Bill Ackerson was a twice-a-year church-goer at most (Christmas Eve services and maybe Easter Sunday). For the eulogy she simply recounted his life story, his childhood in Maine, the Peace Corps service in the Pacific Islands, his years as a book scout and then a bookseller in Manhattan, meeting his first wife and having a son, his wife's brave battle with cancer, then his return to Maine and his second marriage. She talked about his love of the coast of Maine. "Alice spoke to me about Bill's need to see the ocean every day. How it grounded him. He found his true and spiritual home here in Kennewick, and for that we should all be grateful."

Alice dipped her head next to Harry, and covered her face with her hands. He slid toward her and put an arm around her narrow shoulders. Behind him he could hear stifled crying.

After the eulogy, Carl Ridley walked gingerly to the pulpit, a trembling sheet of paper in his hand. Tears already streaked Carl's papery cheeks before he even spread out the sheet of paper in front of him. There was a long pause, Carl smoothing back his thinning hair, but then he was speaking, saying how Bill's office was decorated by two things: stacks and stacks of books, and one poem, tacked onto the wall. The poem was "If," by Rudyard Kipling (he pronounced it "Kiplin' "). Harry had heard the poem before, or at least the line that went, "If you can meet with triumph and disaster, and treat those two impostors just the same," but he'd forgotten that the poem was a message from a father to a son. Harry tensed his jaw. His aunt, from behind him, put a hand on his shoulder, making it worse. But then at the end of the recitation—"You'll be a man, my son!"— Paul leaned close to his ear and said, "Jesus, salt in the wound," and Harry quietly laughed, feeling better.

When the final hymn was sung and the closing prayer spoken, Harry finally turned around to see a sizable crowd, much larger than he'd thought. In the receiving line, many of the people who shook his hand and muttered their sympathies were strangers, but some were cousins and second cousins whom he barely remembered. No one knew what to say, so everyone said how sorry they were, and Harry nodded and thanked them.

While speaking to a man who referred to himself as Ackerson's Books' best customer, Harry noticed a dark-haired woman, probably in her twenties, who had remained seated in her pew, toward the back of the church. Harry thought she was staring at him but couldn't be sure; maybe she was staring at the reception line in general, wondering whether she should join in. She was vaguely familiar to Harry, and he wondered what her connection was to his father. Was she the daughter of a friend? As though she felt Harry's eyes on her, she suddenly tilted her head away, revealing a strong jawline and an upturned nose, and Harry remembered where he'd seen her before. She'd been walking along the road near his father's house on the first night that Harry stayed there. She'd been wearing a headband and had been looking at the house, as though she knew what had happened there.

"Are you also interested in books?" said the man still speaking with Harry.

He was standing too close, his breath sharp with the

bitter smell of coffee. Harry willed himself to not lean backward, said: "Not the way my father was, no. But I do like books."

"Not obsessed, eh?"

"No. Not obsessed."

The man moved along, and so did the line. When Harry looked for the dark-haired woman again, he couldn't spot her anywhere.

Alice's best friend, Chrissie Herrick, had skipped the service in order to set up food and drinks at Grey Lady for a small memorial gathering. There'd been talk back and forth on whether it should be at her house or a restaurant, but Chrissie had talked Alice into the house option, saying she would take care of every detail.

When Harry, Paul, and Alice got home, some guests had already arrived and were milling silently around the spread of cold cuts and salads on the dining room table. Chrissie had purchased a guest book for people to sign and had put together a slideshow of pictures of Bill on a laptop. "At least there's beer," Paul said, and pulled two bottles of Shipyard from a cooler filled with ice. Harry told himself that he should talk to his cousins, most of whom he hadn't seen for two years. But before he could approach them, John Richards cornered him and asked if Alice had broached the subject of him helping out at the store this summer.

"She did," Harry said.

"Oh, good. And you can, I hope?" John was a local widower, and a retiree, who had asked to volunteer at Bill's store. Bill had taken him on just for a few hours a day, but John had made himself indispensable, both as an employee and as a late-in-life friend.

"I can help for the summer. You want to keep the store open, then?"

"I don't know about that, but I do know I can't just shut it down right away. We've got special orders to fill, and cataloguing. Even if we decide to close it, it's still a lot of work."

"No, I know. What about the store in New York?"

Harry had actually been surprised that Ron Krakowski, who had bought out his father's share in the original Ackerson's Rare Books in Manhattan, had not come to the service. Ron had been Bill's closest friend for many years, a true savant with an encyclopedic knowledge of the rare-book trade. Harry did remember hearing from his father once that Ron had become one of those city dwellers terrified to step off the asphalt island of Manhattan. That was probably the reason he hadn't made it to Maine.

"What *about* the store in New York?" John asked, confusion in his voice.

"I thought maybe they'd buy up your stock, if you decided to close shop."

"Oh, right. I hadn't thought of that, but they probably would. When can you come in?"

Harry told John that he'd come and help out in the store on Tuesday. The thought of going in the following day was just too much to stomach. John looked visibly relieved that help was on the way.

His beer gone, Harry checked in briefly with Aunt Anne's kids; all three were milling around the food, demolishing a bowl of Ruffles and some French onion dip. It was clear that he remembered them better than they remembered him, or maybe they were all at that stage of teenage boy in which conversation and facial expressions disappear. Aunt Anne came over and helped out, repeating to Harry several times that he could come visit whenever he wanted to and for however long. While talking with his aunt, he kept an eye on Alice, who was sitting on one of the T-back chairs, a plate of untouched pasta salad on her lap. Carl Ridley stood next to her, a hand on the back of her chair, while a familiar woman—was she a librarian?—bent at the waist to offer Alice her condolences.

"You should get back to Mather," Harry told Paul,

who had just extricated himself from what looked like a stilted one-on-one with Billy Herrick, Chrissie's husband and one of those men who had married a talkative woman so that he, himself, could retire from the act of small talk.

"You sure?" Paul said.

"Yes, please. I wish I could come with you."

"You could, you know."

Harry made a face. "Not really. I mean, Alice . . . and even if she didn't mind, I don't think I could stand hanging around with a bunch of drunks celebrating graduation."

"You wouldn't have to go to any parties. We could just hang out one last night in my dorm room. Kim would obviously love to see you."

Harry briefly considered it. Telling Alice that he needed to tie up a couple of loose ends at college, making sure that Chrissie would spend the night so she wouldn't be alone, and then leaving with Paul, back to college for one more night before the rest of his life began. The thought was tempting, but also exhausting. More concerned people, more condolences. What Harry really wanted to do was to go up to his room, shut the door, strip off his too-tight suit, and crawl under the covers. And there was also a part of him that wanted to stay close to Alice, to not leave her alone in the house. He told Paul he thought he needed to stay, then waited while Paul said good-bye to Alice.

He walked Paul to his car. They hugged good-bye. "You're not alone, buddy," Paul said, and Harry was briefly spooked to hear the words, realizing that had been his primary emotion since hearing of his father's death. He'd felt alone, the world emptied of his family.

"Yeah, well," Harry said, and began to back away.

"Something wrong beside the obvious?" Paul asked.

"What do you mean?"

"You've been not quite yourself this whole year."

"What are you talking about?"

"Never mind. Now is not the time, obviously. I'm just worried about you, and so is Kim."

"You Kim's spokesperson now?"

"Sure, why not?" Paul said, pulling a pack of cigarettes from his jacket pocket. "I'm off. You need anything, like for me to come back, or someone to talk with, just text, okay? And hang in there."

The Prius's wheels spun on the crushed shells, then the car was speeding out onto York Street. Harry watched as Paul drove out of sight, a trail of cigarette smoke coming from his lowered window. The air temperature had cooled, and the sky above was dark with crosshatched clouds. Paul's obvious pity annoyed Harry, and he took several deep breaths. Harry considered going back into the party, saying his good-byes, then retreating to his room, but once he'd walked back through the front door he found himself going immediately to the stairs. He'd talked to everyone he needed to talk to, and no one would blame him for wanting to be alone.

In his room he thought again about the dark-haired woman at the funeral service, wondering who she was. It was easier to think of the mystery of her and not the greater mystery of his father's death. Maybe Alice knew who she was. Alice, as far as he knew, had always lived in Kennewick, and she knew a lot of people. He'd ask her tomorrow. It would give them something to talk about.

Chapter 6

Then

A week before Alice graduated high school, Edith announced that she wanted to throw a graduation party. Alice initially refused—telling her mother that the last thing she wanted was any kind of party—but finally agreed to a nice dinner at home.

"Invite your friend Gina," Edith said. "She's never been here, has she?"

Alice wanted to say, *For good reason,* but instead told her mother she would check and see if Gina was free, but she doubted it.

The date was set for the Friday night before the Saturday morning graduation. Even though Gina knew all about Alice's mom—how all she did was drink and take pills, and it was always a small miracle if she made it through dinner without passing out—Alice still wasn't sure she wanted Gina to actually witness it. Besides, that wasn't her real life. Alice's real life was the dinners for two at the French restaurant with Jake—more frequent now—and the nights they spent together watching television, her mother barely even conscious.

Sometimes, when the three of them were together, Alice constructed elaborate fantasies in which Jake and she were married, and Edith was their sickly child. A burden, but one they bore together. But mostly, Alice imagined that it was just the two of them, just Jake and her, living a perfect life together, years and years passing. Somehow, in these daydreams, Alice got older but Jake stayed the same. No one would mistake them for father and daughter. Maybe one day they'd even have their own child. A daughter. Alice sometimes saw her in her mind, and it was as if she were real, an actual child being remembered. She'd love swimming in the ocean, and grow up speaking both French and English because of all the time they'd spend in France. Genevieve would love her mother, but she'd love her father most of all, doting on him.

"My mom is making a big fancy dinner for the night before graduation," Alice told Gina.

"Are you inviting me?" Gina laughed.

"Thinking about it."

"I'll come. I need to see the real Edith in action."

Alice clenched her jaw, suddenly wishing she'd just told her mom that Gina was busy that night. "Sorry, Al," Gina quickly said. "That was a rude thing to say, but, yes, yes, I want to come to dinner. What is she cooking?"

"Cornish game hens, I think. I told her about a hundred years ago that they were my favorite, so . . ."

"Who else is going to be there?"

"Just you and me, and Edith, and Jake. Should be a hoot."

"It's perfect, because my mom is inviting half my family for that whole entire week, including the cousins I told you about, the NASCAR ones, and I'm going to need some time out by Friday night, and there is no way my mom will say no to me going to your house for dinner. But you gotta promise me one thing, Al. We'll go to that party afterward, at Justin's house. You don't have to stay, but you have to come with me. I'm not going alone. You promise? *And* I get to pick what you wear."

Alice promised. Gina, now that she had other friends besides Alice, including a dim but nice boyfriend that she'd met doing the yearbook, was always trying to get

Alice to come to parties, or hang out with other kids. Alice would occasionally agree, not really because she wanted to, and not really to make Gina happy, but because she saw it as practice for the adult world. It was important to know how to talk with someone in a social situation, even if that someone was a dumb high school boy with a can of beer in his hand. And now that Alice was a senior, the incident with Scott Morgan from freshman year was ancient history. Alice was no longer the slut from Biddeford who would give it up to anyone. She'd changed all that, and now she was known as the aloof girl, too sophisticated for high school boys.

"Yay!" Gina said. "I'll tell Justin. He'll pee himself."

According to Gina, Justin Lashaway, another friend of hers from cross-country, had a huge crush on Alice. "Whatever. I'll go with you, but I'm not staying long. You agree to that, right?"

"Yeah, fine. What time at your mom's house?"

On the day of the dinner party, Alice stayed home all day helping her mother. They'd cleaned the already immaculate condo, made the hors d'oeuvres—asparagus wrapped in ham—set the table, and done all the prep for the dinner. It was four o'clock, three hours before Gina was supposed to arrive, and everything had been done. Edith hadn't been drinking, at least not that Alice could tell, but she was talking a blue streak, and grinding her teeth, and it was clear she was on *something*.

"You okay, Mom?" Alice asked.

"Of course I'm okay. I want to make a perfect dinner for my perfect daughter to celebrate her graduating from high school and becoming a woman."

"You're just so jumpy."

"Am I?" Edith said. Then, with a wide, lunatic grin on her face, she began jumping up and down, her shoes clacking on the tile floor. Alice just stared. She was used to seeing her mother passed out, mouth open, but she wasn't used to seeing her act unhinged. She was clearly on some kind of drug.

"Mom. Stop. You're freaking me out. Maybe you should have a drink."

"What time is it?" Edith asked, glancing at an imaginary watch on her wrist. At least she'd stopped jumping. "I told my Jakey that I'd wait till he got home before having a drink because I think he's worried I'm going to embarrass you in front of your friend."

"You just seem a little wired. Let me make you a drink. What do you want?"

"Just so long as you tell Jake that it was your idea, and not mine, if he gets upset. Let's have some champagne together. I bought it for both of us. Thought it would be okay for you to have a little bubbly on your birthday."

"Sure," Alice said, not correcting her mother that it was a graduation, and not a birthday party.

They drank champagne together on the deck so Edith could smoke. She went through four of her cigarettes— long, thin menthols—in about thirty minutes, talking the whole time about nothing. Alice was just relieved that she seemed to be getting a little bit calmer, but she barely paid attention to the words her mother was saying. Instead, she stared out toward the beach. It was a warm, gusty day and there were whitecaps on the ruffled surface of the ocean. As she listened to her mother talk about how when she'd graduated high school her *only* option had been to go and work at the mill—a story Alice had heard countless times—Alice wondered if she'd *ever* loved her mother. She must have loved her when she'd been a baby, back when her very survival depended on it, but since then, and definitely since the settlement, Alice felt almost nothing when she thought about Edith. Her mother was an alcoholic who looked twenty years older than she was. She'd been pretty once, but the cigarettes and the alcohol had wrecked her looks, and now she was a boring, rotten waste of space. Just like that dry rot that Jake had found in the wooden stairs that led from the first floor down to the garage. He'd ripped it all out so it didn't spread, and then hired someone to build new stairs. That was what Edith was. Dry rot that was never going to get better. The only good thing she'd done was marry Jake, and Alice truly didn't know why he'd stayed with her. She didn't like to think about it, because if she thought about it too much, she'd become convinced that Jake would disappear from their lives as fast as he had entered into them, and then it would just be her and her mother again, the dry rot spreading from mother to daughter.

When the bottle was empty—Alice had only had one glass—Edith declared that they should do final preparations for the arrival of the guest. She told Alice to light the candles and fluff up the pillows in the living room while she prepared the stuffing in the kitchen. The champagne had taken the edge off whatever pills she'd taken earlier. Alice thought her mother seemed back to normal—her voice slightly slurry, and her face slack—and she knew that before she started on the stuffing, she'd build herself one of her health drinks in the kitchen.

Jake arrived home first. He was in his navy blue suit, wearing his tie with the little anchors on it, and he had two bottles of wine in the crook of his arm. "Smells good in here, ladies," he said loudly.

Gina arrived not long after, wearing a shimmery blazer over a white T-shirt and tight jeans. She'd done her hair, teasing her bangs, and was wearing eye makeup in addition to the lipstick and rouge she usually wore. Jake looked her up and down when he saw her. "I can't believe it. You were a little girl yesterday," he said. Gina smiled, and Alice was pleased that a little bit of lipstick was stuck to one of her big front teeth. She hadn't even considered that Jake might be attracted to Gina, but of course he would be. He hadn't seen her for at least a year, and she looked like a movie star now.

The jealousy went away when Gina grabbed Alice, and said, "Show me around. I can't believe I've never been here." Then added, in a whisper, "How's the momster?"

"Still standing," Alice said.

She brought Gina up the stairs and showed off her room, and her own bathroom, then they went out on the deck, and Gina smoked one of Edith's cigarettes.

"So I thought you'd like to know, but now it's official. I'm going to NYU." Gina had been wavering between NYU and the University of Maine. Alice knew that Gina would pick New York City, and that once she got there she'd look for a modeling agent. "Why don't you come with me?"

"To where? To New York?"

"Yeah. We could live together, and you could take classes and apply for a degree program."

"I'll come visit. How about that?"

Alice had already decided that she was going to take classes at the southern campus of the Maine Community College System. She had told Gina that she was worried about leaving her mom alone, but, in truth, she didn't want to stop living with Jake.

"You promise?" Gina stubbed out the skinny cigarette in the ashtray. The filter was imprinted with her lipstick color, a dark plum.

"I do," Alice said, but didn't really mean it, and didn't really think that Gina would remember the promise once she arrived in New York.

Jake shouted, "Girls," from downstairs, and they joined Jake and Edith for appetizers and drinks in the living room. Edith had calmed down, and was her usual slow-motion self, smiling beatifically at both Alice and Gina as though they had done something a lot more impressive than graduate from Kennewick High. Jake kept the conversation going, asking Gina lots of questions about her plans. Alice was slightly jealous again, and actually glad that Gina would be leaving Maine and probably never returning. After appetizers they moved to the dining room table, where every plate was adorned with a Cornish game hen stuffed with wild rice, and a pile of honey-glazed carrots. They looked nice but they'd gone cold. Alice and Gina were allowed to keep drinking wine, and Edith had switched to what looked like vodka on the rocks, her speech getting more incomprehensible by the minute. Edith kept pushing the tiny hen around her plate, occasionally taking a small bite. Gina ate ravenously as she always did, concentrating on her food until all that was left on her plate was a small pile of bones. Alice knew that growing up with four siblings had left her with the constant feeling that there would never be enough to go around.

"You girls should get going to your party. Ed and I will clean up," Jake said. He'd eaten only about half his food, and Alice thought that was strange. He looked embarrassed, probably because there was a new witness to his wife's behavior. He didn't know that Gina had been prepped for the spectacle.

"It was delicious," Gina said, refolding her napkin and placing it on her plate.

"Sorry about . . . My wife sometimes drinks too much."

Edith perked up, and blew a raspberry in the direction of her husband. "I've had three drinks tonight, a lot less than some people around here. But don't worry, don't worry, I'll clean up." She stood up suddenly, went to steady herself by grabbing hold of the chair, missed it, and sat down hard on the floor. Everyone around the table jumped up, but Jake got to her first, helping her stand and bringing her to the couch in the living room. While he got her settled, Alice and Gina brought dishes into the kitchen. Alice whispered: "I wasn't exaggerating, was I?"

"No," Gina said, smiling, but her eyes looked concerned.

At the door, Jake said, "Be extra-careful tonight, you two. Look after Alice, okay, Gina?"

"I'm only staying half an hour, tops," Alice said, as Gina took her by the shoulders and pushed her out the door.

"Thank you so much for dinner, Mr. Richter," Gina said, "and please thank Mrs. Richter for me."

"I will," Jake said, and he swiped at a damp eye. Alice had never seen her stepfather cry. She opened her mouth to tell Gina that she was staying home, but she was already being led down the hall.

Chapter 7

Then

Justin Lashaway lived in a deck house in the woods on the outskirts of Kennewick Village. The long driveway was jammed with cars, kids milling around drinking cans of beer. Justin's parents were home, but they'd offered up the entire bottom floor, a large rec room, for the party. They'd put out tons of food, and buckets filled with soft drinks, but the majority of the kids at the party—almost the entire graduating class— had spilled out into the surrounding pine forest, where most of the drinking and pot smoking was taking place. After checking out the rec room, Gina eating two cook- ies and a piece of cake, they headed out to the edge of the woods and found Justin manning a keg. Alice knew that Justin had a crush on her, had had a crush on her for at least two years now. He'd asked her to the senior prom, and she'd let him down easy by telling him that if she had any interest in that sort of thing, he'd be the guy she'd want to go with.

"Alice! No way," he said. He was filling plastic cups for the swarm of students.

"You got a keg?" Gina asked.

"My brother's home and got it for me. My parents are pretending they don't know."

Justin got them both a cup of beer that seemed to Alice to be mainly foam. She drank it while Gina went to find her boyfriend. When she was finished with the beer she told Justin that she was heading home, that she really just came by to say hello.

"Aw, man. Don't go," Justin said. "Besides, how're you getting home?"

"I'll call my stepdad from inside. He'll come pick me up."

"I can drive you. At least let me drive you."

Alice agreed, and Justin took off to try and borrow a car: "My car's buried, but Brad's around here some-where." Alice thought about trying to find Gina and saying good-bye, but knew that Gina would give her a hard time for leaving so soon. Justin returned, breathless, holding up keys. "Brad's Mustang. I had to fight him for these."

Justin drove slowly, cutting over to Kennewick Harbor, then driving along the shore. At first Alice thought Justin was driving slow because he'd been drinking and was worried about being pulled over, but then she figured out that he just wanted to spend more time with her. He was asking constant questions, wanting to know how she felt about graduating, what classes she was going to take at MCC, why he never saw her at high school parties. She answered as best she could, and laughed when he drove right past her condo. "I thought you might want to go out to the lighthouse, take a little walk," he said, shrugging.

"Sure. Why not?" she said. Part of her just wanted to see what it felt like, spending more time with a boy who seemed to like her. And he was harmless, that much she knew.

There were no other cars parked out at Buxton Point. They walked down the short jetty and sat on a flat slab of granite close enough to the water so that the spray from the crashing waves occasionally reached them. She let Justin kiss her, and unhook her bra, but stopped him when his hand plucked at the top button of her jeans.

"I like you so much, Alice. You have no idea."

"I have a boyfriend," Alice said. It was a lie, but as she said it, she pictured Jake.

"You do?"

"He's older. You don't know him."

"How much older?"

"Just a little bit. I'm sorry, Justin."

"So why are you here with me?" He had leaned back, and in the bright moonlight looked genuinely upset. *He's a nice guy,* Alice thought, *but just a boy.* He was halfway cute but his eyes were too close together, making him seem a little inbred, and his dark hair was already beginning to thin at the front. He'd probably be completely bald by the time he was twenty-five.

"I shouldn't be, Justin. I don't know what I'm doing. It's a bad time for me, and my mom isn't doing well, and I should be home now. I should never have let this happen." It was a trick she sometimes pulled on Gina, suddenly getting emotional to get out of something. She knew that because she was so stoic all the time, when she made herself sound upset, people paid attention. It worked with Gina, and it worked now with Justin. He drove her back to the condo, and dropped her off. She kissed him hard once on the mouth, their tongues touching, then quickly exited the car. The least she could do was let him think it was hard for her to say good-bye.

As soon as she unlocked the front door of the condo

and stepped inside, she knew something was wrong. It was quiet—just the sloshing sound of the dishwasher running in the kitchen—but the house had a bad smell. She could see her mother supine on the couch, but the television wasn't on. She hung the house keys on the hook and walked toward her. The smell got sharper, and as her eyes adjusted to the darkness, she saw that her mother had thrown up. Vomit had pooled on the couch and was streaked down her mother's cheeks. It had happened before, but always when her mother's head had been turned to the side. This time her mother's head was tipped back, crusted lips parted, her eyes partly open.

Alice watched her, frozen for a moment, and then her mother's chest bucked, and she made a sound like a wet cough. Alice stepped backward, alarmed. Her mother was choking in front of her eyes, probably dying. Alice wondered if all she needed to do was step forward and turn her mother's head to the side so that she'd be able to breathe again. But Alice just watched instead. She was revolted, not just by the vomit and her mother's gargling, halted breaths, but disgusted by everything about her mother. She was so incapacitated that all she had to do was turn her head to live, and she couldn't even do that. It was pathetic. Edith bucked again, but didn't make the coughing wet sound.

Alice realized she'd been balanced on the pads of her feet, as though she was about to move forward. Instead, she settled slowly back onto her heels. She didn't want to watch anymore, but she couldn't take her eyes away. A strange relief spread over her; her mother was being ushered away from her and to a better place. Alice's body lightened, and her scalp tingled. Her mother had stopped moving and Alice knew she was dead. Still, she watched some more, aware of the blood rushing through her body. She felt dizzy and her chest was cold. A thought went through her: *I got my wish.* And then another thought: *There was nothing I could do.*

Something caught at the corner of Alice's eye and she turned toward the stairwell.

Jake was on the bottom step, his face half shadowed, watching what had just transpired.

Chapter 8

Now

Harry woke, groggy and disoriented, just past eleven, having stayed in his room for the entire evening, dozing on and off, and finally falling into a deep sleep filled with terrible dreams that, now he was awake, were just out of his mind's reach. He was incredibly hungry for the first time since he'd heard about his father. There was a text on his phone from Kim that had been sent at four in the morning. *WHY AREN'T YOU HERE?* Five minutes later she'd sent him a photograph of Paul, and Paul's current boyfriend, Rich, both asleep, fully dressed, on her bed. Then she sent a photo of herself, her lips puckered in a kiss, the makeup around her eyes smudged. He turned his phone off and got out of bed.

Downstairs had been thoroughly cleaned, with no sign left that there had been thirty people here the day before. There was a note from Alice on the island in the kitchen:

Harry,
I'm at Chrissie's house this morning. Please CALL
if you need anything.

Love, A

He felt relief that he had the house to himself for the first time since he'd arrived back. He swung the refrigerator door open; it was packed with leftover food, and Harry made himself a ham and cheese sandwich. There was some of yesterday's coffee in the pot, not a lot, but he poured it over ice, added milk, and brought his breakfast out onto the front steps of Grey Lady. A cool, gentle rain was just beginning. There was no sound, except for the chatter of birds, and Harry could smell the ocean. That was not always the case in Kennewick Village, far enough inland that, depending on the wind, it didn't feel any more like a seaside town than New Chester, Connecticut. But when the wind was right, the air had that unmistakable tang of salt water and tidal mud. He'd grown up in Manhattan, but Harry had spent enough summers in Maine to consider it a kind of childhood home.

He finished his coffee and his sandwich, then went back inside. He thought of going into his father's office but decided against it. He wasn't prepared for a room so filled with memories of his father. Instead, he wandered into the living room, a room that with its beige color scheme and watercolor seascapes seemed more Alice than Bill. The one indisputable item of Bill's, besides the dark grey wing-backed chair, was one of his cherished barrister bookcases, each shelf with its own pull-down glass front. Harry looked at its contents, all hardcovers, including a shelf of Agatha Christies. Harry lifted the glass front and pushed it back into its slot so he could look at the books. There was a hardcover copy of *After the Funeral* next to a hardcover of the same book with its American title, *Funerals Are Fatal*. Harry, who'd inherited some of his father's immense love of mystery novels, tended to like American crime writers more than cozy English golden-age mysteries, but he'd gone through a brief Christie phase in middle school after his father had given him *Ten Little Indians*. He could still hear his father's voice from then: "Now, if you decide to read all of Agatha Christie, just keep in mind that some of her books have more than one title, so don't read them twice." He'd then gone on to catalogue the many different title changes in her publishing history, like another father might tell his son about the year-to-year batting champions in the 1930s and 1940s. Harry, at twelve, had been impressed, but now he wondered if his father had wasted his life in the trivial pursuit of something only he (and a smattering of other misfits) cared about. How many useless facts and complicated plots got wiped out the moment he died?

Harry was looking at a hardcover of *Five Little Pigs* when the doorbell rang. He slid the book back into its place on the shelf and walked to the front hall. There was a tall figure visible in the frosted glass that ran along the side of the front door, and Harry felt a brief flutter of concern.

He swung the door inward. On the other side of the screen door stood a man in a tan suit. He was holding up a badge.

"I'm Travis Dixon with the Kennewick Police Department," he said. "I'm looking for Alice Ackerson."

"She's not in. Can I help you?"

"Are you Bill Ackerson's son?"

"Uh-huh."

"Do you mind if I come in and ask you some questions? It pertains to your father's death."

"Okay," Harry said, pushing open the screen door so that the detective could enter.

"Thank you—is it Harry?" he said as he stepped into the foyer, ducking his head slightly, and offering a large, knuckly hand. Harry shook it.

"It is," said Harry. The shoulders of the detective's light suit were speckled with rain. The sky was darker than it had been earlier that morning.

"Is there some place we can talk?" the detective asked.

Harry led him into the living room, where they sat on opposite-facing sofas. "What's going on?" Harry asked.

"We got a preliminary report from the crime scene investigators this morning, Harry," he said, hands on his knees. "And although we are not ruling out an accident, we are presently treating what happened to your father as a suspicious death."

"Oh?"

"It's inconclusive right now, but there is a possibility that your father was hit on the head before he fell off the side of the path."

"You think someone hit him?" Harry said, trying to absorb what he was hearing.

"That's what we think."

"What does that . . . ?"

"What does that mean? It could mean many things. He could have argued with someone along the path. It could have been an attempted mugging, although your father was found with his wallet on him. It's possible that some kid threw the rock that hit your father and it was a complete accident. We just don't know. That's why I'm here, just to ask you some questions."

"Okay," Harry said, then added, "Should I text my stepmother? Should she be here?"

"I'd like to hear from you right now."

"Sure," Harry said. He watched as the detective pulled a spiral-bound notebook and a pen from the inside of his jacket. Harry thought that he couldn't have been more than forty years old, although he had a receding hairline, noticeable even though his hair was cut very close to his scalp. He had a long nose and thin lips, and his dark eyes were set deep in their sockets.

"Can I ask you some questions about your father?" he said.

Harry nodded.

"Had anything changed in his life recently? How was his marriage?"

"Honestly, I don't know that much about my father's marriage."

"How long had they—"

"Since I went to college, so about four years."

"Can you think of anyone who might have had a reason to harm your father?"

"No."

"Disgruntled customers from the store? Old girl-friends?"

Harry shook his head.

"Do you know anything about your father's financial situation?"

"You mean, did he have money?"

"That. Or did he have money problems? How was the store doing?"

"Fine, I think. My father did okay in his business, well enough to send me to college. He had some family money, as well, I think. And my mom had some money from her parents. My biological mother."

"Your mother is . . . ?"

"She died. About seven years ago."

The detective jotted that fact down in his notebook, as though it was the first thing he learned that he hadn't known already. "How did she die?" he asked.

"Of lung cancer."

"Did your father have close friends here in Kenne-wick that you knew of?"

"He was friends with John Richards, who works for him."

"What do you know about him?"

"Not much. He's a retiree who started out by volunteering to help out at the store, but now he pretty much co-manages it with my father." Harry stumbled over the words, aware he was using the present tense.

"And they were friends?"

"Oh, yeah. I don't know if they were social with each other, if they did things outside of the store, but my father relied on him."

"What about other employees?"

"I know that he sometimes got someone to help out during the summer, when there was the most foot traffic in the store, but they were usually teenagers or college students."

"You never came up and helped out during a summer?"

"No," Harry said.

"Okay. What about other friends? Did your father and his wife socialize with other couples at all?"

"I don't really know, but I don't think so. Alice has a friend named Chrissie Herrick—that's where she is right now—and she's married but I don't know if they did 'couple' things together."

The detective pulled a vibrating phone from his pants pocket. He checked the screen, then put the phone into his suit jacket pocket. "Sorry," he said, then slid forward fractionally on the sofa. "Anyone else you can think of that your father had regular contact with? Anyone he kept in touch with in New York?"

"His old business partner, Ron Krakowski, was there, and they were still close, but he never even leaves the city."

He jotted the name down on his pad, then put it back in his suit jacket. It was clear that he was getting ready to go. "You've been very helpful, Harry," he said as he stood.

Harry stood, as well, and accepted the card that the detective was holding out to him. "If you think of anything else, even if it seems insignificant, give me a call. That's my cell number on the card," the detective added.

At the door, Detective Dixon asked Harry if he was planning on staying in Kennewick awhile.

"I have no other plans," Harry said. "I'll probably help out at the store."

As soon as the detective turned to go, Harry watched as he pulled his cell phone out, thumbed the screen, then lifted it to his ear. He was talking as he got into the maroon Impala and shut the door behind him. The car's glass was tinted.

Harry turned back into the house and thought of calling Alice but quickly decided against it. Instead he wandered back into the living room and looked out at the rainy day, trying to wrap his head around the new information. He felt as though his body was reacting to the news faster than his mind was; his chest hurt, and his limbs felt electrified, like he needed to do something physical. He realized the feeling was anger. His father might have been killed. Harry's mind flashed on the young brunette woman that he'd seen outside of the house and at the funeral. He remembered that he was going to ask Alice about her today. He stared at the window. It was still raining, but a streak of blue sky had appeared over the tree line to the west. Harry suddenly needed to get out of the house. He grabbed one of his father's raincoats from the row of pegs in the front hall, and stepped through the door onto the front steps. He felt instantly better, breathing in the damp air. He walked to the end of the driveway, then arbitrarily turned right and began to walk, head down, the diminishing rain pattering on the hood of his father's coat.

Chapter 9

Then

Edith Moss's funeral was held at a church in Biddeford, and she was buried in a family plot. Alice wondered if that was what she would have wanted, considering the way she talked about her family, but Alice also knew it didn't matter. Her mother was dead and would never know the difference.

Edith's two brothers were there, and some of their kids from assorted girlfriends and ex-wives. Alice hadn't seen any of them since they'd moved out of Biddeford to Kennewick. "Good riddance to bad rubbish," Edith had said. Alice actually liked her uncle Claude, even though he was supposedly the worse of the two Moss brothers; he rarely worked, and drank all day. But he was always in a good mood, and when Alice was a little kid, he'd give her packs of fruit-flavored chewing gum. Her uncle Theo, who never gave her anything, was a construction foreman with a bad back who was now on disability. In the receiving line, he said to Alice, "Guess you get all that Saltonstall money, now, eh?"

"I guess," Alice said, resolving to never see any of her Biddeford relatives again.

A few of Jake's friends from the bank came but no family. Gina came, of course, and so did Justin, and a few other kids from high school that Alice barely knew. Justin couldn't take his eyes off Alice during the brief, terrible reception in the church's basement. She wondered if he was trying to figure out if her "boyfriend" was there. Would he know she'd been lying? She didn't particularly care one way or another. She hadn't thought she'd ever see him again after the party at his house, and she was pretty sure that now she'd never see him again after her mother's funeral.

Everyone kept asking Alice what her plans were. Was she going away to college? Would she come back to Biddeford? She told them she didn't know yet, but she *did* know. She wanted to keep living with Jake. She'd take classes at MCC, just for something to do, but now she had Jake all to herself. She pictured them trying new restaurants up and down the coast, maybe even traveling together.

After the reception, Jake drove Alice back along Route 1 from Biddeford and through Kennebunkport. "I don't want to go back home quite yet," he said.

"I don't, either."

They went to the Brasserie for an early supper. Alice was wearing a Laura Ashley dress and more makeup than she usually wore. Jake ordered a dinner for both of them and a bottle of wine. The waitress brought the bottle and two glasses and never asked Alice for ID. Alice hadn't touched any of the deviled ham sandwiches or potato salad they'd served at the church, and she was starving. She ate all the bread herself, soaking it in the garlic butter from the escargot. She tried her steak rare, the way Jake ordered his, instead of medium, the way she usually got it, and it tasted better, much better, especially if you didn't think about the pool of bright red juice on the plate.

They hadn't talked about Edith's death since the night it had happened. As soon as Alice, having watched her mother choke to death, had turned to find Jake watching her, she'd immediately said, "We need to call an ambulance," and Jake had gone to the wall phone and dialed 911. After hanging up he rushed to Edith's side and pressed two fingers against the side of her neck.

"She was like this . . . she was like this when I got home," Alice said, her whole body beginning to tremble.

"When did you get here?" Jake asked.

"Just now. Just a minute ago. How long have you been down here?"

Jake took Alice by her shoulders and moved her backward away from her mother's body. "I thought I heard something and came down the stairs. I'm so sorry, Alice. Your mother was drinking, and I shouldn't have left her down here."

"No, no. I shouldn't have even left the house to-night."

"Shhh," Jake said, pulling Alice into his arms and holding her while her trembling turned into uncontrollable shaking.

When the EMTs arrived, one of them asked Alice if this was how she'd found her mother.

"She wasn't moving," Alice said. "She was just lying there."

After dessert, Jake said, "Let's stay here tonight. I can't face going back home. I'll get us two rooms."

"Okay," Alice said.

He left Alice alone at the table while he went to the front desk to book the rooms. She wanted to tell him that he could get just one room, but her voice had stopped working. He came back with two keys. The front desk had also sold him two toothbrushes and a tube of toothpaste.

Both of the rooms were nice, but one of them—the one that Jake insisted that Alice take—faced the ocean and had an outside deck. Jake had bought a second bottle of wine from the restaurant to take upstairs, and together they sat on the deck, the night getting cooler, and drank it. Alice took small sips, not wanting to get drunk, not wanting to be like Edith had been, but the wine tasted good, and was making all her muscles tingle and relax.

"You were brave today," Jake said.

"Was I? I didn't do anything."

"No, but you were there. You came. How are you feeling?"

She thought for a moment about what to say, then decided not to lie. "I feel nothing. I feel cold."

"Cold isn't nothing."

"No, I feel cold right now. It's cold out here." She laughed, and so did Jake.

Inside the room, he pulled her into his arms, and hugged her. His skin smelled of cologne, and he was tall enough that his chin rested above her head. She tilted her head and kissed his neck, and he brought his hand up to her chin, tilting it so that he could kiss her. He brought her to the bed, his hands sliding up her thighs to the elastic top of her stockings. She lifted her hips as he pulled them off.

Afterward, in the black darkness of the room, he said, "No one, absolutely no one, can know about this."

"I won't tell anyone," Alice said. "I don't even want to know anyone else. I just want to know you."

"I feel the same way," he said.

Alice woke at dawn to the sound of gulls. She was shivering. They'd left the door to the balcony cracked. She got up to close it, just as the door to the hallway opened up and Jake was coming back into the room. She startled, not aware that he had left. "Where'd you go?" she asked.

"The other room. I made it look like someone had slept there. Just in case. I didn't want it to look . . ."

"No, I understand."

He was staring at her, and Alice realized she was naked. She stood, letting him look, and then he came to her.

They returned to the condo that afternoon. They walked the exterior stairs up to the front door. Alice used her key, but before she could step inside, Jake said, "Wait." Then he lifted her into his arms and carried her, like a bride, over the threshold.

Chapter 10

Now

Harry got back to Grey Lady at just past three. He had walked for miles, eventually winding up at York Hill State Park, where he'd climbed a muddy trail to reach the top of York Hill, less than seven hundred feet of elevation but enough to see the White Mountains to the west and the Atlantic to the east. The rain had stopped completely by the time he got to the summit; the sky was half clear, half darkened by clouds. He was alone, his shoes soaked through, and he felt like screaming at the top of his lungs. But he couldn't bring himself to do it; a voice at the back of his head was laughing at how clichéd it would be. Instead he sat on a boulder, wondering what would happen if he simply lay back and didn't move. Would he freeze to death in the middle of the night? He tried it, his shoulder landing in a shallow puddle of rainwater, then immediately sat up again. He couldn't even fall apart properly, and he decided that he would go back to the house to hear what Alice had to say about the latest developments.

He was surprised to find her in the kitchen, ingredients spread out on the butcher-block island. "Oh, good," she said when she saw Harry. "I'm starting to prepare dinner. You'll be eating here, I hope?"

"Sure," Harry said, then added, "Did you talk to a detective today?"

"I did. Did you?"

"They think it might not be an accident."

"Well, that's what they say. I don't know what to think except that either way, he's still gone, Harry."

"I know. But if someone had something to do with it—"

"Maybe someone was just trying to mug him, and your father fought back. Maybe it was still an accident."

"If someone was trying to mug him then it wasn't an accident."

"No, I know," Alice said, beginning to slice an onion. "The police will figure it out."

"Where did they talk with you?" Harry asked.

"Who? The police? They found me at Chrissie's house. I think you must have told them I was there. Chrissie wasn't surprised, either. We both thought that someone else might have been responsible."

"But who?" Harry asked, trying to keep his rising irritation at Alice's lackadaisical attitude from showing. "Did they ask you if you had any idea who might have been involved?"

She stopped slicing and looked directly at Harry. "They did ask me. I told them I had no idea." Her eyes held his, almost challenging him to call her a liar. He felt she was holding something back, but he didn't say anything. "It doesn't matter, though, Harry, does it?"

"What do you mean?"

"Your father's dead. He's not coming back."

"I know that. But that doesn't mean I don't want to know what happened to him." He had spoken too loudly, and Alice put her head down, staring at the perfect slivers of onion on the cutting board. When she looked up again, Harry could see bright spots of red on her cheeks.

"You're right. I'm sorry. It was a lot to take in this morning, and right now I just want to make dinner and not think about it. It's enough that he's not here, and now to know that . . . that . . ." She turned away, her shoulders beginning to shake, and Harry went and gave her a hug. She sobbed into his shoulder while he stroked her back.

"I'm sorry," Harry said. "Dinner tonight sounds great. What time?"

She pulled away from him, and with a look of almost childish joy on her face she said, "Seven o'clock? Maybe a drink at six thirty? Have you had lunch? I can make you a snack."

Harry accepted an apple, which Alice cut into slices and put on a plate for him, then he went up to his room.

He didn't come back down until six thirty. He unpacked some more things, looked through his father's books, picking out an Ed McBain novel he hadn't read before, one of the 87th Precinct books called *Sadie When She Died*. He didn't think he'd be able to read, but he tried anyway. He kept thinking about how it had felt to hold Alice in his arms while she cried, the way her body had shaken, and the feel of her skin against his. He tried to stop himself from imagining the hug suddenly becoming sexual, one of her hands sliding down into his jeans, her telling him that it would be the only thing that would help her grief. He started the book, reading a page without understanding any of the words, then started again, and managed to get into it. He'd read half before he realized it was nearly six. He showered and went downstairs. There was music playing—a David Bowie album, the one with "China Girl" on it—and something was cooking in the oven.

Alice had changed her clothes. She wore a long dress, in a fabric that looked hand dyed. It was scoop necked and cinched at the waist. "What can I do to help?" Harry asked her.

She'd been assembling a salad and she jumped a little when he spoke. "Nothing, nothing," she said. "No, actually, you can make us each a drink. Do you mind? A martini for me."

Harry went to the side table in the dining room, where the booze was kept. It was obvious that Alice wanted some semblance of a normal evening, despite the fact that her husband was dead. Harry decided that it might be a good thing. He'd read a book this afternoon, so maybe life just needed to go on. And if Alice relaxed enough, then maybe she'd open up to him. He still thought she was holding something back.

He found a large bottle of Plymouth gin, his father's favorite, and Harry, who'd watched his father drink his single, large martini every night at six on the dot, knew how he liked it. Shaken very cold, no vermouth, and served in a tumbler with three cocktail onions.

"How do you like your martini, Alice? Same as my father?"

"Yes, but with olives. And about half the size of the drinks your father used to make, please."

Harry made the drink, got a beer for himself, then asked again if she needed any help and was told to take a seat on one of the stools around the island. There were snacks out—baby carrots with hummus, and crackers with port wine cheese.

"Your friend Paul is so nice," Alice said, turning away from her salad, and sipping at her drink.

"It was great he came. He skipped graduation, you know?"

"No, I know. It's good to have a friend like that. They're easier to make when you're young, you know, than in real life. Let me tell you."

The timer made a tinny buzz, and Alice pulled a large baking dish from the oven. "It's chicken cordon bleu casserole," she said. "Have you had it before?"

"No, but it sounds delicious. My appetite, though—"

"Oh, I know. I haven't been able to eat a thing." She pinched the bridge of her nose. "Anyway, I just wanted to cook, just to have some semblance of . . . normality. Keep myself busy."

Alice turned back to the casserole, poking at it with a fork, while Harry finished his beer. There was a silence, and Harry tried to think of something to say that didn't revolve around his father's death. He remembered the stranger at his father's funeral, and said, "I saw this girl at the memorial service yesterday. She had dark hair down to her shoulders, and was wearing a grey dress. She didn't come through the receiving line."

Alice frowned. "Was it Ginny Wells?"

"No, I know Ginny. This girl was there alone, toward the back of the church. And she had a red purse with her. I just didn't know who she was, and it's strange, because I thought I actually saw her Friday when I arrived here. Out on the street."

"Out on our street?"

"Yeah. I think I saw her from my window upstairs."

"That's odd."

"That was why I was asking. I'm sure it's just one of Dad's customers."

"Most of his customers were old men like he was, but I don't know. I don't remember seeing her. Should we eat in the dining room?"

Alice let Harry bring the hot casserole and the salad to the long dining room table, constructed from renovated barn wood. There was a trivet waiting on the table, and he put down the casserole, large enough to feed an army. Places had been laid with wineglasses and two forks—one for the salad, Harry supposed.

"White wine okay?" Alice said, entering with an unopened bottle.

"Oh, sure."

"Can you open it up and pour us some, Harry, and then we'll finally eat."

Despite having lost his appetite again after that morning's visit from the detective, the food tasted good. It was clear that Alice was not in the mood to talk about serious matters. She asked Harry rapid-fire questions about his future plans, all of which he deflected. She picked at her food and took small sips of the wine, her pale cheeks becoming flushed.

"And what about a girlfriend?" she asked, after bringing him a butterscotch sundae from the kitchen. "Anyone special you left behind?" The words sounded rehearsed.

"No. Not really."

"Boyfriend, then?" Harry thought she was trying to sound casual, but she punctuated the question with an odd laugh, and her flushed cheeks had become almost mottled with red.

"No, I don't have one of those, either."

"I hope I didn't . . . I just wondered because I thought maybe Paul—"

"Yes, Paul is gay."

"I'm prying."

"No. It's fine."

They were silent for a moment. Harry asked, "Did my father wonder?"

"Wonder what?"

"Did he wonder if I was gay? Is that why you were asking?"

"If he did wonder, he never brought it up with me. And honestly, *you* knew him. More interested in what was happening in one of his books than what was happening around him. And he wouldn't have cared. You know that, too."

Harry finished his dessert. Alice was drinking the dregs of the wine, and rubbing her finger absentmindedly on the wooden table, her eyes slightly glazed over. In the light from the flickering candle, she looked not a whole lot older than Harry. Her skin, except for around her eyes, was entirely unlined. She tapped her finger on the table and shifted her gaze, catching Harry watching her.

"You look tired," he said. "Let me clean up, since you cooked the dinner."

She sat up straight. "No, I'll clean. I want to. You can help me bring the dishes into the kitchen, but that's it. I insist."

Harry did as he was told, leaving Alice cleaning dishes in the large double sink. He said good night and was turning to go when she reached out a hand. He took it and felt a slight tug, and she leaned over and kissed Harry on the cheek. Her skin was slightly damp from the steam of the hot water. "Thank God for you, Harry. I don't know what . . ." She didn't finish the sentence.

"Thanks again for dinner, Alice."

"And, Harry, one more thing. I talked with John today and he really needs you to help him out in the store tomorrow. Could you . . . Do you mind?"

Harry said he didn't mind.

Back in his room, he cracked a window and tried to get back into the Ed McBain book, but he kept thinking about Alice, her damp cheek on his as she kissed him good night. He also kept thinking about her refusal to discuss what had happened with her husband. Was it because she knew more than she was saying, or was she simply someone who didn't want to think about anything unpleasant? He realized how little he knew about her. Was it because he'd never asked, or was it because his father had never offered? And now here he was, living for a summer with this strange woman, and she was practically all the family he had left.

He fell asleep above the covers, and woke up cold. He got up and shut the window, then got under the comforter. He listened to the house, so much quieter than his dormitory, where he could lie in bed and listen to the muffled sounds of its other inhabitants. Here, all he could hear was the occasional sound that old houses made, the almost unnoticeable ticks and sighs. He didn't really like it, the enormity of the quiet, the way it made him feel more alone than he usually did. He felt the negative thoughts rolling toward him, and knew if he let them in he wouldn't be able to sleep for hours. He recited the Lord's Prayer to himself, even though the words had long been meaningless to him, but it was too late. The horrible dread—this now familiar feeling of insignificance—coursed through him. As always, it felt more like fear than sadness. He knew it would pass, and he concentrated on relaxing his body and focusing on his sensations, listening to the house.

After a while, he was beginning to fall asleep again when he heard the creak of the stairs, maybe Alice coming up to bed. Then he heard faint sounds just outside his door. He listened intently, sometimes hearing them and sometimes not. Moving slowly and quietly, he got out of the bed and took three steps along the worn rug to stand in front of the door. He turned his ear toward the door and listened. It was unmistakable. He could hear Alice breathing just on the other side of the door. He shifted his weight, and a floor plank made a squeaking sound. He listened to Alice's footsteps as she retreated quickly down the hall.

Chapter 11

Then

After Edith's death, Jake and Alice settled, quickly and naturally, into a new life together. Alice, as planned, enrolled in classes at the community college, commuting back and forth. She kept her own bedroom at the beachside condominium but spent every night in the master bedroom with Jake, even though there were so many reminders of her mother around.

"Should we pack some of these things away?" Jake asked one morning. He was holding up a half-empty perfume bottle while Alice toweled herself dry in the en suite bathroom.

"I don't mind," she said. "I mean, do what you want. You can throw that perfume away. I'll never use it."

Jake shrugged and put the perfume back on the shelf where he'd found it. He watched Alice dry herself.

"What are you looking at?" she said, smiling. She was bent over, drying her calves.

"You don't know what you have there, do you?"

"What I *have*?"

"What you are. What you look like. Right now, you are absolute perfection in every way. You know that? Youth and beauty."

"And I'm wasting it on you." She straightened up and smiled so that he knew she was kidding. Even so, she caught a brief look of concern cross his face, like a wisp of a cloud crossing the sun.

"I would never keep you here," he said.

"I will never leave."

He pulled her from the bathroom to the bed. As always, what they did together started out slow and reverent, Jake treating her with something akin to worship, and it always ended in an animalistic frenzy, Jake taking complete control. Later, Alice would find bruises on her skin that she didn't remember getting.

She was as happy as she had ever been. It was a month after the funeral.

When Alice was alone in the house, which was fairly often, she occasionally looked through her mother's things, sorting through her clothes and shoes, her books, and her few mementos. Some of it Alice wanted to keep, a decent cocktail dress for example, and the Gucci bag that Edith had bought from the fancy secondhand store in Portland. But most of it was junk, and Alice would fill grocery bags with clothes, bringing them down to the condo Dumpster out back and throwing them away, a little at a time. For some reason, she didn't want to do this in front of Jake, even though she thought it would please him. Still, he must have noticed that there were less and less of Edith's things around, and that more and more of Alice's things were making their way into the master bedroom.

At the bottom of the bedroom closet was an old liquor store box filled with some of the more personal effects that Edith had kept, including her Biddeford High School yearbook. Alice had seen pictures of Edith when she'd been young, but never pictures of her as a teenager. There she was in black and white, her hair in a bouffant, looking prettier than any other girl in her graduating class. Alice also found a picture of her in the cheerleaders' squad, and one candid of her at a car wash fund-raiser. She wore tight white shorts, and a cute sleeveless top, and she was smiling, not at the camera but at another girl. Both had soap bubbles in their hair, and Edith was holding a hose. Alice couldn't stop looking at the picture, partly because her mother looked so beautiful and so happy, but mostly because of how much she looked like Alice did now. How had she gone from that to what she became, that sloppy, drunken wreck drooling on a couch?

Alice looked through the rest of the box. There was a cheap stuffed monkey that looked like it had been won in a fair, a second-place ribbon beginning to fray, a Bible with a white cover and Edith's name inside of it, and two letters, typewritten on thin, oniony paper, that Alice was shocked to discover were from Gary Shurtleff, Alice's biological father. Both were postmarked from San Diego, California. Both were short and apologetic, although in the second one he called Edith an uppity bitch for not writing him back. Neither of the letters mentioned a baby, even though Alice assumed he'd written them after he'd gotten her mother pregnant. Edith had once told Alice that her father had scampered out west as soon as he found out he was going to be a father. Now Alice wondered if her father had ever known about her. She also wondered where he was now. In California still? Then she put the letters back in the box with the yearbook and the Bible and the few other sentimental items that Edith had kept, and brought the whole box down to the Dumpster and got rid of it.

The first winter after high school—the first winter that Alice was alone with Jake—was long and particularly cold. From January through most of March, the coast was pounded with an almost weekly storm, the temperatures rarely above freezing. Alice didn't mind. When she wasn't at college, where she'd enrolled in the business administration program with an accounting concentration, she was happy to be at home, warm in the condominium, with its views of the grey ocean, mirrored by its grey sky. The weather made her lazy and hungry. Every day she'd eat macaroni and cheese for lunch, then drowse on the couch, a textbook open across her lap, soap operas playing on the television in the background. She didn't really pay much attention to them, except for *General Hospital,* but she liked the background noise. Jake always called before he left the bank, and it would give her time to take a shower, put something nice on, apply a little makeup. On the first real warm day of spring—sometime in mid-May—she met Jake at the door wearing her favorite pair of shorts and a bikini top.

"Summer's here," she said.

He squeezed her skin just above the waistline of the shorts, and said, "I'm surprised you can still fit into those things."

That night, after Jake had fallen asleep, Alice slid from the bed naked and went to the bathroom and weighed herself. She *had* gained weight, ten pounds at least. Of course, since high school had ended, she no longer ran. She never really exercised at all, so it was no wonder she was getting fat.

The following day, after Jake had left for the bank, she put on a one-piece bathing suit, and walked down to the water's edge. There were a few shell collectors out, but they were dressed in jeans and sweatshirts. It was going to be a warm day but it wasn't warm yet, and the water numbed her anklebones. Still, she remembered what Jake had said, and she slid into the icy water, swimming hard for twenty minutes till her lungs burned and her arms were heavy and useless. Walking back across the firm sand to the condominium, Alice told herself that she would swim as long and as hard as she could every day. Her body would return to normal. She wondered how long it would be before Jake noticed that she was starting to lose weight. She imagined him looking at her one evening as she changed out of her clothes and into the lingerie she slept in, imagined him reaching out a hand to touch her flat stomach and telling her how amazing she looked.

It didn't happen exactly like that, but after swimming every day for a month, there was a night in June when Jake asked Alice to slowly strip for him in the living room while he sat on the couch and watched. It wasn't the first time he'd asked Alice to do this, but it was rare, and usually after they'd come back from a nice dinner out. That night in June they'd driven all the way into Portland to go to a new French restaurant that had recently opened. The food was good, but when Jake had ordered a bottle of wine for the table, the waitress had asked for Alice's ID. "Oh, I'm sorry," Jake had said. "I don't think you brought it, did you, Alice?" The waitress, slightly flushed, had suggested to Jake that "your daughter can order something else."

"We'll both have water," Jake said, his jaw tensing.

That night, after Alice was naked, Jake asked her to sit on his lap, and said, "You are perfect."

"Thank you," Alice said, thinking of the daily, lung-burning swims in the cold ocean.

"I have something to ask you," Jake said, his voice a little hoarse. "You don't have to do it if you don't want to, but I'd like to take some pictures of you, just as you are now."

"What do you mean, naked?"

"Just for me, I promise. No one else will ever see them."

"Why do you want pictures when you can see me whenever you want, just like this?" She leaned back a little on his lap, nearly slipping off, and opened her arms.

"Here's the thing, Alice, and I understand that you'll never grasp this at your age, but the way you look now, you are not going to look like this forever. And you'll want to preserve it somehow. In pictures. Trust me."

"Do you want to take the pictures right now?"

"No, not right now. I just wanted to make the suggestion. If we do it, I'd want to make everything perfect. The lighting. Everything."

"I don't mind, but I don't want anyone to see them except for you. Ever."

"I promise," he said. "They will just be for me. And for you. One day, you'll cherish them."

That weekend they took the pictures. Jake bought a fancy-looking camera for the occasion, plus a light meter, and Alice posed on the bed in the master bedroom. At first she was nervous, and self-conscious, but then it started to get fun and sexy. Jake was surprisingly quiet the whole time; Alice thought he might have specific ideas for how she should pose, but he didn't—he let her do what she wanted. When she thought they were done, however, Jake said, "Let's take some in your old bedroom."

"Why?" Alice asked.

"It's more you," Jake said. "In here it looks like you're playacting. In your room it will look more natural."

She did what he asked, feeling a little strange posing on her single bed underneath the Duran Duran poster, and the small shelf that held her cross-country trophies. But it made Jake happy, and after he put the camera away, they had sex in Alice's old room for the first time. Afterward, Alice asked, "Where will you get the pictures developed?"

"I have a friend at work with a darkroom, and he said I could use it."

"You won't show him?"

"No, of course not. Those pictures are just for us."

"I don't want anyone else to see me like this. Ever. Just you."

"One day you will. One day I'll be too old for you— I'm probably too old for you now—and then you'll find someone else, someone younger. I won't mind. It's natural."

Alice didn't say anything right away. It was not that she didn't know that Jake, almost fifty, was considered too old for her—although she thought about Rich-ard Gere in *Pretty Woman,* and how hot he was—but she had somehow never imagined him getting *older.* She imagined *herself* getting older, but him staying the same. "I don't know about that," she said.

"You will," Jake answered.

They lay on the bed a little longer. "Did you always want this?" she asked.

"Want what?"

"Want me. Want me more than you wanted my mom."

Alice heard the faintest clicking sound. It was Jake, tapping his teeth together, something he did when he was thinking. "Yes," he finally said.

That whole first winter after her mother died, Alice had successfully avoided any contact with the kids she'd known from Kennewick High. All except Gina, who wrote frequent letters from New York City that Alice would occasionally answer. At the end of her freshman year at NYU, Gina had, predictably, gotten a modeling contract that was going to keep her in the city through-out the summer. But in August, she came home for two weeks, and showed up unannounced at Alice's house on a Thursday afternoon.

"I knew you wouldn't answer my calls, so I just

thought I'd come over." She held out a bottle of Boone's Farm Strawberry Hill wine.

Alice suggested they go to the beach, but Gina said it was too hot. They ended up drinking the wine in the living room, and eating Triscuits with port wine cheese. Gina was skinnier, and prettier, than ever. She'd lightened her hair, and it had been styled so that it lifted off her forehead, then cascaded down her back. Her dark, thick eyebrows had been shaped, and her nails were painted a neon orange.

"Tell me about modeling," Alice said.

"You want to hear the good parts, or the sordid details?"

"What do you think?"

Gina told a few stories. The first time she tried cocaine ("It made me act like my little sister, or like Stephanie Richmond from cross-country, remember her?"), a slew of parties, endless proposals from older men, one of whom offered her ten thousand dollars to sleep with his wife while he watched. "They're so gross," she said. "The older they are, the grosser they are."

"Do you have a boyfriend?" Alice asked, hoping to change the subject from older men. Gina hadn't mentioned Jake yet, but she knew she would. She'd alluded several times in her letters over the winter that she thought it was strange Alice was still living with him, that she thought Alice should move to New York City and stay with her for a while. It was only a matter of time till she brought it up. And it was only a matter of time till Jake came home. He was always home by five, and sometimes earlier, since the bank closed its doors at four.

"Let's go swimming," Alice said, after Gina told her she didn't have a boyfriend in New York.

"I don't have a suit," Gina said.

"Borrow one of mine."

"Okay. I guess."

Alice went to go upstairs, and Gina got up to follow. Alice suddenly realized that it might be obvious to Gina she was sharing a bedroom with Jake. Half her clothes were now in his bedroom, and the bed in her old room hadn't been slept in in months.

"I'll bring you down some suits to try," Alice said, bolting up the stairs.

"Sure," Gina said, shrugging.

Alice changed into her favorite bikini upstairs, and brought down a few extras for Gina to try. She was shocked when Gina stripped down right in the living room. Gina must have read Alice's face because she said, "Sorry. Model life. I have zero modesty."

"That's okay."

Gina picked a black bikini that had white lace trim. The bottom fit fine, but the top was too big for her flat chest. Alice got her a T-shirt to wear over the suit, and together they walked across the softened asphalt of the parking lot and the scalding sand to where the waves were breaking against the shore.

"It's cold," Gina squealed as they waded in.

"You'll get used to it," Alice said, jumping as a wave rolled up against her. She dove under the water, and came up just as Gina tentatively lowered herself into the froth. They swam out together past the breaking waves, then both lay back, spreading out their arms, riding the swells. Gina's white T-shirt billowed around her.

"Okay, this is nice now," Gina said. "Maine's not so bad."

"Better than New York?"

"God, no. I'll come back and visit here, in the summer, but other than that . . . no thanks."

Alice didn't immediately say anything, and Gina said, "Sorry, that was a little harsh. I'm just talking about for me, of course."

They rode together up a high swell, then slid down its backside. Alice's mouth tasted salty. "So you're done trying to get me to move to the city?"

"How will you know you don't like it if you don't try? We'd have so much fun, Al. I mean it. I'd introduce you to my manager, and I bet you could get some modeling work yourself, probably not runway stuff because of your size, but I bet there'd be something. I mean, look at how gorgeous you are."

Alice laughed. "I'll think about it," she said, just to shut Gina up. What she really wanted to say was, *Why would I go somewhere where everyone is looking for a better life, when I've already found it? I have the fairy tale ending already.*

"Is that your stepdad?" Gina suddenly said. She was shielding her eyes with her hand and looking toward shore. Alice did the same thing. Jake was there, just beyond the waterline, looking out toward the swimmers. He still wore his suit—the light blue linen one.

Alice almost denied it, but it was obviously him. Instead, she waved to catch his attention, and said, "Yeah. There's Jake."

"God, you are sleeping with him, aren't you?" Gina said, as they both bobbed in the water, watching him wave back at them.

Chapter 12

Now

You think he had any enemies? Disgruntled customers?" Harry asked John. They were taking a coffee break after a morning spent packaging orders that had come in through the Internet.

John finished his sip of coffee, holding the chipped mug in both hands. He thought for a moment. "Enemies, no. Disgruntled customers, not really, either. If someone was upset with the books we sent them, we'd always give a refund. Besides, even if we didn't . . ." He made a face that suggested a disgruntled rare-book collector was not a likely murder suspect.

"And there was nothing strange about that day?"

"Not that I can remember. It was business as usual, and he left a little early, but just because he wanted to get a walk in before it got dark. He did that a lot of days. Do they think this was a premeditated thing?" His cataract-clouded eyes showed concern, as they had ever since Harry had told him what he'd learned the previous day.

"No, I don't think they have any guesses, except that he was hit on the head."

"Just hooligans, maybe," John said, as though the hooligan problem in Kennewick was well documented. Then he said, "What's Alice say?"

"Nothing. She doesn't really want to talk about it."

John tapped his fingers together, thinking. Harry looked at his large, strong hands and concluded, not for the first time, that John looked more like a retired farmhand than a retired financial advisor. He was almost completely bald, and his pate was speckled with sun damage. He was wearing a dark pin-striped suit and a pink tie, knotted tightly at his neck. He always wore suits, always a little too big for him, remnants from his years in business. "I wouldn't worry about it, Harry," he said at last. "She's probably in shock, and not wanting to process it yet. Plus, she has to be wondering about the rest of her life. My sweetheart died quite young, and afterward I didn't think I'd ever know a moment of happiness again. And then one day, I felt a little better, and then over time I became myself again. It always happens that way. Otherwise, no one would keep going. Sorry, Harry, didn't mean to . . ." John rubbed at his white mustache, the tremor in his arm more noticeable than usual. Harry wondered if he had Parkinson's, or if he was just old, his muscles weakening.

"That's okay, John."

"Police will find whoever had to do with it. They have ways. Back to work, I think."

Harry watched as John stood up, then lowered himself to one knee by one of many unopened packages, and slit the tape with a box cutter. Lew, the cat, sidled up and rubbed against John's thigh. Harry, tired from that morning's work, wanted to sit awhile longer and finish his coffee. How old was John? He had to be in his midseventies, at least, possibly closer to eighty.

Harry remembered the story his father had told him, how John had shown up shortly after he'd opened the new store, asking if he could volunteer for a few hours per week, maybe straighten the shelves, or deal with customers. He was a retiree, with time on his hands, and Bill had reluctantly agreed to let him come in for a few hours each week. The next day, John had shown up at opening time, and stayed until Bill sent him home sometime in the afternoon. It continued like that, John learning every facet of the business, until Bill finally insisted on paying him. They haggled and settled on the minimum wage. After that, John was always at the store, always wearing a suit and tie; he'd made himself indispensable.

Harry finished his coffee and went to help stack the new books on one of the two card tables in the store's back room. There were about thirty of these unopened boxes, all containing books from one estate sale that Bill had purchased sight unseen, making an offer over the phone after hearing that the man who had died had collected hardcover Wodehouse novels. Harry's father had started book scouting when he was still an undergraduate at Columbia, studying English literature and hoping to become a writer. One of his professors had gotten him into it, sending him upstate to garage and rummage sales the summer before his senior year. He taught him what to look for, and how to negotiate. One of the lessons was to never bicker over single volumes at estate sales. If there was something in the shelves that was worth money, then you would always make a fast offer to buy *all* the books. The children of the deceased were almost always thrilled and relieved, and you never knew what other gems might appear.

Bill had fallen in love with book scouting—"treasure

hunting for the unadventurous," he called it—and for ten years after college made a meager living at it, sticking to the East Coast, and selling his finds at the then-myriad selection of used bookstores in the city. By the time he was thirty he could barely navigate his single-bedroom Greenwich Village apartment because of the stacks of books he'd accumulated. He got a loan at a bank and opened Ackerson's Rare Books. His first employee was a shy Barnard College grad named Emily Vetchinsky. They married three months after he hired her, and nine months after that Harry was born.

"Junk, mostly, so far," John said, slitting open another box and peering at its contents.

"How can you tell?" Harry asked.

"You learn, over time." He was holding an interesting-looking hardcover edition of *Jaws*, with a black cover, and the image of a white, stylized shark. He put that one to the side. "Although I double-check myself, take a look at prices on the Web. Your father didn't need to do that."

The bell sounded, indicating that someone had entered the store. "Do you mind seeing if someone needs help?" John asked, and Harry went out front, stood behind the cash register. The customer was an elderly woman, dressed in a long winter coat and a wooly hat even though it was nearly seventy degrees outside.

"Can I help you with anything?" Harry asked, and she looked up, startled.

"Oh, I didn't see you there. I've been here before, of course, but I've forgotten . . . Can you tell me where the mystery stories are?"

Harry stepped out from behind the counter and brought the woman to the mystery section. It was, except for plain fiction, the largest in the store. Crime had been his father's favorite genre, both to read and to collect. He'd had a sizable personal collection of first editions, plus what he claimed might be the only entire collection of "mapbacks"—midcentury paperbacks issued by Dell, almost all crime novels, each with an illustrated map on its back cover. It had been his pride and joy. "They're not worth a lot of money," he told Harry once, "but the day I got the final one in the series was one of my top, top days. Silly, I know."

"Oh, so many," said the woman looking at the mystery shelves.

"There are more in the back," Harry said. "If you're interested in collectibles and first editions."

"I don't think so. What I like is a murder story but I *don't* like violence."

Harry was about to go get John for a recommendation, but decided he could handle this himself. He was not a fanatic like his father had been, but Harry did read a lot. He found three books for the woman—two by Jacqueline Winspear based on their covers alone, and an M. C. Beaton that she thought she hadn't read yet. He brought the books back to the register and rang up the sale himself, relieved that she was paying in cash so he wouldn't have to use the credit card reader. Afterward, he told John he'd just managed his first customer interaction. John put one of his large hands on Harry's shoulder. "Thank you, Harry. Honestly, I don't know what I'd do right now without you."

The words made Harry feel wanted but were also discomfiting. How long would he be expected to help out? Was there a future plan for the store now that Bill had died? He assumed Alice now owned it, including all its stock. She'd occasionally worked in the store, although Harry didn't know how much she actually knew, or cared, about the business.

It was clear that John had learned an enormous amount from Bill, but he was just an employee—and how much longer could he expect to work at his age? Was Harry being groomed to take over forever? The thought knotted his stomach, briefly. *This is my life now.* Then Harry told himself to calm down. His father had died less than a week ago, and there was plenty of time to figure everything out. He found his own cutter and began opening boxes.

Toward the end of the day, the bell sounded, the front door opening to a customer for just the fourth time that day. As John had explained, the store did 90 percent of its business online and very little from the actual physical store. Harry went to his post at the cash register. The customer was the woman from the funeral, with the short, dark hair. She was wearing the headband again. Harry felt his cheeks flush at the sight of her. She spotted him and walked right over, almost too purposefully.

"Hello," she said.

"Hi."

"I was wondering if you're hiring. I know there isn't a sign out front, but I thought I'd check, anyway. I just moved here, and I love books, and so I thought . . ."

Her cheeks were flushed, as well. She was nervous, and the words she'd just said sounded rushed and unnatural.

"Didn't I see you, on Sunday, at—"

"Oh, that," she said. "Yeah, I was at the funeral. I saw you, too. You must be—"

"I'm his son."

"Right, his son. I'm very sorry for your loss."

"You knew my father?"

She looked startled. "Oh, no. I didn't. It's going to sound strange, but I just arrived here, and I'd heard of him. I've actually been to the Ackerson's in New York, and I was going to check and see if there was a potential job up here, and then, of course, I heard what had happened. So I went to the funeral. It was a weird thing to do, I know."

"No, no," Harry said. "Funerals are public, right? They're not just for people who knew the person who died."

"No, really, they kind of are." She smiled, some of her nervousness dissipating.

"I guess so," Harry said, smiling back. "Don't worry about it. What's your name?"

"It's Grace. And you?"

She reached a hand over the counter, and Harry took it, telling her his name. Her hand felt small in his, her fingertips cold. Harry knew she was lying to him, or misleading him, about her reasons for going to the funeral, about her reasons for coming to the store. Had she known his father? And if so, then why was she hiding it?

"Why'd you move up here?" Harry asked.

"I was sick of city life, and I'd been here before, the Maine coast, anyway, so I decided to be impulsive."

She laughed, more like a nervous punctuation mark. Her hair was auburn, bordering on black, and her eyes were blue with a little bit of green in them. She had a small nose that turned up a little at the end, and a narrow mouth with a thin top lip and a plump lower one. She had thick, dark eyebrows and faint freckles on her forehead, and Harry figured she could be anywhere from his age to somewhere in her early thirties.

"You just up and moved here without having a job?" Harry said, and immediately regretted how the question sounded.

"I did."

"Where are you living?"

"Just up the hill past the inn. You know that large brick house with the weedy front yard? I'm in there. It's from Airbnb, just a room, my own bedroom, but it's actually bigger than the apartment I rented in New York. What about you? Are you working here now, in the store?"

"I'm helping out. Probably for the summer, then I don't know. Maybe move to New York City?"

"Don't do it." She laughed.

"Okay."

Grace's cheeks darkened. She pulled at an unpierced earlobe. "No jobs here, then?"

"Oh, right. I don't know. It's probably too soon to

make decisions about what's going to happen here, but I can find out and let you know."

"Okay. That would be good. Kennewick Inn's looking for a hostess, but I thought I'd try here first."

"Should I call you?"

"Sure," she said, and Harry handed her a pen. She turned over an Ackerson's bookmark and wrote her phone number. "Thank you. I knew it was a long shot, and I don't expect anything, so—"

"I'll find out and let you know."

"Okay. I'm going to browse around a little."

"You should."

She wandered off into an aisle where Harry couldn't see her. It was such a strange interaction that for a moment Harry stood, just going over the conversation in his mind. Something she had said had struck him as particularly odd. For a moment, he couldn't place it but then it came to him. She'd asked, "Are you working here now, in the store?" How had she known he'd just started working there? Then Harry remembered the funeral, the minister saying something about how proud Bill was of his son, who had recently graduated from college. That must have been it.

John came out from the back room. "Just cracked the last box," he said. "Finally found the Wodehouse editions. There are some firsts. American ones, but still, not an entire loss."

Harry's weariness must have shown on his face, because John said, "Go home. You've done more than enough here today."

The bell sounded as the door opened. It was Grace leaving.

"Did you see the woman I was talking with?" Harry asked.

"When? Just now?"

"Yeah. She just left."

"No. Why?"

Harry told John how she'd been looking for work. He found himself hoping John would say that an extra hire would be good for the store, but he just shook his head. "I don't think so, do you? We can handle it, especially when Alice decides she wants to come back in and help."

Harry walked slowly home from the store. He wasn't sure he was up for another intimate dinner with Alice, and was relieved to see an unfamiliar car—a dark blue Jetta—parked next to his Civic in the driveway. The license plate read, CSHORE7. He thought maybe it was Alice's friend Chrissie, who almost certainly would have a vanity plate. Harry went up to the front door, which was decorated with stained glass, and was about to enter when he peered, instead, through the one unstained piece of glass in the design. He could see partially into the kitchen, where an older woman was standing, her back to the door, but Harry could see that she was still wearing a raincoat and had a bright red scarf wrapped around her head. She was in profile, her lips moving as though she was talking rapidly. She wasn't immediately recognizable. Harry stood for a moment, frozen on the front stoop, trying to decide if it was possible to enter the house and go straight up to his room. Maybe if he opened the door as quietly as possible. But, no, the strange woman was only twenty feet away in the kitchen. Harry would have to be introduced.

Instead of entering the house, Harry went around to the backyard, where there was an old, dilapidated barn on the property that had been one of the reasons Bill had originally been interested in the house. It was a small barn, unpainted, the wood weathered to the point where there were inch-wide cracks between the planks, but the roof was solid. Bill's plan had been to restore it completely and eventually use it as storage for even more books. That had never happened, of course. Bill's true passion had been the acquisition of books. Finding places to put them was a chore that he only got around to out of desperation.

The barn's wide front doors were open, and Harry walked across the muddy yard and stepped inside, letting his eyes adjust to the dark, cool interior. He could hear the flutter of starlings high up in the rafters. In one corner was an old lathe, left by the previous residents. Harry remembered his father taking a look at it, telling him that maybe he'd take up furniture making and that way he could make his own shelves. "Can you imagine this place filled with books?" he'd said.

But except for the lathe, plus an assortment of lawn furniture and old dining room chairs, the barn was empty. Harry sneezed. The air in the barn, even with the wide doors flung open, was dusty and still, the floors pocked with bird shit. He wanted to get out of there, but instead of exiting the way he had come, he traversed the barn and stepped through the regular-sized back door.

Not ready to go back to the house, Harry sat on the doorjamb. There was a view out over the marsh that abutted the property. Harry felt a sudden and revolting sense of pure grief. It swept through him like an attack of nausea, an absolute knowledge that he was all alone and life was meaningless and devoid of joy. His heart fluttered, and for a moment Harry wondered if he was dying, as though his sudden awareness was bringing on some kind of attack. But then he felt a prick on his arm, and rubbed at it. He looked down and saw that he'd killed a mosquito, leaving behind a smear of blood.

His heart slowed, the terrible thoughts dissipating as rapidly as they had come. Still, he remembered a very stoned conversation he'd had in his dorm room a few months ago. He was with a junior named Tyler whom Harry had met through the cinema club. They'd been listening to a Sparklehorse album, and Tyler had suddenly started to talk about how short our time on the planet was, and how, in the blink of an eye, we would be dead, and everyone who ever knew us would be dead, and that was it. He'd spoken as though he was the first person ever to have had, or voiced, those thoughts. Fortunately, Paul had dropped by, changed the music to a Henry Mancini compilation, and forced Tyler to drink a cocktail. Harry thought of that conversation now, thought of how the deaths of both of his parents had erased a whole portion of his own life that existed solely as their memories. He was half gone, already, more than half gone.

The queasiness and fear returning, Harry made himself stand up. He walked back through the barn and to the front of the house. The car was still there, but the woman he'd seen in the kitchen was now standing on the front stoop, framed in the doorway, saying good-bye to Alice.

"Harry, this is Viv. I don't know if you two have met."

The woman turned to Harry, her dark eyes searching his face. She was very thin, her cheeks hollowed out, and suddenly the head scarf made sense. She must be sick with cancer, going through chemotherapy.

"I'm sorry about your father, Harry," she said, her voice an unsurprising rasp. "I'm afraid I missed the funeral; I've been away."

"That's okay," Harry said, then added, "Thank you." His voice sounded shaky in his own head, probably because of the intense way she was looking at him. He willed himself to not look down at the ground.

"Thank you for coming," Alice said, gently putting a hand on the small of the woman's back, and walking her to the car. The woman moved fast, as though to escape Alice's touch, and got into the car without saying anything else.

Harry stepped into the house and there was the smell of cooking. The table was set for two again.

Chapter 13

Then

Alice didn't see Gina again that summer, not after that time they went swimming. She had denied that she was sleeping with Jake, of course, but it was painfully clear that Gina didn't believe her, especially when, after they'd come in from the water, Jake had acted so strange, insisting on wrapping Alice's towel around her. He'd also stared a little too long at Gina, barely covered by Alice's bikini bottoms and the T-shirt plastered to her chest.

That fall, Jake and Alice drove to Canada, visiting Montreal and Quebec City. "Almost as good as France," Jake said. "And a lot less expensive." It was one of the few times that Jake ever mentioned money. Alice had always assumed that because Jake worked in a bank and wore nice suits, and their condo had a view of the water, they were rich and that money would never be a problem. It didn't matter. Montreal was the most sophisticated place Alice had ever been to. They walked the city in the daytime, stopping into shops, and went to the best restaurants at night. Quebec City was even better, almost magical. They stayed at Le Château Frontenac, more of a castle, really, than a hotel. They ordered wine everywhere they went, and no one ever questioned Alice's age. Maybe some of the hotel staff and waitresses looked at them together and thought they were father and daughter, but no one ever said anything about it. On the final night of their trip, on the boardwalk in Quebec City, Jake put his arm around Alice's shoulders as they walked, something he'd never done before. "Let's come back here next year," Alice said. "This is better than France."

"Don't you want to visit other cities? You haven't been to New York yet, have you?"

"Ugh. No thanks," Alice said, thinking of Gina, and what it would be like to run into her if she was with Jake. She still couldn't get the image of Jake, and the way he'd looked at Gina on the beach, out of her mind.

Over the winter, Alice got a part-time job at a drugstore in Kennewick Center. Jake had brought it up, asking Alice if she was bored just taking classes and spending time at home. "No, not really," she said.

"It doesn't bother you that you spend so little time with other people?"

Alice frowned and thought about it. "I spend time with professors, and I talk with other students, but you know I'd rather be here with you."

"I know, I was just . . ." He trailed off.

"Everything okay?"

"Everything's great. I just wanted to make sure that everything is great with you as well. Just wanted to make sure you didn't think you were missing out on things other girls your age do. Like go to parties. And have jobs."

"I *definitely* don't miss going to parties. That's for sure. I hadn't really thought about a job. Do you think I should get one?"

"I think you should if you want to. You don't need to, obviously, but I had the thought. They're hiring at Blethen's Apothecary."

She'd applied and been hired at the end of her interview by a manager not a whole lot older than she was, a stutterer named Jeff who was almost skeletally thin. She'd thought she'd hate the job, especially after Jeff informed her that treating customers with respect was her number one priority, but she turned out to love it, even the menial tasks, like restocking the shelves, making sure that everything along the row was displayed neatly and perfectly. She liked this part of the job actually better than running the cash register, but she didn't even mind that. Her favorite part was cashing out at the end of her shift, adding up the register contents against the receipts, making sure it balanced. She didn't mind dealing with the customers, but she didn't like when people recognized her from high school, either old classmates or past teachers. They always asked her what she was doing now, and she'd say that she was taking classes at MCC, and sometimes, though not often, they'd ask her where she was living, and she would simply say that she was still at home. A couple of times, she saw the memory that her mother had died pass across their features. They would blush, or avert their eyes, not knowing what to say. It was awkward, but it didn't last, and most of the time she never saw them again.

That was not the case with Mrs. Bergeron, Gina's mother, who came in frequently and always sought out Alice, asking her how she was doing, and telling her all about Gina as though the two of them were still best friends. "She had to drop out of NYU because she just couldn't keep up with her courses and her modeling schedule at the same time. My husband said that she should have dropped some of her modeling work, but I said, well, she can always go back to school and finish, and she won't always be able to be a model. I mean, strike while the going is good, right?" She reminded Alice so much of Gina, the way her words would speed up while she was talking, ending her sentences by taking a deep breath.

Once, when Alice was working in the deodorant and bodywash aisle, Mrs. Bergeron, visibly elated, approached her holding the latest copy of *Cosmopolitan*.

"You're not going to believe this, Alice," she said, thumbing the issue open to an ad for Jordache, and there was Gina, in high-cut shorts and long socks with two other girls in what was supposed to be a high school cafeteria. The ad was selling a new line of knitted socks, and Mrs. Bergeron said, "She also did a session for jeans, but doesn't know if they're going to use those pictures yet. Can you believe it?"

Alice *did* believe it—she'd always known Gina was going to be a star—but shook her head at Mrs. Bergeron and said, "Amazing."

"I know, right? I might have to buy every last copy."

Gina's mother ended up buying most of the copies, but not quite all of them, and Alice took one home with her, first reading the magazine cover to cover while

Jake watched a hockey game, then later, cutting out the ad, and hiding it in the desk in her old bedroom. She kept wondering if Gina was happy, and if she had a nice boyfriend now that she was a model. It was a possibility, but she doubted it. Gina looked very skinny in the ad, and Alice wondered what kinds of drugs she was taking.

Over the following year, Gina went from appearing in the Jordache socks ad with two other models to appearing in a denim campaign all by herself, wearing skintight jeans and an unbuttoned silk blouse. Mrs. Bergeron informed Alice that Gina had started to book runway shows, and magazine layouts, and was going by the professional name of simply Bijou. "You should visit her, Alice," she would say. "She'd love that."

"I'm pretty busy up here," Alice would reply.

"I'm sure they'd let you take a few days off from work, and your stepfather . . . he wouldn't care if you spent some time in New York, would he?"

Whenever Mrs. Bergeron mentioned Jake—always calling him "your stepfather"—Alice could hear the disdain in her voice. It was obvious that Gina had told her mother that she thought Alice was sexually involved with Jake, and that her mother disapproved. "I have school, too," Alice said.

"Not in the summer you don't. Look, if it's money,

I'd be happy to buy you a train ticket to go down. Tell the truth, you'd be doing me and Don a favor, just to have you check on her. She could use a friend from home, I'm sure."

"I'll think about it," Alice always said, the words that would end the conversation.

In truth, Mrs. Bergeron's pleas to Alice to visit her daughter in New York made Alice feel good. It was clear that something was wrong, that the modeling life wasn't all nice restaurants, and handsome men, and glittering New York parties. Was Gina falling apart? Alice began to imagine visiting her, finding her drug addicted and abused in some grungy loft apartment downtown like the ones in *Desperately Seeking Susan*. Gina would be miserable, track marks up and down her arms, constantly crying. This became one of Alice's favorite stories to tell herself, so much so that she began to seriously consider visiting Gina in New York, to make it actually happen.

She never went, but in early fall, before the beginning of her junior year at college, Mrs. Bergeron came into the drugstore to tell Alice that Gina was coming home for a few weeks, that she was simply exhausted from all the work and needed a break. "You'll come over some night, won't you, Alice?"

"I'll think about it," she said.

"Okay," Mrs. Bergeron said. "But I'm going to keep asking, whether you like it or not." She waved a finger at Alice but she was smiling, an impossibly wide, toothy grin that Gina had inherited. She did keep asking, and finally Alice relented, a Friday night in late September, because both Mrs. Bergeron and Gina showed up at the drugstore and begged her to come over for dinner that night.

"Do you have plans?" Gina asked. "If you have plans, then . . ."

Alice did have plans, but only with Jake. It was a Friday night, which meant he would return home with flowers or a nice bottle of wine. Sometimes he would stop at the new video store that had opened up over in York and pick out a movie to watch. But, even so, he'd probably be okay with Alice going to dinner at the Bergerons'. Well, not okay, exactly, but he'd be stoic about it. Alice just wanted to go in order to get it over with. If she didn't go tonight, they would keep pestering her. "Okay, I'll come tonight," she said.

"Yay," both Gina and her mother said at the same time.

"God, it's sloppy joes tonight, but they're homemade, at least," Mrs. Bergeron said.

"My favorite," Gina said, stretching out the vowels.

That night Jake came back from the bank with a

large bottle of white zinfandel but no flowers and no movie. He seemed tired, and when Alice told him she was thinking of going over to the Bergerons' for dinner he made a face but didn't say anything negative. Right before she left, however, he said to her: "You won't tell them anything, will you? About us?"

"I won't, but don't you think . . . I mean, it's been two years, and I'm a grown woman now."

"Trust me, Alice, they won't understand. They'll think that I'm taking advantage of you. We live in America. We were founded by Puritans. In other countries, they would totally understand what was going on between us, but not here."

"I won't tell them anything. I wouldn't have, anyway. It's none of their business."

Alice drove Jake's car across town, listening to the tape he'd left in the deck. It was *Genesis,* Phil Collins singing the word *Mama* over and over again. She got tired of it, and sped ahead to "That's All." After she pulled into the Bergerons' driveway, she listened to the rest of the song, the sky a deep, dusky blue over the Bergerons' house, its first floor brick and its second story painted yellow, the windows with black shutters. The front yard was brown from the summer drought, and with a scattering of orange pine needles. As the song finished, Alice wondered if tonight was the beginning of the story of Gina's fall from grace. What had Gina's mother said, that she was "exhausted"? Alice shut the car off.

Gina didn't seem exhausted during dinner. If anything, she seemed a little hyper, constantly interrupting anything anyone else was saying to get her own word in, pushing her food around the plate, cutting her sloppy joe into bite-sized pieces with her fork and knife, something the rest of the family made fun of her for.

"You want chopsticks for that, G?" her father asked. "She eats sushi now," he said to Alice.

"Everyone eats sushi, Dad," Gina said.

"Not in Maine. We cook our fish up here."

"High five," Gina's youngest sister said and slapped Mr. Bergeron's palm.

Alice kept mostly silent during the meal, except when she was asked direct questions, either about her job at the drugstore or the courses she was taking at MCC. No one asked her about Jake, and what he was up to, at least not at the dinner table. She felt strange during dinner, not uncomfortable exactly, but like an alien that had been dropped into a typical American family, full of inside jokes and overlapping conversation. It was different, so much louder, than what she was used to with Jake, just the two of them, everything perfect and civilized. A small part of her was jealous, only because there

was something relaxing about not always being the center of attention, not always having eyes on you, but then
Alice looked at Gina, the way her eyes were darting
between members of her family, her fingers tugging on
one of her earlobes till it had turned an angry red, and
she thought: *No, family life is messy, and unpredictable.
Who would want that?*

After dinner, when the two youngest girls were tasked
with clearing the table, Alice caught Gina giving her
mother a quick glance, then saying, awkwardly, "New
rule: the grown women get the night off cleaning."

"New rule?" Mr. Bergeron said.

Gina was standing. "Come on, Alice, let's go outside
a minute."

"Gotta get her fix," said Gina's younger sister, pan-
tomiming taking a puff of a cigarette.

"I'll come, too," said Mrs. Bergeron, as Alice rose
from the table, suddenly nervous.

It was balmy outside for September, the dark sky
filled with stars. Gina did light up a cigarette before the
back screen door slammed shut, then took a seat on one
of the patio chairs. She offered the pack to Alice, who
turned it down.

"Smart girl," said Mrs. Bergeron, leaning against
the outdoor table.

Alice sat next to Gina on the very edge of a chair.

She said how much she'd enjoyed dinner, then immediately asked about Gina's oldest brother, Howie, who hadn't been there that night. She just wanted to keep asking questions to avoid the discussion that she felt was coming. Mrs. Bergeron said that Howie was doing the backpack thing in Europe, and she wondered if he'd ever return. While she spoke, Alice felt Gina's eyes on her. She turned toward her just as she was snuffing the butt of her cigarette out against the bottom of her sandal.

"You should—" Alice began, but Gina interrupted her.

"Alice, I want to talk about Jake."

"So do I," said Mrs. Bergeron.

"Okay," said Alice. She could feel the blood rushing into her face, her skin heating up.

"We both think it's really strange that you're still living with him," Gina said, removing another cigarette from her pack of Parliaments. "I know that he's your stepdad, but it's not like he was with your mom for a really long time. You've lived with him longer than he lived with your mother."

"Where else am I supposed to go?" Alice said, anger causing her chest to tighten, and her words to come out sounding slightly pinched. "I don't have a family. He pays for my classes, Gina."

"We're not judging you, honey," Mrs. Bergeron said. "We're worried that Jake is taking advantage of you, and if he is, we want you to know that you have options."

"What do you mean?"

Gina said, "You remember Maddy, right? She said she saw you at a restaurant in Portland with Jake and that you were acting like a couple."

"What does she mean we were acting like a couple?"

"That doesn't matter," Mrs. Bergeron said. "What we want to know is that you are comfortable with whatever situation you're in. That's all. If you tell us that you and Jake are happy together, I mean, who are we—"

"I don't care if you are happy together," Gina said, shouting a little. "It's gross, Alice. You're a young, beautiful girl, and you let that fucking creep have his way with you."

"Gina . . ." said Mrs. Bergeron.

Alice stood up. She felt tears pricking at her eyes, and really didn't want to cry. She quickly scanned the fenced backyard, like a cat looking for an exit, then began to walk toward the latched door that led onto the driveway. Gina ran after her.

"Sorry, Alice, come back. We just want to talk with you."

Alice kept walking, not trusting her voice. When she reached the door, Gina grabbed her shoulder. Alice, without thinking, spun and grabbed Gina's hand, pulling it to her mouth and biting down at the base of Gina's thumb. Gina screamed and yanked her hand back. For a moment, they both stood there, Gina grasping her hand, and Alice frozen, shocked that she'd actually bitten Gina. Mrs. Bergeron had jumped up after hearing Gina scream, and was coming toward them, saying, "What is it? What happened?" Alice pushed through the door and ran to the car. She could taste Gina's blood in her mouth.

When she got back home, Jake was still up, glassy-eyed, watching television, a snifter with brandy on one of his knees. "How was it?" he asked.

"Fine," Alice said.

"What did they serve?"

"Sloppy joes," she said, and Jake smiled. "It was kind of a scene, honestly, everyone talking over everyone else. I missed being here."

"Well, you're here now," Jake said, adjusting the chair so that he could get out of it comfortably, almost spilling his drink. "Let's get into bed."

Alice went up the stairs, feeling good about controlling her feelings in front of Jake. During the drive back in the car, she told herself that she'd barely even bitten Gina, that her teeth had only just broken the skin, and that it had been Gina's fault anyway. *Gina* was the one who'd grabbed her violently, and she had just been trying to get away. It was nothing. And then she told herself that the conversation in the backyard hadn't actually happened, and that the night was merely annoying. If she believed that, it kept the anger she felt toward Gina from rising up in her and making her want to scream. She brushed her teeth, then changed into pajama bottoms and a threadbare T-shirt.

Under the covers, she carefully composed her body, shut her eyes, and began to try to relax. *It had been a nice dinner at Gina's family's house. Nothing more.* But the words she'd tried to erase kept coming back. Gina calling Jake "that fucking creep." Mrs. Bergeron's condescending tone, talking to Alice like she was some little girl. And then she remembered the feeling when she'd bitten down on Gina's hand. Her body was so tight that it was beginning to tremble. While Jake was applying his face cream in the bathroom, Alice slid out from the covers and got off the bed. "Want anything from downstairs?" she asked Jake, and he shook his head.

In the kitchen she made herself a White Russian, heavy on the vodka, and told herself to drink it slowly, to not be like her mother. She drank half of it in short, small sips, and began to feel better. Of course they'd be critical. They didn't know what she had with

Jake. Or maybe they did know, and they were just jealous. That made a lot more sense. As she was making herself a second drink, she heard a very light tapping and thought for a moment that Jake was coming down the stairs. She stepped out into the living room. There was the tapping sound again, and she realized someone was knocking on the door. She went and peered through the eyehole. It was Gina.

Chapter 14

Now

Every time the front doorbell rang at the store the following day, Harry thought it might be Grace, returning to find out more about a possible job. He didn't really believe she'd return—why would she when he'd told her he would call?—but he found himself disappointed, anyway. He'd been obsessing over their conversation the previous afternoon, telling himself that maybe she was just what she said she was—new in town, and looking for a job. But she wasn't, was she? She had obviously come in for some purpose other than a job. Why else would she have been at the funeral, and walking past the house on his first night back in Maine?

But each time the bell rang, it was either a customer—usually coming to offer condolences instead of buying a book—or Alice, who stopped by at lunchtime to bring chicken sandwiches and then again midafternoon, because she was shopping and wanted to see if Harry or John needed anything. Dinner at home the previous night had been less intimate, and less awkward, than the night before, but only because Harry told her he wasn't feeling well, passed on a drink, and ate in record time. He spent the evening in his room, finishing the Ed McBain and starting another, but mostly just thinking about his father and what might have happened on the path that afternoon. He also thought of Alice, sexualized images of her flashing unwanted through his mind. He kept picturing her from that first summer when she was married to his father. The green bikini top and the denim shorts, so short that he could see the bottom curve of her buttocks. He realized that four years of college hadn't managed to shake that image from his mind.

At four thirty, when it became clear that Grace wasn't going to drop by the store again, he got out his phone and punched in her number, adding it as a contact. He was about to call her, but decided to text instead.

This is Harry from the bookstore. Want to get a drink tonight?

He pressed Send, wondering anxiously if he was misleading her about the job possibility. Lew leapt onto Harry's lap, startling him. Lew was not generally a lap cat, unless you'd ignored him for some time, and then he'd find a way to pounce into your lap when you weren't looking. With one hand, Harry stroked Lew's matted fur, writing another text to Grace with his other.

No job here, at least not yet. Just wanted to get a drink.

He shook his head rapidly at the two dumb texts. "You okay, my friend?" John asked. Lew flattened himself onto Harry's lap, purring.

"Oh, sorry. I'm looking at my phone." Harry held it up, and as he did, it vibrated in his hand. It was Grace, texting back.

Sure. When?

They agreed to meet at the Village Inn in one hour. Harry left work early, considered going home to change out of his black T-shirt into something a little more date-like, then decided his time would be better spent waiting for Grace at the bar.

The Village Inn was a large Colonial house refurbished into a small hotel. Harry had been inside a few times, to eat dinner with his father, or his father and Alice. He'd seen the bar, but he'd never had a drink there. It was a small alcove off the main lobby, wood paneled and with just eight padded stools along the bar. It was empty when Harry arrived, not even a bartender. He sat on a stool. The oak bar gleamed with polish, and low lighting illuminated the high-end bottles displayed behind the bar. Harry was used to college bars with Budweiser mirrors and Jägermeister dispensers. While he was trying to decide what to drink, the bartender came out. She was a heavyset woman with old-timey tattoos on both arms. Her hair was dyed a bottle blond and she wore thick glasses. She startled a little when she saw Harry.

"Where'd you come from, sweetie?" she said, as Harry asked her if they were open yet.

"We're open. What can I get you, and can I see an ID, please?"

Harry fished out his driver's license, showed it to the bartender, and ordered himself a bourbon and ginger ale. She made his drink in a low tumbler, garnishing it with a thin sliver of lemon, then fiddled with her phone, which was attached to the speakers, selecting a song, a man's deep voice over drums, bass, and a saxophone. Harry looked at his own phone as she began to prepare the bar, shifting bottles around, cutting up fruit. It was half an hour before Grace was due to show up. Harry told himself to sip his drink, and make it last. He was anxious to see Grace again, and he wondered what she thought about his invitation. He didn't know what to think of it himself. Had he invited her out on a date, or was he trying to find out what connection she might have had with his father? Both, probably, although it was easier for Harry to consider it a fact-finding mission.

Harry had had two major relationships in college. The first had been with Florence Lee, a girl he'd met his first week at Mather when they were both volunteers at the student-run movie theater. Their first night together they had stayed up till dawn talking about the French new wave and Vonnegut novels. She'd done most of the talking, actually, but it was like she was speaking both his thoughts and her own out loud. The next night they stayed up till dawn having sex. Those two nights combined to convince Harry that Florence Lee was the one and only true love of his life. They were inseparable until the following spring, when Harry discovered that she'd never stopped fucking her high school boyfriend back on Long Island. Harry had been inconsolable, even considering leaving Mather. Paul Roman, claiming he'd never liked Florence, had finally gotten Harry out of the funk.

Then Harry had started spending time with Paul's friend Kim, so different from the cerebral, depressive, highly sexual Florence. She was a very sarcastic theater major who wore retro dresses and smoked American

Spirits. They stayed close all through sophomore year, Harry coaching Kim through her own complicated, emotionally abusive relationship with a fellow theater major named Antoine. When Kim finally shed Antoine, at the beginning of junior year, Harry and Kim started fooling around, jokingly at first. They agreed to keep it quiet, and they agreed to take it slow, each having been damaged by previous sexual relationships.

"How slow?" Harry asked, the first morning after Kim had spent the night in his bed.

"When it snows we'll do it. How about that?"

Harry pulled up his dorm room's blind and looked out at a blue sky. It was early November, and most of the trees were still holding on to their changed leaves.

"First snow, really?"

"Sure. Sounds about right. When it snows I'll let you put your penis in my vagina." She was hooking her bra behind her back and smiling widely.

"Promise?"

"I promise."

By the middle of December, there hadn't been so much as a snow squall, and the weathermen were predicting a decidedly nonwhite Christmas. The mild fall had become a constant joke between Harry and Kim, the weather conspiring to keep them apart. On the last night of fall semester, Harry had one paper left to write, five pages on the Protestant Reformation. He was just finishing up when he received a text from Kim.

Done yet?

Almost.

Come over when you're finished.

After giving the paper one last reread, then e-mailing it to his professor, Harry wrapped a scarf around his neck and walked across campus to Kim's single in Hubbard Hall. It was cold, the sky filled with stars. He checked his watch before knocking on her door—it was just past midnight—but he knew she'd still be up. She opened the door, her eyes bright and nervous. Harry walked into a room entirely plastered in cutout snowflakes—it must have been hundreds—taped on the walls, the ceiling, even scattered on the floor.

"Ta-da," she said, her voice quavering, and Harry knew instantly that the waiting had been a mistake. He felt it in his stomach, and put a smile on his face that he hoped looked genuine.

Kim threw him onto the bed—also covered in snowflakes—and told him to "make love" to her, and Harry felt all desire leave his body. Whether it was the gimmickry of the moment, or the fact that he'd never had intense feelings for Kim in the first place, he knew it wasn't going to work. Still, he tried, and by dawn, when it was clear that nothing was going to happen, he pretended to fall asleep, listening to Kim quietly cry into the pillow next to him.

The following semester, Harry and Kim agreed to just be friends. It was awkward for a while, but eventually they went back to the way they'd been before. Harry told himself that their failed consummation had been a product of a mismatch—that they never should have tried—but secretly he worried about it. Was he only sexually attracted to the girls who didn't want him, or to the women he could never have, like his stepmother?

Toward the end of senior year, Harry and Kim had begun to occasionally fool around again, and one night, Kim, as drunk as he'd ever seen her, told him that he was the only boy she'd ever loved. Harry responded with silence. The following day Kim claimed she'd blacked out the night before, but Harry wasn't so sure. He told himself he needed to stop misleading her, and he had, for the most part. But now it didn't matter. She was doing Teach for America for a year in Baton Rouge, and Harry was in Maine.

"Same again?" the bartender asked.

"Uh, sure," Harry said, checking the time on his watch. It was exactly the time that Grace and he had agreed on. He turned and there she was, walking into the bar, wearing a dark blue dress, the hemline over her knees.

"Fancy," she said, looking around as she slid onto the stool next to Harry.

The bartender placed his drink in front of him, and asked Grace what she wanted. She glanced toward the small selection of draft beers, and ordered a Shock Top.

"Any luck on the job front?"

"Not yet. I'm not in a rush, though. How's the bookstore?"

Harry, partly from nerves, found himself telling Grace not just about the work he'd been doing at the store, but also about his anxiety regarding the store's future. His own future, as well.

"You're not interested in taking over?" Grace asked.

"No, not really. And if I was, I'd be interested in working at the Ackerson's in New York, even though it doesn't belong to my father . . . didn't belong to him, anymore. I guess I'm not interested in living up here in Maine, with Alice, for the rest of my life."

"Alice is your . . . stepmom?"

"Yes, sorry. She's my father's second wife. My mother died when I was in high school."

"So what's Alice like?" Grace had finished her beer, and must have signaled the bartender, because a full one was being placed in front of her, along with a small bowl of Chex Mix.

"She's . . ." Harry searched for a word, finally coming up with ". . . fine."

Grace laughed. "Faint praise."

"Honestly, I just don't know her that well. She married my father just as I was getting ready to head off to college. It was pretty much all about me, then, and I didn't really bother to get to know her"—a flash of his father's young bride in her bikini went through Harry's mind—"at least not in any significant way. She's very sincere, and that's always made me a little bit uncomfortable. My father was always closed off about his emotions, my mother not so much, but she was also sarcastic, and that goes a long way. Alice doesn't really have a sense of humor. I sometimes think my father fell in love with her because she reminded him of Maine, and he really wanted to return here."

"Why did she remind him of Maine?"

"I don't know. She's straightforward, not complicated, or neurotic. She's old-fashioned. She took care of him the way his mother took care of him, maybe. This makes him sound terrible."

"Not really," she said, licking some foam from her upper lip.

"Tell me about yourself," Harry said, sipping at his drink, surprised to find it was nothing but ice.

"Do I have to?" Grace said, and laughed.

"You don't have to do anything. I'm just curious. How old are you?"

"You're not supposed to ask that, but I don't mind. I'm twenty-five."

"Where did you grow up?"

"I grew up in Michigan, then I went to school in New York City, and now I live right here in Kennewick, Maine."

"And you dream of working in a bookstore?"

"Truth is, like I told you, I know the Ackerson's in New York City. I used to live on the same block and go in all the time. I like old books. And I knew that there was a second Ackerson's here, and that's partly why I picked Kennewick. Not to work at the bookstore, although obviously I would love to do that, but because I wanted to move to the coast of Maine, and when I found out that the bookstore on my block had a sister store in Kennewick, it felt like fate. That's why I picked here, and that's why I went to your father's funeral. You look like you don't believe me."

"Do I? No, keep going." But Harry had been having trouble believing her. Her story sounded rehearsed, and as she told it, her eyes shifted back and forth, never settling on any one point. She was lying.

"That's it. That's my story."

"Why did you leave New York?"

"Why do you think?"

"Boy troubles?"

"Ha. That's one way to put it, but yes, that is why I left New York."

The bartender asked Harry if he wanted another drink. He hadn't eaten since the chicken sandwich at lunch, and the two bourbon and ginger ales had felt pretty strong. He ordered a beer instead, the same kind that Grace was drinking. After serving it with an orange slice on the rim of the pint glass, the bartender pointed a remote and turned on the flat-screen television built into the bar. Red Sox players were running onto the field at Fenway.

"You a baseball fan?" Grace asked, clearly hoping to change the subject.

"Fair-weather, I guess. When the Red Sox make the playoffs I start to pay attention. My dad was a huge fan." And suddenly Harry realized that his father would never see another Red Sox game again, never read another box score, or complain about a pitcher. "How about you?"

"Not really. I'm a football fan. Soccer fan, I mean. I follow Man United."

"How did that happen?" Harry asked.

He listened to her talk about soccer, how she'd played

her whole life, and how she'd started watching the Premier League games when they'd begun airing them on American television ten years earlier. She talked about players as though Harry had heard of them. Now that she wasn't hiding anything, she was making eye contact, and her voice had altered slightly. She'd relaxed and Harry could see her at fifteen, a feisty, freckled soccer player with long dark hair on some playing field in the Midwest.

Harry finished his beer and ate the orange slice.

"You hungry?" Grace asked.

"I am. I should go home, probably, because I'm sure that Alice has cooked a three-course meal. It's what she's been doing since my father died."

"I should eat something, too."

"I'd invite you, but—"

"No, no. Please. I have food at home. I should get going as well."

Outside, it was still light, but the sun was hidden behind a bank of dark clouds coming in from the west. There was a distant roll of thunder. "I'll walk you home," Harry said.

"You don't have to."

"It's sort of on my way."

They walked up the hill from the village, stopping outside the large redbrick Victorian where Grace had rented the room. There was an old Mazda RX-7 in the driveway and Harry wondered if it was hers.

"Let's do this again," Grace said, as a few fat drops of rain started to hit the sidewalk.

"I'd like that," Harry said.

He turned and began to walk toward home, wondering if he'd get there before it really began to rain hard, when he heard Grace's footsteps following him. "Wait up," she said, and he turned.

For one brief moment, Harry thought she was going to keep coming and kiss him, but she stopped, a little breathless, and said: "I did know your father, a little bit, from down in New York. From Ackerson's."

"Oh," Harry said.

"I felt bad lying to you about it."

"Why did you?"

"I don't know. I didn't want you to think . . . We didn't know each other well."

"That's okay."

"Good night again," she said, walking backward, smiling, nodding her head slowly, a gesture that seemed to say that she felt better now that she'd told the truth. But she hadn't told the truth, at least not the whole truth. Harry was sure of that.

Chapter 15

Then

They sat on the beach together, up near the wall, each on one of the flat stones that clustered along the high-tide mark. It was high tide now, an occasional wave lapping at their feet.

Gina had wanted to come inside the condominium, but Alice had stepped out through the door, pulling it shut behind her, and said that they should go talk on the beach. It was clear that Gina was either drunk or seriously messed up on some kind of drug. Her eyes were red rimmed and unfocused, and her words sounded gluey in her mouth. Alice held her arm as they walked toward the water.

"I'm sorry, Al," Gina said, "but I *had* to say something, because if I hadn't then I'd keep thinking it, but now it's ruined us and you're my only friend in Kennewick, only real friend, and now you hate me."

"I don't hate you," Alice said.

"You don't know what it's like in New York. I, like, don't trust anyone. *Anyone.* Everyone tells me I'm beautiful, and everyone tells me how I'm this big star, but I'm not, Al. Margery, you know Margery?"

Alice didn't, but nodded anyway. They were near the beach, the ocean's pulsing roar muffling Gina's words. Alice let her talk. She told a long, rambling story about her manager, Margery, and how she'd thought Margery was the only one she could trust, but how it turned out that she couldn't trust anyone. While she spoke, Alice looked at Gina's hand where she had bitten her. It had been swaddled in a white bandage, and even in the dim moonlight, Alice could see dark spots where the blood was seeping through. *I did that,* she thought. She remembered what it felt like, her teeth sinking into Gina's flesh.

"But I trust *you*," Gina was saying. "And that's why I can't lose you, Al. I can't lose you, and I don't care what you're doing with your mom's husband. That's not my business and I should never have brought it up. I mean, do what you want, right?"

"We're not doing anything."

"Hey, I get it, Al. He's hot. I'd do it with him."

For a brief moment Gina's words provoked in Alice an urge to pick up the nearest rock and drive it into Gina's face. Instead, she said, "Let's go swimming."

Gina swiveled her head toward the black expanse of the ocean, almost as though she was just realizing that it was there. "Really?" she said.

"Sure, why not?"

"It'll be freezing."

"It won't be. You're just scared. It'll be amazing."

Gina stared toward the water for a moment, then said, "Sure. Okay." She smiled, leaning in toward Alice. Her breath had an almost chemical smell to it, like rubbing alcohol. She stood. "Let's go swimming. It can be symbolic, like our fresh start." She pushed her jeans down her long legs, almost slipping on the rocks, then pulled her shirt and sweater over her head. Alice, still wearing just the pajama bottoms and the T-shirt, pulled them off, feeling awkward and exposed, but wanting to get into the water. Gina's eyes quickly scanned Alice's naked body, and Alice resisted the urge to cover her breasts, which suddenly seemed awkward and fleshy next to Gina's flat chest and small, dark nipples.

"I can't believe we're doing this," Gina said. "It's

going to be freezing." She pulled the bandage off her hand and tossed it on the sand.

"The water's probably warmer than the air right now," Alice said, stepping from the rocks onto the hard-packed wet sand. As soon as she was ankle high in the water, she realized the water temperature was probably exactly the same temperature as the air. It felt like stepping into nothing. She waded out, as Gina flew past her, spinning her arms and screaming, crashing into the surf. "Chicken," she yelled back at Alice.

Alice kept wading forward. Everything was dark except for the foam of the breaking surf. A large wave was rolling toward her and Alice dove under it, swam underwater, then came up next to Gina. "This feels fucking amazing," Gina said, tilting her head back so that her hair was in the water.

Alice found herself annoyed to share the sentiment. She'd never swum naked before and the grasp of the ocean water on her skin made her feel incredibly alive. "Let's see how far we can swim out," she said.

"Maybe we'll get eaten by sharks," Gina said, then laughed drunkenly, swallowing some water then coughing it out.

Alice took a deep breath, filling her lungs, her feet planted on the dense, sandy bottom. The moon emerged from behind a cloud and shone silver on the water. "No, it will be great. Trust me." Alice began to swim, Gina beside her. She went slow, not wanting Gina to fall behind. The water turned colder and calmer the farther out they went. She could hear Gina starting to breathe hard, snorting out water as she turned her head every other stroke. "You okay?" Alice asked.

"Yeah. A little tired." Gina spun onto her back, her breath sounding ragged.

"If we go a little farther there's a sandbar."

"Yeah, let's keep going," Gina said, spinning and beginning to swim again, her arms slapping the water. Alice remembered what Gina had been like at cross-country practices, always willing to slow down if Alice was behind, but always making sure that she would be first to finish. Alice swam by her side. She was beginning to breathe heavily, too, but her arms felt strong, slicing through the water, propelling her. She felt like she could swim forever. She sped a little ahead of Gina, steadily moving away from shore, the water now much colder.

"Stop, hold up," Gina yelled, her voice hoarse, and Alice stopped, spun, and swam back toward her. The lights along the shore seemed far away and insignificant. "I think I'm cramping," Gina said, and there was some panic in her voice.

"Just rest for a moment," Alice said.

"Have you felt the sandbar yet?"

"I haven't, but I remember it, unless it's moved." Doggy-paddling, Alice could feel the water tugging at her legs. She'd wondered if they'd hit a rip current, and it felt as though they had. There really had been a sandbar out this far from Kennewick Beach, but that had changed after the storm-filled winter the year after they graduated.

"I shouldn't have come out this far," Gina said, her chin submerged in the water, the words sputtering.

"No worries. We'll rest a bit, then turn back."

"Okay."

Alice, staying afloat just by scissoring her legs, said, "I am having sex with him, you know. With that fucking creep." The moon was back behind a cloud, and it was dark again.

Gina took a breath, then said, "I don't care," the words sounding like exhalations.

"You do care, Gina. You want me to stop."

"I don't, really. Alice, I think I need help."

"Okay," Alice said. She was starting to tire now, too, and began to swim in a crawl, her arms struggling to get out of the water, so she switched to the breaststroke. There was a definite pull in the water, a current tugging her away from the shore. Panic coursed through her, squeezing her chest, but she took a breath, and told herself to swim parallel to the shore for a while, till she was out of the current.

"Alice, help," Gina shouted, and Alice turned to see her wave a hand above the water, her head submerging then coming up again. She was drowning, her words sputtering.

Alice felt a burst of strength and began to swim north, toward the lighthouse on the bluff, stopping occasionally until she no longer felt the pull of the current. Then she turned toward shore, her lungs burning, her arms as weak as jelly, and began to breaststroke home. After what felt like an eternity, the water began to swell again, and suddenly she was being pushed forward by a curling wave, her chest and thighs scraping the rock-strewn shore. She crawled forward and collapsed, her body shivering, her lungs pumping. When her breathing returned to normal, she stood, stumbling a little, then worked her way along the shore, making sure to walk near the waterline and not where the sand was dry. She didn't want to leave footprints.

The moon came out again and she was able to find the two small piles of clothes, Gina's and hers, up near the rocks. She pulled her pajama bottoms and T-shirt back on over her damp, sandy skin. She was now shaking uncontrollably, her teeth starting to chatter. A car went by on Micmac Road; she crouched under the sweep of its headlights, seeing Gina's clothes briefly illuminated. The tide was now going out, but the sand was smooth and wet right up to where her sandals lay. There were no footprints visible.

Despite how cold she was, Alice crouched and watched the ocean for as long as she could, scanning its surface when the moon was out from under cloud cover. She knew that Gina had drowned—she must have gone under right after Alice had swum away from her—but still she watched, just to make sure. She tried to feel her way across the water, to sense Gina still struggling to stay alive, but there was nothing. The ocean had swallowed her.

Alice took the cement steps back up to the road, crossed it, and jogged toward home. She pushed the door open, glad she'd remembered to leave it unlocked, and stepped into the quiet interior, lights still on in the kitchen and the living room. She turned them off, and went upstairs. Passing through the bedroom, she could hear the rhythmic staccato breathing of Jake that meant he was in a deep sleep. She undressed, bundling her clothes together and pushing them toward the bottom of the laundry basket, then got under the hot pulse of the shower, letting the water warm her up, soothe her muscles, and wash away the sand that ran off her body in dark rivulets. She shampooed and conditioned her hair and soaped herself completely with Jake's Irish Spring twice. She stopped shivering, and the taste of salt in her mouth went away, but she turned the water off and stepped out of the shower only when her legs felt like they could no longer support her.

In a fresh set of pajamas she got under the covers quietly and lay on her back, and told herself she needed to make some decisions. When the police came to question her—and they would come—she'd tell them that Gina had come to her door, and that Alice had told her she was too tired to talk, and that Gina was very drunk, and maybe on drugs. She'd wanted to go swimming but Alice refused, and so she left. They couldn't prove otherwise, not after Alice laundered the pajamas and took another shower to make sure there was no other evidence. She could do that early in the morning, before Jake woke. How soon would the police come? How soon would Gina be missed?

She closed her eyes, and she was back in the cold, deep water, Gina asking for help. Alice told herself there was no way she would have been able to save her, even if she'd wanted to. She'd barely saved herself from the tide. And Gina was incapacitated. She'd gotten what she wanted—all the beautiful lies about fame and money and the world telling her how special she was—

and it had clearly been killing her. And maybe because her own life was such a shit show, she'd decided to mess with Alice's life, to pass judgment, because Alice had actually found someone to love who loved her back.

No, she couldn't have saved Gina even if she'd wanted to. She'd be dead now, too, if she'd tried to save them both. Gina would have dragged them both under the water. There was nothing Alice could have done.

Satisfied with these thoughts, Alice turned over onto her stomach and fell happily asleep.

Chapter 16

Now

Harry slept late again the following day, coming down to find a note from Alice saying she had gone out to do errands and wouldn't be back till noon. Harry suddenly relished the idea of some time alone in the house, some time to think some more about what had happened to his father, and his strange date the evening before with Grace. He called John at the store and let him know that he wasn't feeling great, and could he just come in during the afternoon.

"You don't have to come in at all, Harry," John said. "I can handle things here."

"Okay, but I'd like to come in. If I feel better I'll drop by, and if I don't feel better, I guess you won't see me."

"Okay. Take care, son."

There was half a pot of lukewarm coffee left and Harry poured himself a mug, adding milk, then heating it up in the microwave. He brought the coffee back up to his room and logged on to his laptop. He was hoping to find out something more about Grace; he knew she had lied about her relationship with his father. Were they having an affair? And if so, was that why she had come to Maine from New York? For the funeral? Then why was she sticking around?

He realized he didn't know her last name, so he Googled "Grace" and everything she'd mentioned to him the night before. "Ann Arbor, Michigan." "New York University." He even tried "Ackerson's Rare Books." Nothing came up, and it made him realize how little he'd learned about her. On a whim, he decided to call the Ackerson's in New York and see if Ron Krakowski was there. He got the number from their website and called on his cell phone.

"Ackerson's Rare Books." It was a female voice.

"Is Ron available?"

"Let me check. Can I ask who's calling?"

Harry gave his name, knowing that Ron, phobic

sometimes about talking on the telephone, would take the call.

A half minute passed before Ron's voice said, "Jesus, Harry, I can't fucking believe it."

"I know," Harry said, suddenly happy to hear Ron's voice. He was a prickly presence, but a constant one. Harry had known him his whole life.

"I left a message for Alice, but I haven't heard back. You in Maine now? Of course you are. What are they saying? He just slipped and fell and died, just like that?"

"Actually, no. Now they're saying that maybe he was hit first. That's what killed him."

"Like someone killed him? Jesus H. Christ. How do they know all this? Maine CSI, I guess, right? They know who did it?"

Harry told him they didn't, and that the police had been by to ask him if he knew anyone who might have had a grudge against his father.

"You told them no, I hope. I like to say that your father had few friends but no enemies. I would have said that at the funeral if I'd, if I'd . . ."

"Don't worry about it. I understand. It was a long way to come."

"Yeah. Older I get, anything farther than ten blocks seems a long way to go." Ron was no older than sixty years old, Harry thought, but let it go.

They talked some more. About Alice, and about what might happen to the store up in Maine, then Harry said, "I've got a strange question, Ron. Do you know someone named Grace? I don't know her last name but she knew my dad, and she said she met him down in New York at your—"

"Irish girl with pretty eyes? Her last name's McGowan. You know the apartment on Third that Jim Mills sold to me for a thousand dollars in 1978? She's renting that from me."

"Still?"

"Far as I know. She's paid up on rent. She's a nice girl, helped us clear books from the basement when Sandy hit. She did know your dad 'cause he was down here then, as well."

"Were they close?"

"Were they close? Who? Your father and Grace? I didn't particularly think so, but it's not like I was paying attention. Why? Does she say they were?"

"No, no. It's just that she came to the funeral."

"No shit. That is a little strange."

"You think they were having an affair?"

The line was silent for half a second, and Harry could almost hear Ron's shrug. "Uh, I would say no, but what do I know? Your father and I didn't talk about that stuff."

"But do you think it's a possibility?"

"Harry, I don't know. Your father seemed like a happy man, but he did come down to New York a lot. She's a pretty girl, Grace, but she's no Alice, I'd say."

Harry wondered for a moment if Ron had ever met Alice, then remembered the time that she'd come down to New York to visit.

"Thanks, Ron," Harry said.

"You need money, Harry?"

"No, no, I'm fine. But I might need some help dealing with this store."

"Call me anytime, okay? Let me give you my home number, too."

After writing it down—not surprised that Ron didn't have a cell phone—Harry asked if Ron knew how to spell Grace's last name. He wrote that down as well.

After ending the call, he Googled "Grace McGowan." There were quite a few, but none that seemed to match the person he was looking for. There were still people— even young people—who didn't have online profiles. He was one of them. Alice was another. His father didn't have much of one, but he had been profiled years earlier in a *New York Times* article about selling books in the age of the Internet. He looked him up now, reread the article, and studied the accompanying picture of his father, looking distinguished and handsome in front of a cluttered shelf of books. Like a young Ted Hughes, all strong chin and thick hair. He killed the screen, not wanting to look anymore, but he kept thinking of his father.

Would he have had an affair with a much younger woman in New York? Maybe Harry was biased, but he would have said no if his mother had never died. But maybe his relationship with Alice had soured, or maybe Grace had thrown herself at his father, and he'd simply been unable to resist.

And if he had had an affair, what if Alice had found out about it? How would she react? Would she have followed him on his afternoon walk, waited for him to reach a secluded spot, and hit him with something? It seemed ridiculous, but *someone* had killed him. Why not Alice? Or for that matter, why not Grace McGowan? Maybe his father had broken off the affair, and she'd followed him to Maine to get her revenge? Harry wondered if there might be some answers to these questions in the house. If Alice had suspected Bill of cheating, she might have hired a private detective to follow him in New York. And if so, there might be some record of it.

Grey Lady was a big house. Before Bill bought it, it had been a bed-and-breakfast, started by a couple that got lonely when their six children all left home. On the second floor alone there were five bedrooms and three bathrooms. The first floor had been renovated at some point so that the modernized kitchen flowed into the dining room, and French doors led into the large front living room with its bay windows. At the back of the house was a wide sunroom, clearly an addition, with views of the barn and down toward the marsh. The two other major rooms on the first floor were Bill's office and Alice's office. Bill's looked more like a storage area than a functioning room; the walls were lined with bookshelves, all filled, and stacks of books covered the floor, creating a strange cityscape in miniature. Bill had left a narrow path through the books that led to the only furniture in the room, a large oak desk, and a faded leather swivel chair that Bill had owned since college. The other office was all Alice, a sunny corner room dominated by a craft table with a sewing machine and stacks of fabric. But there was also a desk in the room, ridiculously neat compared to Bill's, and that was where Harry decided to look first.

The desk, painted a robin's-egg blue, was practically child sized compared to the monstrosity in Bill's office. On top of it was Alice's laptop computer, closed, and cool to the touch. She had a short stack of mail that hadn't been opened. Harry riffled through the envelopes, nothing immediately catching his eye. There were credit card applications, what looked like a bill from Macy's, an alumni letter addressed to William Ackerson from Columbia University.

Harry pulled open the only drawer. He expected it to be as neat and organized as the desk, but inside was a jumbled mess of papers, photographs, a half-filled perfume bottle, a box of thank-you cards. The house made one of its sounds, a wall settling somewhere, and Harry jumped. What would happen if Alice returned home early and found him looking through her things? He cocked his head and listened. The house was quiet again. He told himself that he'd just quickly look through the items in the desk, see if there was a letter from a private investigator, anything that would suggest she had information about his father's affair.

Harry sat down on the chair, painted the same color as the desk. He carefully slid the drawer all the way out. Most of what he found was paid bills, bank statements, an insurance policy for the station wagon. There were no letters from a private investigator. He did find an expired passport that had been issued when Alice was just nineteen years old. He'd never seen a picture of his stepmother when she'd been young. She was makeup-free, her skin as pale as it was now, but her eyes seemed even larger in her face, her face a little bit rounder. She was beautiful, and Harry wondered what she'd been like as a teenager. It was somehow impossible to imagine her any different than she was now. He stared at the picture for a long time, and she seemed to stare back, telling him nothing.

He flipped through the passport to see where she'd been, and a photograph fell out. It was a picture of a young Alice standing with a man Harry didn't recognize on a cobblestone street, a stone building behind them with the word *Funiculaire* in metal letters on its side. Both Alice and the man were wearing long, heavy coats. The photographer had focused more on the building behind them, the rail tracks leading up a steep slope, and less on Alice and the man, both a little blurry. Even so, it was clear that the man was quite a bit older than Alice. His arm was draped possessively over Alice's slim shoulders. Her father, probably. Harry tried to remember if he knew anything about Alice's family, but all he could recall was his own father telling him that Alice's parents were dead, and that she wasn't close to anyone in her extended family.

Bill hadn't talked too much about Alice, except for the time he said she reminded him of Maine. For some reason, that description had stuck. Harry heard a noise coming from the front of the house. He quickly returned the passport to where he'd found it, shoved the drawer shut, and went to look. The mailman had pushed the mail through the front door's slot. Harry picked up an envelope from a bank and a Nordstrom catalogue, and brought them to the kitchen counter. He considered a second cup of coffee but decided he was already jumpy enough. He drank a glass of orange juice instead, flipping through the catalogue, barely seeing the pictures. Then he checked his phone. Nothing from Grace, not that he was expecting something.

He didn't go back to Alice's office, going instead to his father's, and sitting at the desk on the leather chair. He stared at the framed print on the wall, an original signed illustration by Robert E. McGinnis of a girl in a short white dress sitting on top of a roulette table. It had been done for a book cover, Harry knew, but he couldn't remember which one. Something from the 1960s. Harry swiveled in the chair, looking at all his father's books, wondering what would become of them now. He began to think about all the words his father had read, all the plots he'd absorbed, and how they were all gone, but then he stopped himself. Instead, he picked through a stack of books on the desk. At the top was one of his father's moleskin notebooks. He'd always had one going, filling at least two notebooks a year. In a sense, they were his diaries, but instead of filling them with activities and day-to-day recollections, they were filled with lists of books he was trying to acquire, and lists of books he already had. There was also page after page of favorite quotes, plus his current ever-changing lists of top tens. *Ten best Signet paperback covers. Ten best standalone Christies. Ten best crime novels published before 1945.* Harry had flipped through his father's notebooks before. There was never anything personal, not even a shopping list. But, in a way, it *was* as personal as a diary. It mapped his interior world.

Harry flipped to the last entry, which came midway through the notebook. It was a quote, centered on the page:

"It's not dark yet, but it's getting there."

As was sometimes the case with quotes his father wrote down, it wasn't attributed to anyone, probably because his father knew who said it, and these books were only for his father. Harry read the words several times, haunted by them. Maybe it was just some line from a song that his father liked, but it also sounded like a premonition of death.

Harry punched the line into his smartphone, and got an instant hit. It was from a song by Bob Dylan called "Not Dark Yet." He wasn't surprised. Dylan was his father's favorite musician—there wasn't even a distant second, except maybe Frank Sinatra. Bill had spent as much time obsessing over Dylan's lyrics as he did actually listening to his music. His notebooks were filled with Dylan quotes, and sometimes he'd transcribe entire songs.

Still, Harry stared at this particular line from Dylan for another minute. It was the last thing his father had ever written. Then Harry flipped back a page. There was another quote, this one with an attribution:

"That's the worst thing about democracy: there have to be two opinions about every issue."
—Ross Macdonald, *Black Money*

And before that quote was one of his father's lists. This one was titled: *A REVISED list of Ross Macdonald's Lew Archer novels, ranked in order of preference.*

He didn't hear the front door open, but Alice's voice was suddenly in the house. "Anybody home?"

Harry startled, then stood up, putting the notebook down, and stepping out into the hallway. Alice was there, between Detective Dixon, wearing what looked like the same tan suit he'd had on the first time Harry had met him, and another man, much shorter, in a dark suit. Strange scenarios were passing through Harry's mind. Was Alice being arrested? Was there more bad news?

But then Detective Dixon, in a calm voice, said,

"Hello, Harry. Alice came by the station this morning, and I thought I'd bring her home. She's a little upset."

"Is everything okay?"

Alice turned and entered the living room. Detective Dixon stepped forward. "Harry, this is my colleague, Detective Vogel."

Harry nodded in the other detective's direction. He had a wide face and thick, dark eyebrows that almost touched above the bridge of a squat nose. "What's going on?" Harry asked.

"Sam, why don't you sit with Mrs. Ackerson a moment while I talk with Harry."

Detective Vogel nodded and followed Alice into the living room while Dixon grasped Harry's shoulder in one of his big hands and said in a lowered voice: "Alice came to the station today with some new information. She said your father was involved with a young woman here in town. Do you know anything about that?"

"What do you mean, 'involved'?" Harry asked.

"Does the name Annie Callahan mean anything to you?"

Harry, completely expecting the detective to say Grace's name, said nothing for a moment. "You knew her?" the detective asked.

"No, sorry, I didn't. I don't. Who is she?"

"Are you sure? She worked briefly at your father's bookstore?"

"Up here? In Maine?"

"Uh-huh."

"No, I didn't know her."

"What about the name Lou Callahan? Ever heard that name?"

Harry shook his head.

"Okay, thanks. That's all I needed to know. Your stepmother told us today that your father had been involved, romantically, with an employee at the store. That's Annie Callahan. She thinks either she or her husband might have had something to do with your father's death."

"Why is she just telling you this now?"

"Partly because of you, Harry. That's what she said, that she wanted to protect you from finding out that information. She's pretty upset." Just as Detective Dixon was saying those words, the other detective—Harry had already forgotten his name—reappeared in the doorway to the living room, and said, "She's asking to see Harry. You all set here?"

"We're all set," the detective said, placing his hand on Harry's shoulder and leading him toward Alice.

Chapter 17

Now

In the living room, Alice was on the couch, her knees up tight to her chest. Her head was angled down, her eyes squeezed shut, and she was emitting low, eerie groans. Her wet cheeks made it clear that she'd been crying. Harry was paralyzed with inaction for one brief moment, then slid next to her and placed an arm over her shoulders. She instantly adjusted herself, moving closer to him, pressing her damp face against his shirt. He could hear and feel the ragged breath entering and exiting her body. Both detectives stayed standing, but Detective Dixon said, "Alice, I'm going to go talk with this Annie Callahan, okay? And then maybe with her husband."

Harry didn't think she was going to react, but then she shifted her body, turning to face the detective, wiping at her face. There was a damp spot on Harry's shirt where her face had been. The detective pulled at his suit pants above the knees and crouched. "You going to be okay here with Harry?" he asked.

Alice slid her legs off the couch and put her feet back on the floor. She nodded her head, while drawing a wet breath in through her nostrils. Harry kept one hand on her back, nervous about moving it. She was wearing a wraparound dress, and the front had slid open a little so that Harry had a brief view of one of her breasts barely covered by the white cup of a bra. She shifted again, fixing the dress, and Harry moved his hand.

"I don't know if . . ."

"You don't know if what, Mrs. Ackerson?"

"I don't know for a fact if Annie . . . or if her husband . . . had anything to do with what happened to my husband."

"No, of course not. But it's information we should have. We'll check it out." He stood and nodded toward his partner. Harry took the opportunity to get off the sofa and walk them to the door. "We'll let you know if we find anything out. In the meantime, if Alice mentions anything that she didn't mention to us, then . . . you have my card?"

"I do," Harry said.

After they'd left, Harry returned to Alice, who was now standing, smoothing out her dress in the middle of the living room. Her face was dry.

"You okay?" Harry said.

Alice didn't answer the question, but said, "It's this woman's husband, I know it is."

"Who? This Annie Callahan?"

"I was hoping you'd never have to hear that name, Harry. I'm sorry. It wasn't your father's fault. It was all her. She went after him. She saw his store, and she saw this house, and—"

"Tell me what happened between them," Harry interrupted.

She hitched her shoulders back. "Is it too early for a drink, you think?"

Alice went to the sunroom while Harry made drinks: a glass of rosé for Alice and a beer for him. He was really only drinking the beer so Alice didn't have to be alone, but was also happy to be drinking it. He was rattled by the new information.

Once they were settled—Alice on the love seat, and Harry in one of the rocking chairs—Alice said, "We hired Annie as a huge favor. Her husband, Lou, was a fisherman, is a fisherman, and, you know, with the cod restrictions, he'd been out of work for six months. Your father heard about it, and offered Annie a job. It was last fall, when there'd been extra work."

"I didn't know about that."

"Your father was back from a scouting trip with too many books, of course, so he offered Annie a job. Just to help out with cataloguing, but at *twenty* dollars an hour." She shook her head, more of a tremor, at the memory. "And then, before you knew it, she's coming around here to help Bill with the books in his office. I knew. I knew something . . ."

"How old is she?" Harry asked.

"Annie? She looks a lot older than she is. I don't know, somewhere in her thirties."

"And they were definitely involved?"

She tipped her glass back and almost finished her wine. Harry watched her throat muscles swallowing.

"Oh, they were, for sure, Harry. I'm sorry you have to hear this. I was hoping you wouldn't, because I know how you felt about your father, how much you admired him, but it was very clear that something was going on. And I had to force him to get rid of her. And then when the detective told me that your father's death was not an accident, I just knew. I didn't say anything right away, because of you, Harry, but then I decided I had to tell them."

Harry wanted to ask Alice for more specifics. Had she caught them together? Did his father confess to her that they were involved? He didn't know why he was skeptical—especially considering the possibility that his father had also been having an affair down in New York City—but he did wonder if Alice was overreacting.

"So she was fired?"

"She was let go, let's just say that, and that's when her husband finally figured it out. John told me that he came to the store, threatened Bill, told him that if he ever came near Annie again he'd kill him with his bare hands. Something like that."

"John told you this, or my father did?"

"John was the one who told me, because he was worried. I asked Bill about it, and he said it was no big deal, just a frustrated man blowing off steam. Your father could be . . . he could be too charitable at times."

"So you think that Lou . . . ?"

"I didn't think your father had anything more to do with Annie, but who knows? He was always gone lately, and maybe he was meeting her somewhere else. I don't know. Stupid man." She looked at her glass, rolling the tiny amount of wine that was left up one of the sides.

"Can I get you some more?"

"Okay," she said, holding out the glass for Harry to take. When he returned with the wine, Alice had curled up in the fetal position on the love seat. Harry gingerly placed her glass on the glass-topped coffee table, as she said, in a fuzzy voice, "Thank you, Harry. I might just take a little nap."

"You should."

"Don't leave me, okay?"

"Okay," Harry said, not knowing exactly what she meant, "I'll be here if you need me." He quietly left the living room, went up to his bedroom, opened up his laptop, and did a search for Annie Callahan or Lou Callahan, but couldn't find anything. Then he texted Grace, asking if they could meet and talk sometime soon. He needed to get the whole story from her, why she had come to Maine. It was clear that she'd had some sort of significant relationship with his father, and the police would need to know about that, as well.

Waiting for a response, Harry paced his small bedroom. He stopped and looked at the packed bookcase, all filled with his father's detective stories. Bill Ackerson would never know that he wound up as a corpse in his own mystery story. Harry almost smiled at the thought. He thought back to the previous Christmas, his father giving him, as he always did, a check, plus one single book, usually his father's favorite book of that past year. This year it had been *A Kiss Before Dying* by Ira Levin. "I missed this, somehow, on the first go-round. It's brilliant."

"Thanks, Dad," Harry had said.

Later that same night, Alice in bed, Harry had started the book while his father finished reading the latest Ruth Rendell.

"Why do you think you like mysteries so much?" Harry asked.

"I'm deeply skeptical of any book that doesn't begin with a corpse."

Harry had heard his father say these exact words, or something close to them, many times. "No, really. Why?"

His father frowned, thinking. "It's my religion, I guess, since I don't have a real religion. The world is chaos, and then a detective comes along and restores order. Or he doesn't, and that's really my favorite kind of mystery story."

Harry had finished *A Kiss Before Dying* by the time he returned to school that year. It turned out to be one of those books in which order is restored, but not before a lot of damage had been done. Harry liked the book, but it had left him feeling empty and sad. Instead of bringing it back with him to Mather, he'd left it in the bookshelf in his room. He pulled it out now, looked at his father's inscription: *To Harry with love from Dad.* He quickly closed the book and put it back on the shelf. A few months earlier, Harry thought he knew his father, inside and out. Now, he realized he didn't know him at all.

His phone buzzed, a text coming through.

Come by tonight any time. Just ring the front doorbell and I'll come let you in.

Harry wrote back—*okay*—then went back downstairs to check on Alice.

She was still in the sunroom, still tucked up asleep on the short sofa in the same position. She looked deeply asleep.

While Alice slept through the afternoon, Harry tidied up around the kitchen, finding a frozen pizza in the freezer, and cooking it for dinner, even though he wasn't hungry, and doubted that Alice was, either. When she finally awoke, she wandered into the kitchen, empty glass in her hand, and asked Harry what time it was.

"Dinnertime," he said. "You really slept."

"I dreamt I woke up and you were gone, and I started to look for you, asking everyone I knew, but everyone told me you'd never existed. And then I was asking about your father, and it turned out he never existed, either."

"Scary," Harry said. "Are you hungry?"

"Maybe in a minute. I'm going to go see what's on the TV."

Alice turned on the television to the only channel she really watched—HGTV. A couple—a striking blonde and her dark-haired husband—were putting an offer on a California ranch house they wanted to renovate and flip. Harry brought Alice a plate with a slice of the pizza on it. "Thank you, Harry. Who knew you were so handy in the kitchen?"

"It was frozen."

"It's what your father used to make for dinner when I wasn't around."

"Oh," Harry said, wanting to apologize. Instead, he said, "So you really think it was Annie Callahan's husband?"

"I know it was. I think I knew it when I first heard what happened to your father, but I didn't trust myself."

"Do you think she was the only one . . . the only other—"

"She was the only one I found out about, but I don't know. I assume she was it. Your father and I had a good marriage, but I think that over time maybe he'd fallen a little bit out of love with me. At least it felt that way; he began treating me more like a friend than a wife."

"I'm sorry about that."

"You don't need to be sorry about anything. It wasn't you. And if it makes you feel better, I can tell you that I think your father only ever loved one woman, and that was your mother, Harry, not me."

Harry didn't say anything right away. He'd never heard Alice talk so openly before. "I think he was in love with you," he finally said. "He said nice things about you."

She half smiled, and something about the expression made her look young and vulnerable. "Thank you, Harry. I appreciate it. Look, I'm exhausted right now. I just want to watch some television for a while. You understand, don't you?"

"Of course. I'm sorry." He got up to leave the room as Alice turned the volume up. He was returning to the kitchen when she said, "You'll watch with me, won't you?"

"Oh. Okay." Harry got himself a beer, and put a slice of the Mediterranean pizza on a plate and returned to the living room. He almost sat in the leather recliner, but it had been his father's chair, so instead he sat on the other side of the couch from Alice. Together, they watched the show in silence, Alice's attention not even wavering during the commercials. As soon as the show ended, another one started up instantly. Same couple, different house. Harry stood, stretched, and asked Alice if it was okay if he took a walk. Without turning away from the screen, she said, "Has it stopped raining?"

Harry tried to remember if it had rained that day. He hadn't been out of the house. "I don't know," he said. "I need a little fresh air, regardless."

"Go, Harry," she said. "I'll be fine." She sounded a little doubtful, though, and for a moment Harry considered just staying with Alice. He felt bad for her, and she seemed to need him. But she had the television, for now at least, and he'd be back soon, he told himself.

He cleaned his plate, looking out through the window that was over the sink. The sky was filled with dusky light and towers of pink clouds. The window was cracked and the air that was coming through it felt cool, almost cold. He went up the stairs to his room, where he changed into his best jeans and pulled a V-neck sweater over his T-shirt, then left the house, the sound of Alice's program still coming from the living room.

Chapter 18

Then

When the doorbell to the condo rang, Alice thought it was probably the police. She was prepared. She would tell them how Gina had come to her door the night before, apologizing and wanting to go for a night swim in the ocean, and how Gina had seemed intoxicated.

But when Alice opened the door, it was Mrs. Bergeron, Gina's mom, standing on the landing. Alice had never seen her without makeup on before, and she almost didn't recognize her. Her skin was blotchy, and she had bags under her eyes. "Is she here?" she asked Alice.

"Who? Gina?"

"She's missing, Alice. I went into her room this morning and she hadn't even slept there." She was stepping into the house, uninvited, and Alice suddenly panicked that Jake was about to come down the stairs naked.

"She's not here, Mrs. Bergeron," she said, "but she was here last night."

"She was? When?"

"I don't know exactly. It was late. She knocked on the door, and she seemed really drunk. She apologized about dinner, and asked me if I wanted to go swimming."

"Swimming?"

"That's what she said. I told her I was tired and going to bed, and she left. That's all I know."

"Why did she want to go swimming? It's so cold out."

"I know. I thought it was strange, too, but she wasn't herself. I shouldn't have let her . . . I should have . . ."

"Jesus, do you think she went swimming by herself? Stupid, stupid girl." Mrs. Bergeron's eyes were jittery. "Can I use your phone?"

"Of course." Alice led her into the kitchen, and to the wall-mounted phone. Mrs. Bergeron plucked the receiver up, then pulled out a card from the front pocket of her jeans, dialed a number. Alice could see that the card was from the Kennewick Police Department.

"Is that Michael?" she asked, her voice panicky. Then: "I think she went swimming. In the ocean . . . Last night . . . Okay, yes. Okay."

Alice watched the conversation from the doorway, and jumped a little when she realized that Jake was standing right behind her. "What's going on?" he said.

"Gina's missing," she said, turning. He was dressed but he hadn't shaved yet. His dark stubble was flecked with grey.

"Since when?" he asked.

"She was here last night, after you fell asleep. She was drunk."

"Did you—"

He was interrupted by Mrs. Bergeron hanging up the phone, and racing out of the kitchen. "I have to go, Alice," she said, moving toward the front door.

"Can we do anything to help?" Jake asked, but she had already left.

Alice went to shut the front door, while Jake went into the kitchen.

"Do you think I should help them look for her?" she asked him as he was pouring coffee into a mug.

"She'll turn up," he said. "I'm sure of it."

Later, Alice heard that they found the clothes on the beach first, then found the body later that afternoon, lodged between rocks north of Buxton Point.

The police, as Alice knew they would, came to the house the following morning. Jake answered the door while Alice was cleaning up the dishes from breakfast. It was just one uniformed police officer, an Officer Wilson, who took his hat off when he entered the living room of the condo. He looked like he was in his early twenties; he had a large balding patch at the back of his head, and he had tried to make up for it by growing a wispy, blond mustache. Alice and Jake sat across from him as he took out a notebook.

"I'm sure you know why I'm here," he said, his eyes on Alice.

"It's about Gina Bergeron."

"Right. Her mother said that she came here yesterday, and you were the one who informed her that Gina had gone swimming on Friday night."

Alice nodded.

"Can you tell me about Friday night? Do you remember what time she was here?"

Alice told the whole story, omitting the part about Gina and her mother confronting her after dinner at the Bergerons'. And definitely omitting the part about biting Gina on the hand. She just said that she left their house and then later Gina showed up, acting drunk and wanting to go swimming.

"Was that unusual?"

"What do you mean?"

"Did it surprise you that Gina was drunk, or that she wanted to go swimming? Was this something she typically did?"

"I don't really know her that well, to tell the truth," Alice said, repeating words that she'd said to herself in her own mind many times. "We were close friends in high school, and then she went to New York City, and she changed. I didn't know her anymore."

"You didn't know her anymore because you didn't see her, or because she'd changed so much?"

"Both, I guess. I barely had any contact with her. I saw her mother more, because she comes into the pharmacy where I work, and she was the one who wanted me to come over for dinner when Gina was back in town. I didn't know why, but I think it had something to do with her being worried about Gina being on drugs, and maybe she hoped I'd be a good influence."

"She said all this to you? Gina's mother?"

"No. It was just what I thought."

"Okay. So what was she acting like when she came here?"

"I couldn't really understand her. She was slurring

her words, and she asked me to go swimming with her, and I said that it was too late, and it was too cold, and that was it."

The officer turned and looked at Jake for the first time. "Did you see Gina when she came here to the house?" he asked.

"Oh, no. That was long after my bedtime." He said it with a kind of faux heartiness that Alice had never heard before. *He sounds like he's lying,* she thought.

But Officer Wilson didn't follow up. He turned back to Alice. "Did you think it was unusual that Gina wanted to go swimming?" he asked.

"Um . . . I guess so. It was late at night."

"Besides it being late at night, did it surprise you in other ways? Is this something she liked to do?"

"Swimming?"

"Yes."

"I guess so. I don't really know."

The officer was writing something. When he didn't immediately ask another question, Alice said, "We'd gone swimming before, Gina and I. The last time that we spent together. It was nice. I think she wanted to repeat the experience as a way to . . . to get back that feeling. She said that swimming together would be like a fresh start."

"She said that here, the night she came over."

"Something like that."

"Why did you need a fresh start?"

"Just like I said, we'd been close before, and now we weren't so close. We'd drifted apart."

"Okay." The officer nodded fractionally and was quiet again for a moment. Alice didn't say anything, either, this time.

"One more thing," he said. "Had Gina ever said anything to you that made you think she might be suicidal?"

"No. Like I said, I barely even—"

"Not just recently, Alice, but when you knew her in high school. Or anytime really."

"Oh." Alice pretended to think. "There was this one time, our senior year, when we were talking about our futures, you know. Where we might be in a few years. And she said something like: 'Alice, you'll still be here in Kennewick. You'll probably be married to some perfect man, and have a baby boy and a baby girl, and I'll still be in New York, and I'll be a rich model with a major drug habit, and about sixteen boyfriends, and I'll be so unhappy that I'll probably kill myself.' I mean, I didn't think anything of it at the time."

"When did she say this?"

"Our senior year. I thought she was just joking."

"You've been really helpful, Alice," the officer said

as he stood. Jake stood as well and walked him to the door. Alice stayed seated, but the officer turned back and thanked her before he left the condo. She felt a sudden emptiness, like she hadn't been ready for him to leave, that there was more she could have said.

"What do you think that was all about?" Jake asked after shutting the door and turning back into the living room.

"What do you mean?"

"It felt like they were putting you through the third degree."

"I guess so," Alice said.

"If it didn't bother you, it didn't bother me. I was worried you might be upset."

"I'm not upset. I'm just tired. I haven't been sleeping."

"I'm sure. Go take a nap," he said, just as Alice knew he would.

She went upstairs and into her old bedroom, and shut the door. It was an unspoken code that was used between her and Jake. When she went to take a nap in the bedroom they shared together, it meant that Jake would join her. When she went into her old bedroom, he wouldn't. They'd only ever had sex in that room once, right after he'd taken the pictures.

In her bedroom with the door closed, Alice took out

the folder that contained all the magazine photos of Gina, the clippings she'd saved from the past few years. She spread them out on the nubby bedspread, finally arranging them in a way she liked, with her favorite picture of Gina in the middle. It was from one of her last published photo shoots, one in which she'd gotten to travel down to Miami. In the picture, she was wearing a yellow one-piece bathing suit and holding a lit cigarette. In the background was a ramshackle beach house, painted in neon colors, and a sexy man asleep in a hammock. Gina was looking directly at the camera, her face almost in a frown. *Look at all I have,* that face was saying, *and look at how miserable I am.* Alice ran her finger down the picture, as though she could feel Gina through it. The paper felt cheap. The shot was published in one of the lesser fashion magazines, a magazine that she'd had to pick up in Portland, since Blethen's didn't even carry it.

She looked at the other pictures, then gathered them up and put them back in the folder. She stretched out on the bed and looked at the ceiling. She listened to Jake coming quietly up the stairs, then heard him turn around and go back down. He'd seen the shut door of her bedroom. *Why had he been so concerned about the policeman's visit?* She hadn't been bothered by it. They were just trying to decide if it had been a suicide or an accidental death. And it was going to be easy to confirm. Gina was unhappy and on drugs. Why else would she swim out into the cold ocean water? It was so sad, really, when she thought about it. All that youth being swallowed up by all that water. Poor Gina so alone in those final moments. Alice really was a little bit sleepy, and she closed her eyes, then gently massaged her temples, hoping she wouldn't get one of her headaches.

Before she fell asleep, though, Alice got up and slipped from her bedroom into the master bedroom she shared with Jake. The bed was still unmade. She pulled her clothes off and slid under the warm, familiar sheets. Maybe Jake would come up and check on her again.

Chapter 19

Now

Outside, the air was crisp and smelled of loam. The pink that had just suffused the clouds was now gone, the light draining from the sky. Harry walked through the village, noticing movement behind the big window at the bookstore, the silhouetted figure of John hunched behind the checkout desk. The police would probably be questioning John as well. He'd clearly known Annie when she'd worked at the store. Had he known what was going on with the two of them? He must have had some idea.

Harry almost considered popping in to see him, to ask him directly, but he wanted to see Grace first. He headed up the rise of the Old Post Road, passing the inn, then arriving at the house where Grace had rented the room. It was mostly dark, except for some dim light in one of the second-floor windows. At the front door he rang the bell. There was a chime inside the house. He looked at the door while he waited; ornate wooden scrollwork framed a circular piece of glass. Below it was a visible remnant of what had been a number attached to the door—22—and two nail holes where the numbers had been affixed. Harry looked to the side of the door where *37 Prospect* had been stenciled in dark red paint. Either the street number had changed or the door had been moved from another house. He pressed his finger to where the numbers on the door used to be, then pulled his finger back as the door swung inward, Grace looking a little startled, as though she was surprised to see him.

"Sorry," she said. "I forgot Mrs. Whitcomb isn't here, so I didn't immediately get to the door. Come on in."

Harry followed Grace as she led him up the stairs, carpeted with a threadbare Oriental runner, and to her rented room. It was as large as she'd said it was, the wide double bed looking out of place against the far wall. It was as though the house had once upon a time been split into a two-family, and this had once been the upstairs living room. A couch and two wooden chairs made a semicircle around a fireplace; Grace sat on the couch and Harry took a chair.

"What's going on?" Grace said, pushing her hair back off her forehead. Her eyes were bright, almost jumpy. She was wearing a pair of jeans and a striped black-and-white shirt. Her feet were bare, her toenails painted green.

Harry opened his mouth to speak, and surprised himself by saying, "I don't believe that you only knew my father a little."

"Uh-huh," she said.

"We just found out . . . I just found out that my father hadn't been faithful to his wife, and, and I wondered what your relationship with him was."

As Harry spoke the words, a deep flush of red spread across Grace's face.

"What do you mean you just found out?" she asked.

"I just found out that my father was having an affair with someone here in town."

She shook her head rapidly. "He wasn't."

"I think you need to tell me what's going on."

She exhaled, and rubbed at an eye with the heel of her palm. "I was involved with your father. Down in New York. Who told you he was having an affair here?"

"My stepmother."

"Alice?"

"Right. She said he was involved with a married woman who worked at the store, and she thinks that the woman's husband might have had something to do with my father's death."

Grace was shaking her head again.

"Look," Harry said. "Just tell me what the fuck is going on. Stop shaking your head."

Grace lifted her head and met Harry's eyes. In the lamplight of the room her eyes looked more green than blue.

"Okay," she said, and took a breath. "You know how your father used to come down to New York all the time to visit his old store?"

"Uh-huh."

"I know Ron, the owner of the store. He owns the apartment I rent."

Harry was about to tell her he already knew that, but let it go. He wanted to hear the whole story first.

"I used to help out in the bookstore a little bit. That's how I met your dad, about two years ago. This was right after Hurricane Sandy, and the store's basement flooded and wrecked a bunch of books. Your father came down to help out."

"Yeah, I remember," Harry said.

"I was helping out as well, and we spent a lot of time

together. Ron was pretty useless—you know Ron—and two of the employees couldn't even get into Manhattan that week, so it was just us. And, basically, I fell in love with your father."

She paused, and Harry said, "Okay."

"I know it sounds strange."

"It's just that the age difference . . ."

"I can try and explain it if you like, but the truth is, I don't know if I can. I was coming off a shitty relationship with someone my age who turned out to be a worthless human being. Your father and I . . . it was almost instant, like when you feel you've known someone your whole life five minutes after meeting them. And he was kind, as you know. But he was married, and even if he wasn't, he was nearly twenty-five years older than me, so it's not like I thought there was potential. But I let myself fall in love, even became a little obsessed. I think he knew—no, I *know* he knew—and I think he decided to not take advantage of it. But whenever he came to the city he'd take me out to dinner. We had a place, a Spanish restaurant, that we always went to. We'd started going there when we first met because it was the first restaurant we'd hit when we walked out of the blacked-out portion of the city to where there was still electricity. And we kept going there. We even had our own special table, not that we always got it, but we usually did, and the owner and his wife treated us like we were a couple."

"But you weren't yet?" Harry said.

"Well, not yet, but then we were. It wasn't casual, Harry. It was serious. That's why I know he wasn't having another affair. I think your stepmother made that up, that maybe she's trying to deflect the police from looking at her."

"You think she had something to do with my father's death."

"I don't really know why I'm here, but yes, I've thought about it, thought about Alice having something to do with your father's death. That's why I came up, I guess, and why I wanted to meet you. To find out if you knew anything."

"Did you think Alice found out about you and my father?"

Grace shifted forward. "The last time I saw your father, about two and a half weeks ago, he talked about Alice a lot. It was something he never really did, so I thought it was strange. He told me that she'd started acting strange toward him. She couldn't make eye contact, she was totally cold. He kept asking her what was going on, but she wouldn't say anything."

"It sounds like she found out about you two."

"That's what we thought, but we went over it, and there just didn't seem to be any way she could have."

"There could be a thousand ways. She could have found one of your hairs on his coat, she could have hired a detective, she could have just felt it, known it."

"I know. Like I said, it's why I came here. I had to see her, at the funeral. I thought I might just know, from looking at her."

"And did you?"

"I don't know what I know anymore, but I think I should go to the police, tell them I was having an affair with him. Maybe it would make a difference."

"You should," Harry said.

"I will, before I leave."

"That will mean that Alice will know about you."

"I guess. If she doesn't already."

"She already knows about this other woman."

"There is no other woman," Grace said.

"Are you sure?"

"Yes. Your father and I talked. I was definitely the only person he was involved with. He was racked with guilt. He said it was the first time he'd done anything remotely like this."

Harry felt her eyes on him, looking for confirmation. "I don't know what to tell you," he said. "But think about it . . . he was deceiving Alice with you. What makes you think he wouldn't have deceived *you* with someone else?"

Grace pursed her lips, then said, "Because he wouldn't have. I don't believe it. Alice is making it up because maybe she wants the police to look at someone else."

Harry felt a little bit of loyalty toward Alice. He said, "Why wouldn't she just tell them about you?"

"I don't know. Maybe she didn't know about us. Maybe because I wouldn't be a good suspect because I was down in New York City."

They were both quiet for a moment. Harry's eyes traced a water stain in the corner of the bedroom's high ceiling. Finally, he asked, "Were you hoping that my father would leave Alice to be with you?"

"Of course that's what I was hoping," Grace said, her voice loud.

"I just didn't know . . . I didn't know if you saw it as a fling."

"I thought it was just a fling, because he was married, and because he was twice my age, and all those other things, but, like I said, I was in love with him. We got one another. So, yeah, I had fantasies that he'd leave Alice and move back down to the city and in with me. It didn't make me feel good about myself, but I thought about it. I thought about it all the time." She paused, and Harry didn't say anything. "Are you mad at me?" she said.

"What do you mean?"

"I seduced your father. He was a married man. It's possible that I'm the reason he's dead."

"I don't know if I'm mad at you, but I want to know more. About you and him."

"You're just like him, you know. You don't talk about yourself. You just keep asking questions. He did the exact same thing. I thought he was selfless, at first, but I changed my mind. I think it was selfish. I think he didn't want to give anything of himself away, and I think you're the same."

"I don't know what to say to that," Harry said.

"Yeah, that's what he used to say," Grace said, her voice tinged with anger. Then quietly, she said, "What's the name of this woman he was supposed to be involved with?"

"Annie Callahan."

"How did he know her?"

"She worked at the bookstore, the one up here. Alice said that my father hired her because he'd heard her husband was out of work, and she needed the money."

Harry watched Grace, who was chewing at the side of her thumbnail. He thought she looked doubtful, for the first time. He wanted to say more, wanted to convince her that there was a possibility that his father had been involved with two women on the side. Maybe it was a midlife crisis, maybe it was a pattern he'd had his whole life. Harry no longer knew what to believe.

"Grace," he said.

She stopped biting at her nail and looked up at him.

"You should definitely tell the police you're here," Harry said.

She shrugged, and said, "I'll talk to them. They won't believe me, but I'll talk to them." She started chewing at the side of her nail again. He wondered what she'd done today—if she'd left this room, or had anything to eat. He was going to ask her, but instead he said, "I should go. Thanks for telling me the truth about my father."

"Stay a little longer," she said quickly, smiling weakly, her eyes locking on his.

"No, I should go back," Harry said. He stood.

"Okay. I understand."

Harry didn't immediately move. "Are you going to be okay?" he asked.

"I will be. I'll be fine."

"I'll check in with you tomorrow morning, okay?" he said. "Bright and early. I think we both need to get some sleep."

"Okay," she said, her shoulders dropping. There was

a sad smile on her face, and she looked defeated. "Be careful," she said.

"I'll be fine. I'll be back tomorrow. We can go to the police, together, if you'd like?"

"Yes," she said. Harry went through the door, shut it behind him, and retreated, hand on a banister, down the dark stairwell, and out the front door, back out into the night.

Back at Grey Lady, he shut the front door quietly behind him. He could hear gentle snores coming from the living room. He took his shoes off by the door, and went and looked over the couch at Alice, sleeping, while another home renovation show, this one with a pair of handsome twins, played on the television.

Harry left her where she was and went up to his own room. It was warm and stuffy, retaining the heat from earlier in the day. He opened a window, took off all his clothes, and got under his single sheet. He cracked a book even though he knew there was no possibility he'd be able to read anything. He stared at the illegible lines of print, and thought about the day, and about how little he'd known his father.

Chapter 20

Then

The police returned the next evening. Not Officer Wilson with his fuzzy mustache, but a woman with a perm of tight curls who introduced herself as Detective Metivier.

"Sorry to come around during dinner hour," she said to Jake at the door, as Alice listened from the living room, "but I have some follow-up questions for Alice."

Jake let her in, offering her coffee that she turned down.

Alice had called in sick at the pharmacy, and was still in her pajamas and her favorite robe. She wasn't sick, but she really didn't want to be out in public, listening to people speculate about what had happened to Gina Bergeron. They must have been gossiping like mad in Kennewick, because they had already begun to gossip in the world at large. Alice had watched *Entertainment Tonight* the previous evening, and Gina was the second story. A promising model who had mysteriously died in the ocean while visiting her family. Alice had been shocked when one of the pictures they chose to show was her own favorite picture. Gina in the yellow bathing suit with the sad eyes. Well, they'd picked it because of how haunted she looked, probably. At the end of the segment, John Tesh had said something like "More to come on this story, for sure," and Mary Hart had frowned and tilted her head. Alice had thought: *Why is there more to come?* Another tragic model, drugs and suicide. What else was there?

After Jake pulled up a chair for Detective Metivier to sit on, Alice, settling on the edge of the sofa, noticed that the detective held a small plastic box in her hands. It looked like a square toolbox, or a piece of medical equipment. The detective caught Alice looking at the box, and said, "It's a kit for making a tooth imprint, Alice."

Jake, still standing, said, "What's going on?"

"Alice, did you bite Gina Bergeron on Friday night?"

"Yeah, I bit her on the hand."

The detective looked a little taken aback, as though she'd been preparing for a denial.

"Can you tell me why?"

"Okay. I went to dinner at the Bergerons' house because Gina's mother invited me. After dinner, Gina and her mother asked me to come outside, and then they attacked me—"

"They attacked you? Physically?" the detective asked, gesturing. Alice noticed that there were no rings at all on any of her fingers.

"Not physically, but they ganged up on me."

"Why did they do that?"

Alice turned and looked at Jake. His normally placid features registered a small amount of concern. She turned back to the detective. For someone who didn't wear jewelry at all, she wore a lot of makeup.

"They didn't like that I was still living with Jake. They thought I should get my own place."

"Alice, you—" Jake began, but the detective interrupted.

"Why did they think that?" she asked.

"You obviously know, because you've talked with Mrs. Bergeron. She must have told you about the bite, so she probably told you all about everything else."

"I'd like to hear it from you, Alice."

"They thought Jake was taking advantage of me. It's sick. I have no family left, and Jake is all I have. He's more than a stepfather to me, more like a real father, and they were telling me that I should get away from him. It was crazy. I took off."

"Why do you think they thought Jake was taking advantage of you?"

"How do I know? Gina got it stuck in her sick head, and she told her mother, and her mother believed her, I guess."

The detective turned to Jake for the first time and asked: "Did you know anything about this?"

"No, I'm hearing this for the first time. It's totally ridiculous. Alice is, was, my wife's daughter. That's all it is. Alice, why didn't you tell me about this?"

"Because I didn't want to bother you. Because it was disgusting."

"So, Alice," Detective Metivier said. "What can you tell me about the bite?"

Alice breathed deeply through her nostrils. Some of the anger she'd felt that night was coming back, and for a brief moment she could feel Gina's flesh between her teeth. "They kept accusing me, and I got upset. We were in the backyard and I decided to just leave. Gina ran over and grabbed me, and I just took her hand and bit it. I wanted her to let go of me, and it worked."

"But Gina came back that night. She came here and tried to talk with you some more, right?"

"I already told the other policeman all about that. Gina was drunk. She came to apologize and wanted to go swimming as a way to restart our friendship, or something. I told her I didn't want to, and she left. That's all that happened."

"You didn't go swimming with her?"

"No. I stayed here. If I'd gone swimming with her she probably wouldn't have drowned. Does her mother think I went swimming with her?"

Instead of answering, the detective asked, "Why didn't you tell us the whole story when Officer Wilson first questioned you?"

"I told you, because I hadn't told Jake about what Gina and her mother were saying. I didn't want to upset him. And it had nothing to do with what happened later. I'm sorry, I should have told you, but I didn't."

"That's okay, Alice," the detective said, and looked as though she was about to stand.

"So you don't need my teeth . . . you don't need to use your . . ."

"I don't, not if you're telling me that it was you who left the bite mark on Gina's hand." She stood, glancing toward Jake, then back to Alice.

"What does Gina's mother think? Does she think

I had something to do with what happened to Gina?" Alice asked.

"She's pretty upset. She says that Gina hated swimming, and would never have gone swimming alone in the middle of the night, especially with her hand the way it was."

"She didn't hate swimming. Like I told that other detective, we'd been swimming before."

"Okay," the detective said. "Thank you, Alice, for clearing up the issue of the bite." Something in the detective's voice and body language told Alice that she'd just decided that there was nothing mysterious about Gina's death. Alice had passed, somehow. But then Detective Metivier turned to Jake and said, "Do you mind walking me out to my car? I have a couple of questions just for you."

"Oh," Jake said, then nodded. "Sure."

Alice was able to watch them talking in the parking lot from the window in Jake's office. They stood side by side near what was probably the detective's tan car, something American, maybe a Chevy Celebrity. It was a grey evening, the air filled with fine mist, and Jake, wearing only a sweater, stood with his arms across his body. The detective had put on a white trench coat with a big, floppy collar. She seemed to be mostly listening as Jake spoke. She nodded several times, then

began patting at her pockets as though she was getting
ready to leave. Jake unfolded his arms and held out a
hand for her to shake. Then she was pulling out a pack
of cigarettes, offering one to Jake. To Alice's surprise—
he'd quit a couple of years ago—he took the cigarette.
The detective lit her own with a lighter then handed
the lighter to Jake. After she drove off, Alice watched
him stand, greedily smoking the cigarette, and looking out across the road toward the ocean, lined with
whitecaps.

When he came back in, his skin was damp with the
mist from outside, and he smelled sharply of the cigarette.

"Why'd you smoke one of her cigarettes?" Alice
asked.

"You were watching us?"

"I saw you through the window, but you smell like
cigarettes."

He sniffed, and rubbed at his nose. "I was just being
polite. She offered."

"What did she ask you?"

"Let me get a drink, and I'll tell you. Why didn't
you tell me about Gina and her mother? Jesus, Alice."

She followed him into the kitchen. "I didn't tell you
because who cares what they think."

"Maybe I would've cared. You have to tell me these things, Alice. I need to be prepared."

"What did that detective ask you?"

He poured whiskey into a tumbler, then added some ice and soda water. It was what he drank when he was drinking a lot, what he drank all day on Sunday when there were football games on.

"She wanted to know what our relationship was."

"What did you tell her?"

"I told her that it was none of her business."

"Why didn't you tell—"

"She said that Vivienne Bergeron told the police she has proof that we're involved, that one of her friends saw us together at a restaurant in Portland."

"That doesn't mean anything. Besides, who cares, and what does it have to do with what happened with Gina?"

"Nothing. Nothing at all. That's what I told the detective and she agreed. She says that Vivienne Bergeron is kicking up a fuss, convinced that because they had accused you that night, somehow you got revenge on Gina. She's been talking about the bite, and how she knows for a fact that Gina would never have gone swimming by herself."

"That's stupid."

"I'm just telling you what the detective told me that Vivienne has been saying."

"So what does she think I did? Does she think I killed Gina and threw her in the ocean?"

Jake shrugged. "She just lost a child. I don't think she's thinking straight. Can I get you a drink?"

They watched TV. Jake let Alice pick what to watch. *Mystic Pizza* was on USA and they watched that, Alice occasionally flipping over to MTV during commercials. Jake went back and forth several times to the kitchen to get a new drink. When the movie was over, Alice turned the television off and said that she was going to bed.

"Wait a moment, Ali, okay?"

Her body was instantly cold. "Sure," she said.

"I'd like to talk with you about something."

Alice's heart fluttered, and she stood up, and said, "How about tomorrow, okay? I'm too tired to talk." She knew what he wanted to talk about. She knew that the police detective bitch had said something to him, and now he wouldn't want to live with her anymore.

"Hey, stop that," he said, his voice too loud, like it sometimes got when he drank a lot. "Come here, okay?"

She came over and stood in front of him. She realized she was still in the robe she'd worn all day, and her hair was probably flat and greasy. No wonder he was kicking her out. "You want me to leave?" she said, and jutted out her lower lip.

"Alice, no. That is definitely *not* what I want. Sit down here."

He patted his lap, and she slid on top of him as he carefully placed his drink on the glass-topped side table. "What I want," he said, "is for you and me to have a conversation about how we need to be extra-careful from now on."

"I didn't say anything to Gina and her mother. They were trying to get me to say something about you, but I swear I didn't."

"I know you didn't. I'm not talking about just you, I'm talking about us. We have to be careful about what restaurants we go to, and how we act, and eventually— not right away—you should get your own place. No, no, don't worry. You should get your own place even though you can keep staying here most nights."

"Maybe we should just let people know about us. It's not illegal."

"I know it's not illegal but it's frowned on. And I wouldn't care except that I have a position at a bank that's important. I advise people in this town on what to do with their money, and they're going to lose faith in me if they think that you and I are together. They won't understand."

"What if we got married?"

"Alice," he said, then took a long sip of his drink, placing the glass back down with a loud clink. "It wouldn't make any difference. In fact, it would probably make things worse. It's not just that you're the daughter of my wife, it's that I'm thirty years older than you."

"I don't care."

"I don't care, either, but other people will."

"Fine. We'll be extra-careful."

"That's all that I'm saying. We have to be very, very careful from here on out. People hate to see other people happy. Remember that."

Alice went to bed first. She was exhausted, brushing her teeth for less than thirty seconds, then slipping out of her robe and under the covers. She wondered if she was exhausted because of the stress of being interviewed by the frizzy-haired detective, or if she was tired because she'd barely done anything all day. She hadn't gone swimming since Friday night, the night that Gina couldn't make it back. Tomorrow she'd swim again. There were only so many days left before it would be too cold, and then she'd have to swim at the Y with the overchlorinated water and the old ladies.

She lay awake thinking about swimming, then listened as Jake got ready for bed, standing for a long time in the bathroom applying his face lotion, as he always did. He climbed in beside her, naked, smelling of vanilla and sandalwood.

He kissed her, the type of kiss that meant he was tired, then said, "I was going to bring it up earlier, but I couldn't find the right time."

"What?" she said, her limbs tingling.

"I woke up on Friday night to get a glass of water. You weren't in bed so I went downstairs to look for you, and I couldn't find you anywhere. I was nervous, so I looked out the window. I saw you coming back from the beach. Your hair was wet."

She didn't respond.

"Alice?" Jake eventually said.

"Why didn't you say something?"

"When? That night?"

"Yes."

"I guessed that it was something between you and Gina, and I didn't want to bother you about it. I went back to bed. You came in and showered."

"I didn't—"

"Shh," Jake said, his face pressed close up to her ear. "I don't want you to say anything, but I wanted you to know that I knew. Don't say anything, okay? We're better off—much better off—without Gina in our lives. Just like we are better off without your mother."

Alice's limbs stiffened at the mention of her mother.

"Whatever you say," she said.

"I love you, Alice. Forever and ever. No matter what happens."

"I love you, too, Jake," she said, and turned away from him.

After he fell asleep, Alice got up and went to her old bedroom, and got under the covers. She could hear the very faint sawing sound of Jake's snoring through the condo's cheap walls. She tried to sleep, but she kept thinking about what Jake had said. Why had he brought up her mother? She'd found her mother dead on the sofa, something she'd have to live with forever. And now she'd lost her best friend. She hadn't been able to save her, and Jake was making it sound like she was somehow to blame.

She flipped over onto her stomach, even though she knew she wasn't going to fall asleep. She thought about Jake, trying to erase the words he'd said to her.

Chapter 21

Now

The bed was moving, the twisted sheet tightening against his ribs.

Harry opened his gummy eyes. It was still night. He was cold, but a warm body was pressed against his back, and an arm had snaked over his shoulder. He heard Alice's voice in his ear: "Just keep sleeping, Harry. I don't want to be alone."

Harry stayed as still as possible, wondering if he could just pretend to be asleep, but he knew that she'd felt his entire body tense when she touched him. She pulled in tighter. There was some kind of satiny fabric between his body and hers, but he could feel the press of her breasts against his back, the rough edge of a nipple. "Alice . . ." he managed to say.

"Shhh. Go back to sleep. You're so cold." She spread her hand across his chest, then brought her legs up so that her knees touched the backs of his thighs.

"I don't think—"

"Just for me, okay. Go back to sleep." He could smell the wine on her breath. She shifted her body back and forth like a bird settling into a nest. She pressed her forehead against the back of his neck.

Harry concentrated on his breathing, keeping it steady. He closed his eyes. It did feel good to have a body up against his, radiating warmth. He listened as her breathing became deeper; he could feel her breath against his skin. His heart rate began to slow.

When he woke, he was on his back, Alice hovering over him, lifting her nightgown past her hips. Harry started to speak, and Alice was kissing him, one hand against his neck, her other sliding down his stomach, and taking hold of his erection. There was nothing he could do to stop it from happening; his body was taking over, and soon they were having sex. Alice kept her head close down to his, her hair spread over his face, and he shut his eyes, the world reducing to darkness and sensation, Alice whispering his name in his ear again and again.

Afterward, he started to speak again, and Alice said, "Don't. Let's not talk about it."

Harry, relieved, stayed quiet, and soon Alice's breath became slow and rhythmic. He turned away from her and closed his eyes. When he opened them again the window had brightened with soft morning light. Alice was still breathing heavily, her mouth now pressed into the hollow between his shoulder and his spine, her lips against his skin. He moved his hips involuntarily, and Alice's fingers fluttered against him. Harry made himself roll away, then sat up on the edge of the bed. He produced a low humming sound to make it seem as though he had just woken up. Behind him, on the bed, Alice stirred. He stood before she could say anything, aware of his nakedness, and quickly left the room, grabbing his jeans and T-shirt from the floor.

He went straight downstairs, where he got dressed, and pulled on the shoes that were still by the door. Then he stood still, listening for the sound of Alice getting up herself. He heard nothing. What had happened in the middle of the night now felt like a vague, dusky dream. How drunk had she been? Was there the possibility that she hadn't known what she was doing?

Harry opened the door quietly and stepped out onto the front step into the cool dawn. Birds were chattering loudly in the trees, and the front lawn was coated in dew. He sat on the steps, his mind replaying details from a few hours ago. His skin shivered and tightened at the memory. It had been a new experience, giving in to the will of someone else, her body taking control of his; she was smaller than he was, but she'd felt larger as she'd drawn him into her. Harry was desperately trying to file the experience into a folder that made sense, but he couldn't. He'd had sex with his stepmother, less than a week after the death of his father. It felt halfway between a fantasy come true and the type of nightmare you wake up from drenched in sweat. He tried to stop remembering it, but kept hearing her whispering his name in his ear, the edge of her teeth against his earlobe.

He had no idea what time it was, but figured it was probably just around five o'clock. He decided to walk to the Dunkin' Donuts over in Kennewick Center, get himself some coffee, maybe something to eat.

It was over a mile to Kennewick Center, but the walk felt good. He began to warm up, the sun rising, the mist burning off. Approaching the Dunkin' Donuts, he wasn't sure it was open yet, but when he got to the front doors, he could make out an employee moving behind the counter. He got himself a large regular—a coffee with maximum cream and sugar—and a blueberry donut.

He sat in a booth, watched through the steamy window as a pickup truck pulled in across two spots. A skinny man wearing a camo baseball cap jumped out of the cab, the truck still running, and strode into the shop. "Mornin', Cody," said the woman behind the counter as she got him a coffee and an apple turnover without asking him what he wanted. Harry kept his eye on the truck, spilling exhaust, and had a brief urge to race out of the shop with his coffee, steal the truck, and just start driving north, see how far he could get.

But he didn't move. The man returned with his breakfast to his truck. Harry kept sipping at his coffee. He ate the blueberry donut, remembering, as he ate it, that it had been his father's favorite. His thoughts shifted again to Alice, and Grace's conviction that she had something to do with the murder. What if Grace was right, and he'd slept with his father's murderer? His stomach flipped. He told himself to breathe, and thought of Occam's razor, something he'd learned about in a probability course in college: *The simplest solution to a problem is most likely the correct one.*

What was the simplest solution?

Probably that his father had been an adulterer who liked to seduce younger women. He'd seduced a married woman and been killed by a jealous husband. Grace was just another girlfriend who had nothing to do with his father's death. Alice was a betrayed wife who was right now trying to grapple with everything that was happening. And she was desperate for attention and affection. Wasn't this the most logical solution? And if that was the case, then Harry had some responsibility because of what his father had left behind. His hand went instinctively to his pocket, looking for his phone, just to check if Grace or Alice had sent him a text, but he'd left it in the bedroom.

He left the shop with his coffee. The sun was higher in the sky, and there were a few cars along Route 1A now. He decided to walk back home; later he would get in touch with Grace again, make sure she told the police what she knew. He walked along the sandy edge of the road. There was a breeze from the east, and the air held the smell of the ocean. As he approached Kennewick Village he was about to veer off toward York Street and back to Grey Lady, but decided at the last moment to walk past the house where Grace was living. It was too early to visit, but maybe if he just walked by . . .

The house looked quiet and empty in the morning light. Harry glanced up at Grace's second-floor window; it was hard to know for sure, but he thought her lights were on. He walked halfway to the door, thinking maybe he'd knock gently just in case she was up. But then he stopped; the door was open. Not by a lot, but it was cracked by about six inches. He almost turned back, knowing suddenly that something was wrong. He stood frozen for a few moments, then continued toward the door. He could peer inside, and listen. When he reached the door, he pressed his palm against it and pushed. The inside of his mouth was coated with the cloying taste of the sweet coffee.

Grace was on the floor of the foyer, her bare feet pointed toward the door. He knew she was dead but said her name anyway, his voice no louder than a croak. He stepped through the doorway. She was wearing the clothes she'd been in the night before. A striped shirt and jeans. One arm was flung over her head, the other down by her side.

"Grace," he said louder, hopeful, but when he took another step inside the house, he could see what had happened to her. Her skull, on the left side, was collapsed inward, her hair sticky with blood. Her purple jaw didn't line up with the rest of her head.

Bile rose in the back of Harry's throat, and he closed his eyes for a moment. He took a step backward, felt the blood rushing from his head, and took hold of the door frame.

He touched his pocket, even though he knew he

didn't have a phone with him. He took one quick look into the foyer again, past Grace's body, and saw a phone on a waist-high table. Keeping his eyes on the phone, he went to it. It was an old landline, squat like a toad, and he half expected it to not have a dial tone when he picked up the receiver and pressed it to his ear.

PART 2
Black Water

Chapter 22

Now

Caitlin McGowan reread the e-mail for what must have been the fiftieth time. It was from Grace, her sister, and it had been sent probably just hours before she'd been murdered.

I know you're going to freak out, C, but I'm in maine. I came up after I heard B died, just after we talked. I found an airbnb and drove up to go to the funeral. I just couldn't stay in new york and pretend it wasn't happening. I needed to see her.

Sorry, I know I'm not making sense. I'll slow down. I'm exhausted and wired at the same time, and I've barely eaten today. B's son Harry was just here. He came by to tell me that there's now a suspect, that Alice told the police B was having an affair with someone in town, and she thinks this woman's husband was the one who killed B. SHE'S MAKING IT UP, and that makes me think that Alice actually did have something to do with B's death. First of all, B was not seeing someone else. I told Harry that and he looked at me like I was deluded, and you're probably thinking the same thing. But he Wasn't. Alice made it up because she found a way to kill him, and now that the police know it wasn't an accident, she needs someone else to blame.

The son is CUTE. He's an age-appropriate B, right down to his pure emotional blockage. When I saw him at the funeral my knees literally buckled and then I saw the way Alice was hovering over him and I wanted to swoop in and save him. I went to the bookstore because I thought Alice might be there and I could see her up close but he was there, and then I was telling him I was looking for a job. I could tell he was into me, or maybe it was just that he could tell that I was lying about why I was there at the store. He texted me, and asked me out for drinks, like a real date. He told me all about his life, and I made up a story about coming to maine to get away from it all, but he didn't believe it (you know I'm a lousy liar) so he came here tonight, and I told him EVERYTHING. And then all I could see was how he was blaming me for what happened to his father, that I started it all, and then I didn't know if I was just projecting my own guilt onto him.

I feel like my skin is on fire I'm so anxious. I just decided to go to the police in the morning and tell them EVERYTHING. Who knows if they'll care, but then I'll be done with it. I have nothing to hide and no one to protect. And as soon as I do that, then I am hightailing it away from maine, and, look, I buried the lead (lede?): Can I come stay with you? Not forever, but for a few days. I'm done with new york, and I can't stay here, and I really don't want to move back in with mom, at least not right now. I know you've told me in the past that I can come anytime but I still wanted to ask. I'll be in boston tomorrow. You're probably asleep but write me back as soon as you get this. xoxo g

Caitlin shut her laptop. She'd shared the e-mail with Detective Dixon, bringing it up on her phone at the station to show him earlier in the day. He'd read it, then asked Caitlin if she could forward it to him.

"What do you think about it?" she asked him.

"I wish she'd come to us earlier," the detective said, and the words made Caitlin's stomach hurt. It must have shown on her face, because he quickly continued, "But who knows if it would have made a difference? It's not a smoking gun. Plenty of people have affairs and don't end up being murdered."

"But the fact that Grace got killed must mean that Bill Ackerson was as well, that it's connected?"

"There's no indication that Alice was even aware of your sister's existence."

"Why? Because she says she wasn't?"

"Can I ask you some questions about Grace?" the detective said, hunching his shoulders forward like he had a kink in his back. Caitlin noticed that he had a scar above his right eye where his eyebrow didn't grow.

"Sure," Caitlin said, and settled back into the molded plastic chair. They were at a small conference table toward the back of the station, in a glass-encased room. There was a whiteboard that had been erased clean of all but a few random, smudged words: *names, cell, separate.* The detective had brought her here to show her photographs of Grace's lifeless face for purposes of identification. Caitlin had received a frantic call from her mother early that morning, telling her that she'd just heard from the Kennewick Police Department, looking for identification of a body carrying a Michigan driver's license in the name of Grace Ellen McGowan. Caitlin volunteered to drive up to Maine. During the hour-and-a-half drive, in a state of unreal shock, she'd alternated between bewildered grief and a desperate hope that it was all a misunderstanding. When the detective put the first photograph down in front of Caitlin, she had had a moment of pure relief wash over her. *It wasn't Grace.* The face they were showing her was a young woman, but with fuller cheeks than Grace had, with puffier eyes.

Caitlin shook her head. "I don't . . . I don't think . . ."

The detective placed a second photograph next to the first one. It was of a tattoo, cursive script across a rib cage: *Do you realize we're floating in space?* As quickly as the wave of relief had swept through Caitlin, a wave of icy recognition replaced it. Caitlin looked back at the face, photographed on a neutral background. Yes, it was her twin, her features reduced to their basic nature, a nose, two eyes, a mouth. She hadn't recognized the face because there was nothing left of Grace in it. But the tattoo, that silly, impulsive tattoo, some line from a song Grace had loved in high school, meant that it was really her sister.

She nodded at the detective, and he produced a piece of paper, proof of identification, for her to sign. She quickly glanced over the sheet, not trusting herself to speak, then signed on the line. The detective put the sheet of paper in a manila folder, and thanked her, then asked if she wanted to be alone for a moment before they talked further. She nodded, and he left, shutting the door behind him. She cried, a hand across her eyes, for several minutes. She'd cried earlier, when she first got the call from her mother that Grace was dead, but this was different. She'd seen the pictures. Grace, unimaginably, was truly gone.

"She was your twin?" the detective asked, after he'd come back, after she'd shown him the e-mail, after she'd asked him repeatedly what had happened, and *why*.

"Yes."

"Identical twins?"

"No. Fraternal. But some people thought we were identical because we looked alike. But really, we just looked alike because we were sisters."

"Were you alike in other ways?"

"Personality, you mean? God, no. Not at all. I was the careful one, and she wasn't careful at all. As you can tell . . . from the situation, and from the e-mail. She was kind of impulsive and didn't really know what she wanted. No, that's not entirely true. She was impulsive, but she always knew what she wanted. It just changed all the time."

"Like the way she wanted Bill Ackerson."

"Yes."

"Were you surprised that she came up here for the funeral?"

"Yes and no. I just found out, when I got the e-mail."

"Did you know him?"

"No. I'd just heard about him. Not even that much, because Grace knew I disapproved. Then she called at the end of last week to tell me that he'd died."

"You said your sister was impulsive. Any history of violence, any outbursts, any mental health diagnoses?"

Caitlin shook her head no.

"How intense do you think Grace's relationship with Bill was?"

"She was in love with him," Caitlin said.

The detective pushed the box of Kleenex closer to Caitlin. She took a tissue, realizing there were tears on her cheeks. "Can I keep you here just a little bit longer?" the detective continued.

"I guess."

"I want to ask you some general questions about your family and Grace's friends. Maybe this had nothing at all to do with Bill Ackerson."

Caitlin didn't get back to her room at the Sea Mist Motel until late that afternoon. She sat on top of the shiny bedcover and reread Grace's last e-mail, then she listened to the three messages she'd gotten from her mother since she'd last checked her phone. She knew she needed to get back to her, to confirm what they'd already known, that the body was indeed Grace's.

She braced herself and made the call.

"Caitlin?"

"It was her, Mom. It was Gracie."

They both cried together on the phone, then once Caitlin had confirmed that her mother wasn't alone—Patrick was there, like he always was, and her mother's sister, Aunt Nan, was coming over later—Caitlin felt better about beginning the process of ending the phone call.

"Mom," she asked. "Can you have Patrick call Dad? I don't think I'm up to it."

"Yes, of course. Patrick can do it. You've done enough, Caitlin. I should have been out there with you."

"No, there's no reason for you to be here. I'm fine. Well, I'm not fine, but you know . . ."

"Did the police say anything else? Do they know who did this?"

Caitlin told her what she'd found out, but left out for now that Grace had been up in Maine for close to a week without letting anyone know. She'd already told her mother earlier about Grace's involvement with Bill Ackerson, a much older married man. Her mother's response had been expected: "I blame your father."

They talked some more, Caitlin ensuring her mother that she would find out when the body was going to be released—she'd forgotten to ask—and how to make arrangements to bring Grace back to Ann Arbor.

"I'll call you later tonight, Mom, okay? I'm exhausted and going to try and get some sleep."

"Okay. Don't go out alone. I still wish Dan was up there with you."

"I'll be fine. Have Patrick call Dad."

They said good-bye, then Caitlin lay back on the bed. The air-conditioning unit in the window kicked up a notch, and the sound jolted her. She sat up again. As she always did when she was overwhelmed, she made a quick mental list of what needed to be done and in what order. Find out when they would be done with Grace's body. Arrange for the body to be transported to McLellan's Funeral Home in Ann Arbor (she had their number on her phone). Call Maria at work and tell her she'd be away for at least a week. Fly back to Ann Arbor herself.

And once she was there, she could finally tell her mom that Dan and she were no longer together, hadn't been for about three weeks. Her mom, who loved Dan and referred to him as her daughter's "fiancé" even though he never was, was going to be crushed. Or maybe it wouldn't bother her, because of what had happened with Grace. But she didn't believe that. She knew how her mom's mind worked, and it was a moment of tragedy, and that meant all hands on deck, and Dan's not being around was going to be a problem. The other problem, of course, was going to be her father. He would have to go to the funeral, of course, and her mother would just have to ignore him. She just hoped that her father would be decent enough to come to the funeral alone, and not bring his new wife and her three children.

He'd left fourteen years ago, the day after Christmas. Until that moment, Mike and Carol (yep, the parents' names on *The Brady Bunch*) had been together since high school, staying faithful all through college, even though Mike had gone to the University of Michigan while Carol went to Barnard in New York City. They got married a week after they had both graduated. They had three children in two years: the twin girls, then Patrick. There were no more children after that, and Grace and Caitlin had often speculated on how their parents had managed to find a Church-approved method of birth control that actually worked.

Then there was that day after Christmas when Mike called the family together, told them that he was leaving to be with Angela Hernandez, a widow who had three children of her own. He left with one bag of clothes, plus his golf clubs. Caitlin and Grace had just turned eleven, and they had opposite reactions to the sudden decampment. Caitlin had made a silent list of what needed to be done, dedicating herself to helping her mother and her siblings get through the ordeal. Grace had gotten mad, at one point sneaking out of their house late at night and bicycling to their dad's new home to throw rocks through their windows. That was why Carol blamed her ex-husband for all of Grace's outbursts and bad relationships, in particular any relationship she had with a man older than she was. Truth was, there'd been a few, but Caitlin, as much as she blamed her father for many things, tended to think that Grace's personality had been formed long before the Christmas when their father had left home.

Caitlin went to the motel's window and stared out into the half-empty parking lot. A gull skimmed by, just a few feet above a parked Suburban. It reminded her she was in a seaside town. Just two days earlier,

Grace had been alive here, maybe falling for another man. Bill's son, Harry, of all people. And it had been Harry who found her body. How was *he* not a suspect? He must have been at least somewhat upset at Grace and her role as his father's mistress. *Mistress.* The word almost made Caitlin laugh out loud. But that was what her sister had been, right? Nothing more than a mistress to a man old enough to be her father. And she'd gotten killed because of it, despite the detective's asking questions as though there might have been some other motive for Grace's death. The whole thing was lurid, and she hadn't been surprised to see the news vans gathering outside of the police station earlier.

She began to have a conversation in her head with Grace, something she'd done her entire life. *Can you believe it? You were murdered.*

I know, right? Grace's voice, so real in Caitlin's head that a feeling of utter desolation swept through her that she'd never hear that voice out loud again.

Caitlin, throat aching, focused on the mental list again. She repeated the items from her earlier list, adding *Get something to eat at the terrible-looking diner across the street.*

Then she added one more item: *Find and talk to Harry Ackerson.*

Chapter 23

Then

Jake Richter, born and raised in Menasset, Massachusetts, was the son of a German immigrant named Peter Richter, a truck driver who made deliveries for a fishing company in nearby New Bedford; his mother, Jocelyn, half Portuguese and half Quebecois, had cleaned fish at the same New Bedford company. They went on three dates before getting engaged on their fourth. A year later they were married and expecting their first child. After Jacob's birth, a labor so traumatic that she made sure to never get pregnant again, Jocelyn quit her job, occasionally picking up housecleaning work for the summer residents who owned five-bedroom cottages down at the beach.

During his interminable childhood, Jake and his parents spent every evening together in the cramped middle apartment of a brown triple-decker in Menasset's town center. They didn't own a television but listened to the radio every night, Peter steadily drinking brandy from a water glass while Jocelyn would eat Nabisco waffle creams and work on her needlepoint, sometimes talking back to the radio but seldom, if ever, speaking to her husband or her son. Peter Richter rarely spoke, either, and when Jacob started kindergarten he was so stunned by the sheer amount of chatter, not just from the other kids but from nervous Ms. Soares, a first-year teacher, that he refused to speak. Suspected of retardation, he was held back a year.

But by the time he reached middle school, Jacob—now known as Jake—was regularly getting high marks and had learned to insinuate himself into conversations with the other kids in his class. Boys talked about baseball and comic books and liked to make up stories about getting into fights, while girls just liked it when you paid attention to them, mainly through teasing. Both boys and girls talked about television—for a while it was *Howdy Doody*—but by the time Jake was getting ready to leave Menasset Middle School for the regional high school, it was all *Candid Camera* or a new show being aired in the afternoons called *American Bandstand*. Jake asked his parents only once if they would consider buying a television. His mother said that she didn't think she'd be able to keep doing her needlepoint *and* watch television at the same time, and his father said that television was a waste of money. So Jake learned to secretly listen in when kids talked about the shows they watched. He memorized what they said, and that way he could pretend he watched TV as well.

When he was fifteen years old, one of the women whose houses his mother cleaned asked her if she knew anyone who could take care of the grounds in the fall. Jocelyn volunteered her son, and in October of that year, Jake began to work one day a week at Mrs. Codd's shingled cottage, two streets from the shore and with a two-acre backyard to take care of. His job was primarily raking, getting rid of the leaves from the massive beech trees and maples that lined her property, but Mrs. Codd always had one or two small jobs for him to do around the house—taking down the storm windows, or moving the patio furniture back into the garage. She'd hover near him while he did these chores, always with a lit cigarette. Her hair, cut into a bob, was dyed a platinum shade of blond; her face was heart shaped, dominated by wide-set brown eyes made larger by heavy streaks of light blue eyeshadow. She couldn't have been more than fifty years old—at most—but her two children were already away at college, and her husband, an insurance executive in Hartford, came out to the house only on the weekends. Like some of the kids at school, and not at all like his own parents, Emma Codd talked nonstop to Jake, even sometimes accompanying him as he raked up leaves, telling him about her two boys at college, or asking him what kids these days were like, what music did he listen to, what did he watch on television.

"We don't have a TV," he said to her, the first time he'd admitted that to someone.

"Well, that's probably a very healthy thing, Jake, although I don't know what I'd do without it in the evenings. It's not that I watch it all the time, but it's nice to have on just for the company, you know?"

"My parents don't really care about my health, it's just that my dad is too cheap." Jake had figured out that Emma Codd, who could talk about anything, liked to talk about other people's shortcomings most of all.

"Oh, I don't know about that," she said. "I bet he's just worried about your eyes, is all. But, really, if it has to do with money, I'd be happy to just let you have my old television set, one of those things they made just after the war, looks more like a radio with a screen in it, but I'm sure it still works. Or, you're more than welcome to come over anytime you want in the evening and watch some television with me. I wouldn't mind the company."

Jake knew that his father would never accept the television, especially from Emma Codd, a woman he often referred to as "that rich bitch," and whose husband he called "cuckold Codd," using a word that Jake didn't understand. But he did mention to his parents that he'd been invited to watch television at the Codd household. He knew there would be no objection. His was a cold and loveless house, but that also meant there was freedom. He could come and go as he pleased; his parents never expressed any desire to have him around, and his father even grumbled sometimes about how much the weekly food cost had increased now that Jake, who'd grown four inches in under a year, was eating so much.

Jake started going to Emma Codd's house weeknights after suppertime, only after the dishes were cleaned, dried, and put away (his nightly chore), and only if he'd finished all his homework. In her large living room, Mrs. Codd and Jake would watch television together while she drank a Tom Collins, and talked over most of the programs. She would move around the room, freshening up her drink, or stretch out on the sofa next to Jake, sometimes brushing his legs with her bare feet.

Back at home, under his covers, he'd allow himself

vague and dirty thoughts about Mrs. Codd, which would always end with him feeling repulsed by himself. Jake had limited knowledge about sex, not having learned anything from either of his parents, and having absorbed a fair amount of misinformation from kids at school. But in all that misinformation he'd never heard about a kid having any kind of relationship with an adult. It never occurred to him that Mrs. Codd would want to have sex with him. Jake knew that married couples did it, and he'd heard stories about spin-the-bottle games, and the two or three girls from Menasset who would let you get away with more than kissing, but he was still utterly surprised when Emma Codd, one night, asked Jake if he'd ever kissed a girl.

"Not really," he said.

"Not really?" she laughed, so loud that it led to a coughing fit. She stubbed out her cigarette in the plate-sized glass ashtray on the coffee table.

"One or two, I guess," Jake said, which was true. Margie Robinson and he had kissed on the lips in the woods behind the middle school playground. She'd claimed she wanted to see if the lipstick she was wearing would get onto his lips.

"No tongue?"

"What do you mean?"

"Did your tongues touch when you kissed? Was it French kissing?"

"No," he said, shifting uncomfortably on the sofa. Just hearing Mrs. Codd say the word *tongue* had caused an instant reaction in his jeans, and he moved so she wouldn't see what was happening to him.

"It's not real kissing, you know, if you don't use the tongue. I can show you if you like? That way you won't be embarrassed when you next kiss a girl."

"Okay," Jake said, his mouth instantly drying up.

As though she could tell, Mrs. Codd passed him her tall Tom Collins. "Have a sip of this. It will help."

He drank the sweet, icy drink, and it did help, at least with the dryness of his mouth. Mrs. Codd slid down the sofa next to him. He was worried, more than anything, that if they got close enough to kiss, she might notice the hardness in his pants. Would she be disgusted, kick him out of the house, tell him to never come back? Would she tell his parents?

"Now just relax," she said, taking the drink from his hand, sipping some herself, then placing the glass on the coffee table. They began to kiss, and just like she'd said, there was a lot of tongue. She tasted of gin and tobacco, and they kissed so long that Jake began to worry he would suffocate. When she pulled away, she said, "Not bad for your first time." Her lipstick was smudged around her lips, and Jake thought of Margie Robinson in the cold, damp woods.

"Now let's try it again, but a little bit closer this time." She turned toward him, sliding a leg across his lap, and Jake shied away.

"Sorry, sorry," he said.

"What for? This?" She put a hand on his crotch, and Jake nodded, feeling so ashamed that he was worried he might start to cry.

She laughed again, a deep, raspy laugh, and said, "That's what it's supposed to do, sweetheart. As soon as we've mastered kissing, I'll give you lesson number two, okay? Trust me, you'll be fine."

"Okay," Jake said, but his voice sounded shaky and pinched.

"Leave it up to me, Jake," she said. "I'll teach you everything you need to know to be a man. Would you like that?"

He nodded.

"Okay. There's only one rule, though, and it's a big rule. You can't tell anyone about us. Anyone at all. That includes your friends at school, even if they're bragging about girls. It's not that I'm ashamed, or that you should be ashamed, it's just that some people would think it's wrong. Do you promise, Jake?"

She was fully straddling him now, her stiff, satiny skirt bunched up around her waist, and Jake, heart tripping in his chest, promised her he would never tell another living soul.

Jake kept his promise, all the while visiting Emma Codd two or three times a week. They would still occasionally watch television, but only after they were both exhausted by the "lessons." Then they would watch together, each in a postsex daze, crumpled on the sofa, naked and sweaty, each drinking their own Tom Collins, and Jake smoking one of Emma's Chesterfield Kings. She taught him everything a boy and a girl could do together, including things he had never even imagined in his dirtiest thoughts. He was particularly astounded, and baffled, by Emma's physical reactions. Sometimes she would shake so hard that he thought she must be having some kind of medical seizure.

A week before Christmas, Emma told Jake that he needed to stay away for the next month and a half, since her boys were coming home from college, and her husband was taking two weeks away from the office.

"I'll miss you," Jake said.

"I know what you'll miss," she said back. "You'll have to find some innocent girl your own age to corrupt. Shouldn't be too hard."

"I would never do that," Jake said.

"Why ever not?"

"Because of . . ."

"Because of what we have? Jake, sweetheart, what we have together is perfect, as you know, but you are a young man and I am an old, married woman. Don't ever forget that."

Jake did as he was told, and stayed away for the remainder of December and all of January. But after a February nor'easter, Jake took a shovel and walked to the Codd house. Emma was alone again, and after Jake dug out her driveway, she greeted him at her front door with a mug of hot chocolate, then led him to the bedroom.

Afterward, she asked him what he'd done over Christmas.

"Nothing," he said.

"No nice young girls?" she asked.

"No. I thought about you."

"You're very sweet, Jake, and you're a smart boy, and I'm going to fill you in on a secret. The worst thing in the world—the absolute worst thing—is growing old. There's not too much you can do about it, but having a lot of money does help some. Have you met Mr. Codd? I can't remember."

"I saw him once, I think, at the Fourth of July parade."

"He's much older than I am, as I'm sure you noticed. He's turning sixty-five this year. He's made more money than he'll be able to spend in his remaining years, of course, but let me ask you: Would you trade places with him? Would you agree to be sixty-five in return for all his money?"

"I guess not," Jake said, thinking that was the answer she wanted to hear.

"Exactly my point. Your youth is worth more than all his money. So cherish it, Jake. Use it. And when you're my age I recommend that you find a way to make enough money so that you can find someone young to be with yourself. When I'm with you, I'm a young girl again. It's not forever, I know that, but it's much better than tennis with the girls, or going into the city to have dinner with Richard and his insurance friends."

"Does he know about us? Does your husband know?"

Emma Codd leaned away from Jake to get to her pack of cigarettes on the bedside table. Jake studied her body, always a little less attractive to him after they'd done it. Her heavy breasts sagged a little, and there was puckered skin on her thighs and buttocks. After lighting two cigarettes and passing one to Jake, she said, "He doesn't *not* know, I guess. He knows I'm not entirely alone out here week after week while he's in Hartford tallying numbers, but he doesn't know about *you*, specifically.

"He's no saint, himself, you know. He used to have a few regular girls, but I doubt he still does. He can't perform, you know, in the bedroom, anymore."

"Oh," Jake said.

"You're my replacement. That's a good thing, not a bad thing, for everyone involved." Emma Codd blew out a plume of blue smoke, then leaned over and kissed Jake on his hairless chest. "Don't grow old, Jake. That's my advice to you. And if it happens anyway, then find someone younger than you. I know of what I speak."

Two and a half years later, at the beginning of Jake's senior year, Mrs. Codd told him that she was having some health problems, and they wouldn't be able to see each other anymore. He objected but was secretly okay with it. He'd found a new girlfriend by then, a plump blond sophomore whose single mother worked afternoons at the town library. Jake taught her everything he'd learned from Mrs. Codd, and decided he liked being the teacher as much as he'd liked being the student. Maybe more.

After his senior year, Jake went to the University of

Massachusetts at Amherst on a partial scholarship to study economics. He came home that first Christmas, and during a silent midday meal with his mother and father, neither of whom had asked him how he liked school, he asked about Mrs. Codd, and if his mother was still doing housework there.

"You didn't hear?" she said.

"Hear what?"

"She died months ago. She had cancer."

"Oh," Jake said, taking a bite of the dried-out turkey.

"The house was sold and everything."

That afternoon, mild for a Christmas day, Jake walked down to the shingled cottage. It hadn't snowed yet, and there were damp, darkened leaves piled all across the yard. The windows were unlit. The cottage had probably been sold to people who wanted to use it only as a summer house.

The next day Jake returned to Amherst, knowing that he would never go back to Menasset. His parents weren't helping out with any of his college expenses, so there was no reason to ever see them again.

Chapter 24

Now

After spending a good portion of the morning discussing the transportation of Grace's body with one of the funeral directors back in Ann Arbor, but mainly trying to come up with a way, any way, to meet and talk with Harry Ackerson, Caitlin went back to the police station to see if one of the detectives could help her.

She parked across the street from the station, about five car lengths down from a news van belonging to what Caitlin recognized as a Boston news outlet, and idly crossed the street. A woman who *had* to be a reporter—shiny blouse, black skirt, streaky blond hair—watched

Caitlin as she approached the front doors of the station. Sensing the eyes of the reporter on her, Caitlin walked with neutral purpose. She knew she looked like Grace, the murdered girl, and if she showed any signs of grief the reporter, smelling family member, would pounce.

But she made it into the station unmolested, and was buzzed past the front desk when she identified who she was and said she was looking for Detective Dixon. A uniformed officer met her in the main room of the station house, told her that the detective was currently busy but would be free soon, and could she wait. Caitlin said yes, and she was brought to a chair in front of what was probably Detective Dixon's desk, which was cluttered but orderly. She wondered if there was information on her sister's death in one of the neat stacks of manila folders. She waited, checking her phone, texting her mother the details and costs she'd gotten from the transportation company.

When she looked up, she saw that the detective, in a light grey suit, was now standing outside of the same meeting room where he'd shown Caitlin the photograph of Grace the day before. His back was to Caitlin, and he was talking with a young man wearing dark jeans and a green Oxford shirt that was untucked and wrinkled. It had to be Harry Ackerson, even though she'd never seen a picture. He was the right age, couldn't have been more than twenty-one or twenty-two years old, and he looked enough like that picture of Bill Ackerson that Caitlin had seen on the Internet. Dark hair, lanky, narrow faced.

She stood and walked toward the two men across the open space of the station. When she reached them, Detective Dixon turned and spotted her, smiled. "I'll be with you in just a moment, okay?"

Caitlin wondered if he didn't use her name because he didn't want to say it in front of Harry. It didn't matter. The young man was staring at Caitlin, his eyes wide, and his mouth slightly open. It was obviously Harry, unnerved by how similar Caitlin looked to Grace.

"Okay," Caitlin said to the detective, then added, "Is this Harry?" She met his stare. There was fear in his eyes, and something else. He looked distraught.

The detective rubbed the side of his nose, then quickly said, "Harry, this is Grace's sister, Caitlin. Caitlin, this is Harry Ackerson."

"Sorry I was staring," Harry said. "You look just like—"

"I look like Grace. I know."

"I'm really sorry," he said, and his eyes now looked sad instead of scared. He had long, thick eyelashes like a girl's, and high cheekbones.

"Thank you. I'm sorry you had to . . ." She couldn't quite bring herself to say *find the body.*

"Caitlin, I'm going to walk Harry out, then we can talk," the detective said. "Should we meet again in here"—he indicated by turning his head toward the conference room—"or back at my desk?"

"Either one. We can talk here. That's fine."

It was clear that, for whatever reason, the detective was hoping to shuttle Harry as quickly as he could away from the police station, so Caitlin said, "Harry. Can we meet, and maybe talk sometime today?"

Detective Dixon answered, saying, "I'd rather that Harry not discuss details of the case."

"We won't. He won't. I just want to talk with him since he was spending time with my sister."

Harry was alternately looking at Detective Dixon and Caitlin, not speaking, and Caitlin thought of someone at a tennis match, watching the ball go back and forth over the net.

"I can't stop you," the detective said, and Caitlin turned toward Harry.

"Will you meet with me?"

"Okay," he said.

"Will you wait for me, outside of the station?"

Both Harry and the detective, speaking at the same time, said that there were too many reporters outside.

"I could meet you somewhere else," Caitlin said. "Just tell me where."

"Where are you staying?" Harry asked.

She told him, and they agreed to meet in an hour at the Agamenticus Diner, near her motel.

"I don't know what you hope to get from talking with Harry," Detective Dixon said, after returning to the conference room. "I'd rather you weren't talking with him at all."

"He was spending time with my sister. I need to know what she was like during her last few days. Is he a suspect? Is that why you don't want me to talk with him?"

The detective hesitated fractionally. "No, not a suspect, but we believe that whoever killed Harry's father also killed your sister."

"And is Harry a suspect in his father's death?"

"No, no. He wasn't here. He was at his college in Connecticut. And he's been very helpful to us."

"You're looking at his stepmother?"

"I'm not at liberty to say, Caitlin, sorry. What can I do for you? Did you think of something we didn't talk about yesterday?"

Suddenly, Caitlin couldn't remember why she had come back to the station, then recalled that it was to find out if she could get contact info on Harry. She said,

"I just wanted to find out if you had any new information."

"Just that your sister's body will be released later today, and we're hoping to get autopsy results anytime now."

"But you know how she died?"

"She most likely died from trauma to her head. It was very fast, like I told you."

"Okay."

They were each quiet for a while. Caitlin's eyes went again to the whiteboard, erased now of all words, although there was a faint trace of two drawn boxes, arrows going back and forth between them.

"Can I ask you to do me a favor?" the detective asked.

"Sure."

"If you do wind up talking with Harry—and I'd rather you not talk about the details of the case—but if you do, will you consider giving me a call and letting me know what you talked about? I'm sure he won't say anything he hasn't already told me, but he might."

"Okay," Caitlin said.

"And one more thing. Please don't talk to reporters, and if you do—"

"I won't. I have no intention of talking to reporters."

"Well, if that's the case, I'm going to show you to

the side door. They're forming a blockade at the front as we speak."

When she got to the diner early, she found Harry already seated in a booth, a cup of coffee in front of him. She slid in across from him, and said, "Thank you for meeting me here."

"You look so much like her. I'm sorry if I stared earlier."

"I know we did look alike. I didn't see it myself, and people who knew us both said we were very different."

"But you're twins."

"We're fraternal twins." Caitlin caught herself using the present tense and almost corrected herself, but didn't. Instead, she said, "Grace was more outgoing, talked a lot, always did whatever she wanted to. She was fearless."

"And you're not like that."

"No, not particularly. Not like Grace was, anyway." Caitlin felt the ache in her throat that meant she was about to cry again, tried to stifle it, but couldn't. She let out one smothered sob then pressed both palms against her eyes. Her chest hurt.

"I'm so sorry," Harry said. "We don't . . ." He trailed off.

Caitlin looked up at him, took a deep breath, and

said, "No, it's fine. I get these waves, almost like I realize all over again that she's really gone, and they just, they just . . ."

"I know. I get the same thing with my father. Like how is it possible that I'll never speak to him again? It doesn't make any sense."

"No, it doesn't," she said, her voice back to normal.

"I can't imagine what it's like for you. At least with my father . . . he was older. I didn't expect him to die, but we always assume our parents will die before us."

The waitress appeared, refilling Harry's coffee and asking Caitlin if she wanted anything. She didn't, really, but asked for a cup of tea.

"Thanks again for meeting me here," Caitlin said, wanting to get the conversation back on track.

"It's fine. I know you're probably going to want to hear if I know how Grace died, and I really don't."

"You found her, I heard."

"I did. I'd seen her the night before, and the next morning I went back to the house she was staying at to check on her, and . . . I was the one who called the police."

Caitlin wondered, not for the first time, why Harry, who had seen her last, and who had found her body, was not being held as a suspect. Although seated across from him now, seeing the gutted look in his eyes, she didn't think he had had anything to do with Grace's death.

Her tea arrived. Caitlin added sugar and took a sip. She said: "The detective seemed to think that whoever killed your father also killed my sister."

"Is that what he said to you?"

"He did. What do you think?"

"I guess that's what I think, too. But I don't really know, and, honestly, I feel like I've been in shock since coming back up here to Maine. I believed Grace, though. She was convinced that my stepmother had something to do with my father's death. That's why she was here."

"I know. You think she was right?"

"Well, no. When I said I believed her, I guess what I meant was that I believed that she really believed my stepmother had killed my father. She was sure of it. I don't know what to think myself."

"How's your stepmother now?"

Harry scratched his jaw. "She's upset. I'm still staying with her. She says that there's a woman my father was involved with—another woman besides your sister— and that she was the one who killed my father, and now she thinks she killed your sister because she was with my father as well."

"Who's this woman?"

"I don't know if I should tell you her name. Only because I think that she's still being investigated."

"That's okay. I understand. Look, I didn't really want to meet with you to pump you for information. I really just wanted to know about my sister, and her last few days. She liked you. She sent me an e-mail that said so."

"I liked her, too. I felt bad for her. I think she really loved my father."

"Is that what you two talked about?"

Harry told her about seeing Grace at his father's funeral, and then how she came into the bookstore and asked about a job. He said they'd gone out for a drink together, and the last time that Harry saw Grace alive he'd told her about the other woman, a local woman that Bill Ackerson had also been involved with, and she'd been upset.

"She believed it?" Caitlin asked.

"No, she didn't believe it at all. She was upset because she thought Alice—that's my stepmother—was trying to mislead the police. And also, she just seemed jumpy that night, agitated. She seemed different."

Caitlin nodded, picturing it. She said, "She could be like that." And then she found herself telling Harry, this stranger, the story of their father leaving, and how Grace had reacted, going to his new house and vandalizing it.

"So it sounds like maybe her affair with my father had something to do with your own father."

"You think?" Caitlin said, and laughed a little.

Harry smiled back.

"Actually," Caitlin said, "I don't think it's that simple. I don't think anything's that simple. People aren't just defined by a single moment in their life, even if it's this huge moment."

"You don't think so?"

"I don't. I'm sure Grace was susceptible to an older man because she felt betrayed by our dad, but it's not like she would have wound up with just any older man. I think she was in love with your father, probably because of who he was, and not just his age."

"I guess so. I don't know anything anymore. I thought I knew my father better than anyone, and now I find out that he was having at least two affairs behind his wife's back. It's hard for me to imagine."

"You don't *know* that he was having two affairs. Grace was sure that he wasn't."

"I know she was, but think about it: if he was willing to deceive his wife with your sister, then why wouldn't he deceive your sister and be with another woman?"

Caitlin sipped her tea. She'd left the tea bag in too long and it was bitter. She added more sugar, while saying, "You're right, of course. Grace could be stubborn. If she wanted to believe something, then she'd keep on believing it."

"I'm sorry she ever got involved with my father," Harry said. "If she hadn't, then none of this—"

"I know."

They were quiet for a moment. The diner's front door swung open, and a loud group of young girls in soccer uniforms entered, escorted by a few parents. Caitlin watched as a hostess seated the group in three adjacent booths.

"What are you going to do now?" Caitlin asked Harry.

He shrugged, frowning, and for a moment Caitlin thought he was going to start to cry. Instead, he said, "I don't really know. I guess it depends on what happens next. Since the second murder, since what happened to your sister, Alice is terrified. She doesn't want to be alone, and I guess I feel some responsibility toward her."

"Just some?"

"She's all that's left of my family, and I don't want to just abandon her. I'm sure she's freaking out, right now, that I'm not home."

"But she *is* a suspect?"

"No one has said that to me except for your sister."

"What do you think?"

"The night your sister was killed, I was home, and so was Alice. She couldn't have killed Grace."

Caitlin watched Harry shift in his seat, itching to leave. She opened her mouth to ask another question, but Harry placed both hands on the table, and said, "I should go, I think."

"Okay."

"When are you leaving?"

"Either tomorrow night or the next morning, depending on when Grace's body is getting shipped back to Michigan. She can either go in a cargo plane and the funeral director will pick her up at the other end, or she can also go on a passenger plane, and I can ride with her. Not *with her* with her, but on the same plane. I know it doesn't make a difference, but I kind of want to be on the plane with her."

"I think it will make a difference."

"You do?"

"Sure. Maybe you'll feel better."

"My mom will feel better, that's for sure. It's silly, I know."

"I think you should travel with her."

Caitlin felt something loosen in her chest, hearing from this stranger what she'd been hoping to hear.

"Okay, I probably will. That means I'm here for at least another whole day, though. That's what they said."

"Do you know anyone here?"

"What, here in Kennewick?"

"Is anyone here with you?"

"No."

"Maybe we could see each other again. I mean—"

"Yeah, I'd like that," Caitlin said.

They exchanged phone numbers, and Harry got up to leave. She watched him through the greasy window of the diner as he walked to his car. In her head, she spoke to Grace. *He's not your type,* she said, and Grace laughed.

Too young, right?

Far too young.

He's all yours, Caity. Besides, as you now know, I'm dead. She laughed again, and the sound was perfect in Caitlin's head, exactly how Grace laughed, loud and breathless, and usually at something she'd said herself.

Chapter 25

Then

After college Jake Richter worked at a succession of banks, first as a teller and eventually graduating to branch manager, before deciding to go back to school for his MBA at the University of Rochester in upstate New York. After graduation, most of his fellow students went to New York City or Boston to look for jobs, but Jake stayed in Rochester, accepting a job as an investment manager at a local bank. He stayed there ten years, buying a brand-new town house and working out at least five days a week at one of the new gyms that had cropped up downtown. He was in his midforties but looked younger, slim but muscled, and with a full head of hair. He left the greying temples alone because he thought they made him look even more handsome.

Some of the women who worked at the bank, mostly married bank tellers, would interrogate Jake on why he wasn't married yet. "Still having too much fun," he would answer, winking. It was essentially true. But the twentysomething girls from the gym that he dated were becoming less and less interesting to him. They were as experienced as he was, already cynical of the dating realm in which they existed. Jake was most attracted to the high school girls who traipsed through downtown after school let out, fantasizing about introducing them to sex.

Sometimes a group of teens, led by Joan Wilkes, the daughter of one of those married tellers, would come into the bank to get lollipops from the dish that sat on the lacquered table in the waiting room. Joan had flawless skin and natural blond hair, and she was always pestering her mother to take one of her fifteen-minute breaks to give her a ride home. On a cold and rainy November day Jake came out of his glassed-off office while Joan was lingering around, waiting for her mother's break. He said, loud enough so everyone could hear, that he had a few errands to do, and did anyone need anything.

"Ooh, Mr. Richter, can you drive me home?"

Emily Wilkes, currently unoccupied at her station, said, "Joan! That's not appropriate."

Jake laughed. "That's fine. I don't mind her asking. And I don't mind taking her, but that's up to you, Emily."

"Please, Mom."

Jake watched Emily think about it. He knew that what she really liked to do on her fifteen-minute breaks was go to the beat-up couch in the employee break room, put her feet up, and read her latest romance novel.

"I guess if Mr. Richter doesn't mind . . ."

After that first time driving Joan home, Jake knew that seducing her would not be a problem. It was clear from her flushed cheeks and stammered answers that she already had a crush on Jake. It was just a matter of figuring out how to begin an affair without getting caught. The answer came around the third or fourth time Jake, always claiming errands, drove Joan home from the bank. She told him how much she liked going to see old movies at the local university's campus theater, how her friends thought it was lame, and she always had to go alone. Jake knew enough to not suggest a date, but he did start haunting the theater, finally running into Joan during a screening of *Shadow of a Doubt* on a wet spring evening. She'd taken the bus to the theater, so Jake gave her a ride home, but only after bringing her to his town house, parking in the first-floor garage, and taking her virginity in the back seat of his Quattro.

They managed to see each other occasionally during the remainder of that school year, and much more frequently during the summer between Joan's junior and senior years of high school. Sometimes they'd meet at the town house, but more often than not Jake would take her to a roadside motel three towns away, occasionally bringing her to a nearby Chinese restaurant that had low lighting and high booths, and would serve Joan mai tais despite her obvious age.

Jake figured that it was at the Chinese restaurant where they were spotted.

In September, the president of the bank, a jowly man named Charles Fitch, called Jake into his office and gave him a terse ultimatum. Jake would leave immediately, not just the bank, but the city of Rochester. Preferably, even, the state of New York. If he did that, and if he did that right away, then the bank would supply a letter of recommendation. If it became clear that Jake had any more contact with Joan Wilkes, then the authorities would be alerted.

"Does Emily know?" Jake asked.

"If Emily knew it would be Mr. Wilkes talking to you, or the police. I'm cutting you a huge break and I suggest you take it."

Jake did as he was told, selling the town house quickly, and at a loss, then relocating to Kennewick, Maine, a town that reminded him of all the good things about Menasset, but with none of the squalor. Charles Fitch made good on his promise, and the bank supplied a reference that allowed Jake to get a job at a bank two towns over, about a third of the size of the bank he'd worked at in Rochester. He slowly rebuilt his life, telling himself that he should find some nice girl, not too young, and settle down. He briefly dated the events manager from a nearby hotel, a lusty divorcée on the wrong side of forty. It was a mostly unpleasant affair, except that Karen Johnson knew everyone in town, and helped him build his client list at the bank. Not that the year-round residents of southern Maine had much money to invest. But some did, and after a year, he got a raise at the bank and was able to move out of the basement apartment he was renting. He bought a condo, much smaller than his previous town house but with a view of the ocean.

All was going well until the first hot day of Maine's brief summer, when he took a walk on Kennewick Beach and spotted Alice Moss in a green one-piece coming out of the frothing surf. Looking at her body, he thought she was probably sixteen, but her face—its blank inwardness, the wide-set eyes that reminded him of Emma Codd—made her look younger. He pivoted, checking his watch as though he had just remembered an appointment, and followed her to where she flopped onto a beach towel on her stomach. He walked past, trying hard not to look at the way her bathing suit had ridden up along the firm buttocks, and sat on one of the rocks that separated the beach from the road. He lit a cigarette, watching her, aware that she didn't know she was being watched. Did she have any idea what her body was doing to all the men in her vicinity? He finished the cigarette, crushing it out on the rock he was sitting on, and watched her flip onto her back, rustle through her beach bag for a book. She was clearly going to stay for a while, and Jake knew he couldn't linger around too long. He wasn't dressed for the beach, didn't have a towel or a beach bag with him. He took a chance and left. It was a Saturday, and the weather was supposed to be hot the following day as well. She'd be back, he told himself.

That night he barely slept, the image of the pale girl in the green bathing suit whipping through his mind like film through a projector. If she wasn't at the beach the next day, then it was a sign that it wasn't meant to be. But if she was there, then it would also be a sign.

The next morning he drove to the outlets in Kittery, where he bought himself a new bathing suit, plus a towel and a beach chair. After lunch back at his condo, he walked to the beach. The girl wasn't where she was the day before, but he positioned himself nearby. He'd brought his Walkman with him, and a book. *It'll be a blessing,* he thought, *if she doesn't show up.* But she did show up midafternoon, the temperature tipping over ninety, in a different suit, a black bikini this time. He hadn't seen her with dry hair and was shocked by how blond it was, straw colored almost, hair color that only the very young possess. She found an empty spot less than ten yards away. She was close enough that he could see the fine white hairs on her arms.

He watched her all afternoon. Clouds built up in the sky during the evening hours, white and fluffy at first, but darkening. Soon there were distant rumbles of thunder, and a few fat drops of rain began to patter onto the sand. The girl packed up her things, peering with annoyance at the sky. After she left the beach, Jake made himself count to thirty before getting up and donning a Panama hat he'd brought in his beach bag. He left the chair where it was and scrambled up the wooden walkway to the road, just in time to see the girl turn off onto a side street. He followed her at a distance, the major rain holding off, and saw her enter a small, nice house. He noted the number as he walked past, then doubled back to the beach.

Finding out who lived in the house was surprisingly easy. Recent real estate transactions provided the name of the resident. Edith Moss, originally from Biddeford, Maine, and apparently unmarried. Jake called her from the bank, introduced himself, and asked if she'd like to open an account locally. She said she'd come in the next day at noon. Jake identified her right away, as she pushed through the bank's glass doors at half past one: an older, worn-out version of the perfect girl from the beach. As he helped her open an account, he could see the past prettiness in her features, now submerged under puffy, alcoholic skin and sun damage. He studied her as she filled out the paperwork, seeing his future life unfold. How natural it would seem that Jake Richter, the newly arrived bachelor, would court and marry an age-appropriate woman who just happened to have a teenage daughter. The thought of living with the girl from the beach, sleeping down the hall from her, was intoxicating.

He called Edith Moss again that night. She answered the phone, her voice thick and slurred, clearly drunk. He thanked her for opening the account and asked her if she'd have a drink with him sometime. She agreed, but sounded confused, as though that day's events had already begun to fade in her memory. Jake made a note that in the future, any plans he made with Edith would need to be made early in the day.

They were married the following summer, and Edith and Alice moved into Jake's condo near the beach.

It was part bliss and part torture. Alice, more perfect than he had ever imagined, paraded sleepily through the condo in too-small pajamas and, during the summer, still-damp bathing suits. And as Edith became more and more addled from the alcohol, and from the pills that Jake persuaded her to take, Alice and he began to form a silent partnership, a family unit stronger than anything he'd felt before. It wasn't just lust anymore, it was love. And Jake now knew that his original plan, to seduce Alice while still married to Edith, was not enough. He wanted more than a cheap affair with his wife's daughter. He wanted to be together with her, in their own place, without Edith. Jake also knew that Alice did not love her own mother. Her disinterest more than anything else showed that to him. It reminded Jake of his own childhood, his own worthless parents, and how he'd felt nothing for them, then or now.

Jake decided that Edith, half dead already, needed to

die, and he wasn't willing to wait for nature to take its own course.

He killed his wife the night of Alice's graduation dinner party. Alice brought a friend, that leggy girl who was bound to end up as some rich man's mistress in some city far away from Maine. Edith, taking more pills than usual, had been speedy all day long. But she began to drink before dinner, and by the time that Gina and Alice were leaving to go to a party, she was her usual self, a drunken, slurry mess. After the girls left, Jake made Edith a brandy and ginger ale heavily laced with crushed Valium. She drank the first one down before he'd even cleared the dinner plates from the table, so he made her another. He didn't know how many pills and how much alcohol it would take to kill her, but if it didn't work, he could always try again later. And if it did work, if tomorrow was the morning she didn't wake up, then it couldn't be more perfect. Gina had been over to dinner, a perfect witness to Edith's inebriated state in case there was any kind of investigation.

When he was done with the dishes, he came into the living room to find her sprawled on the couch, head tilted back, passed out. The glass that had held the brandy and ginger ale was on the coffee table. It was empty, except for three slivers of ice and one swallow of liquid. He swirled the glass, and was able to see the dregs of the crushed pills. He had done a poor job mixing the Valium into the drink, but it hadn't mattered. Edith had drunk it anyway.

He rinsed the glass in the sink, then put it in the dishwasher and started the cycle. He was planning on watching television, waiting to see what would happen to Edith, but he was too keyed up. He turned the television on, just for the noise, then straightened up the living room, returning to the kitchen to do a thorough clean of the junk drawer, something he'd been meaning to do for a while.

He was consolidating rubber bands, twisting them into a tight ball, when he heard the gagging sounds coming from the living room. He entered to find Edith's body bucking slightly on the couch, vomit bubbling up from between her lips. Her head was tipped back, and she was choking. He watched, dispassionately, then heard footsteps on the outdoor stairs, and the click of a key in a lock. He hesitated, not knowing if he should bolt from the room, or try to start reviving Edith. He bolted, going halfway up the stairs into the shadows, as Alice entered the condo. He heard the door shut behind her, her steps, and then heard another wheezing breath from Edith. He thought he'd hear Alice rush to her side, maybe she'd shout for help, but he heard nothing. He moved down the steps as quietly as he could, and watched Alice watch her mother die. There was a peculiar look on her face as she watched—it wasn't indecision or happiness. It looked like pity, and something else. Disinterest, almost. Or disgust.

She turned and caught Jake watching her, and for a sliver of a moment Jake felt like there was a telepathic acknowledgment of what was happening. Then Alice said something about an ambulance and Jake ran to the wall phone.

Chapter 26

Now

Unable to sleep any longer, Caitlin got out of the motel bed at just past six in the morning. She hadn't brought her running clothes or her good sneakers, but she did have sneakers with her, and a pair of khaki shorts that weren't really for exercising but would have to do.

She desperately wanted to go for a run, to exhaust herself physically. She'd slept some the night before, but only in short, troubled bursts, her skin itching with tension and her body aching with grief.

It was cool outside, the sky a flat, milky white. She was vaguely aware of where the ocean was and headed in that direction, not even stretching first. She spotted a sign that pointed her toward Kennewick Village. It was up a hill on a road without a sidewalk that was lined with pine trees. She ran on the gravel embankment, her lungs starting to hurt a little, her muscles stinging. By the time she reached the top of the hill, a thin layer of sweat covered her skin. In the distance she could make out a strip of the ocean, a hazy, half-shrouded sun above it. She passed the few shops and restaurants of the village, then started downhill toward the shore, not stopping even when she felt that familiar pinch in the joint of her left knee.

She stopped only when she reached the beach, a long crescent that ran along a road. It was empty except for one distant figure on the far end, hurling a tennis ball for a dog. She sat on the edge of the stone wall that overlooked the sea, and took deep, ragged breaths. The sun was burning through the thin layer of cloud and causing spots to swim in Caitlin's vision. She was light-headed, and she thought about how little she had eaten in the previous twenty-four hours. Still, she felt better after the run than she'd felt in the past few days.

When her heartbeat had slowed down, she turned and began to walk back toward the motel. She'd made up her mind on the run. She'd travel back with Grace on the plane the following day, if she could still get a reservation. It meant another day in Maine, another day alone in the town where Grace had died, but she could handle it. She'd call her mother as soon as she got back to the motel.

Once the decision was made, she felt relieved. And now that she had a day to kill, she thought about Harry. She wanted to see him again. Talking with him at the diner the previous afternoon had helped her. Some of that had to do with how grief-stricken he seemed, not just by his father's death, but by Grace's as well, and some of that was because she'd felt so instantly comfortable with him. She thought of Grace's last e-mail, in which she'd written how cute Harry was, although Caitlin assumed that she was simply transferring whatever she felt for his father onto him. Caitlin and Grace had never been attracted to the same men. Grace, since their father's abandonment, had always fixated on older men, or, if not older, then men who were quiet and distant, men who were challenging. Caitlin, less assertive, had always been drawn to gregarious boys, sporty types who told jokes, and treated her like one of the boys.

Reaching Kennewick Village, Caitlin spotted a bakery that appeared to be open. She bought a large coffee and a maple scone, then sat outside on a bench and ate the scone while waiting for the coffee to cool down enough to drink. The sweat had dried on her skin, and her legs and arms had broken out in goose bumps in the cool air. She crossed the street to a bench that was in the sun, which had now entirely broken free of the clouds. From her new position she could see a row of shops, including one that had books in the window. *It must be Bill Ackerson's store,* she thought. After warming up in the sun, she walked over and looked through the window. It *was* Ackerson's, and it was dark inside, not surprising this early in the morning. She watched as a bushy cat padded toward the glass front door, looked up at her, and opened its mouth. She couldn't hear the meow through the door. Something about the plaintive look on the cat's face made her feel a sudden stab of emptiness. She thought again of Harry.

She walked the rest of the way back to her motel room, and once she was there, before she did anything else, she sent him a text: *What's the cat's name in your father's bookstore? I saw him this morning.*

When she got out of the shower, he'd texted back: *Lew. You leaving today?*

No. Tomorrow.

Can I see you?

I'd like that.

They made plans to meet that afternoon for a drink

at the Livery bar in the Kennewick Inn. Caitlin was happy that she wouldn't have to spend the entire day alone. She got dressed, then called her mother.

They started on a second round of drinks, and Harry said, "Can I tell you something?"

"Of course you can."

"It might freak you out."

"Okay," she said, suddenly fearful.

They'd met at three in the afternoon in the basement bar, long and narrow and decorated to look like the sleek interior of a yacht. Harry had ordered a bourbon with ginger ale, and she'd gotten a pint of Harpoon. They'd brought the drinks to an alcove near an unlit fireplace. She'd told him about her decision to accompany Grace's body back to Michigan, and he'd told her all about the bookstore, and how it seemed as though his stepmother, Alice, and the man who worked at the store, John, wanted Harry to take over the business. They'd finished their drinks, and then Harry had gotten two more, paying for them at the bar and bringing them over. Caitlin had just been realizing how much you could read on Harry's face, his anxiety, his sadness, and then she'd seen indecision flit across his features right before he asked her if he could tell her something.

"No, maybe I shouldn't," he said.

"You can trust me," she said.

"Okay," he said, taking a sip of his drink, then rubbing at the edge of his lip with a finger. "Alice, my stepmother, is interested in me, romantically, sexually, whatever you want to call it."

"Oh," Caitlin said. It was not what she had expected to hear.

"I think it's the way she's processing grief, or something like that."

"Oh," Caitlin said again. "It's strange. Is it new? I mean, did she act this way before your father died?"

"No, but I also didn't know her all that well."

"Is she coming on to you?"

Harry rubbed at his jawline. There was a little more stubble there than the day before. "Yeah, it's pretty obvious, and now, with what happened with Grace, she's convinced she's in danger, and that I'm in danger, and she wants me to be in the house all the time, or else down at the bookstore. She made me promise that I wouldn't leave her."

"What do you mean, wouldn't leave her?"

"That I won't leave right away. She doesn't want to be alone."

"You can't be with her forever. Even if she was your actual mother. You need to have your own life."

"I know that. I get it. But that doesn't mean that I

should just up and leave before the police figure out what happened to my father and your sister. I owe something to her."

"No, I understand," Caitlin said. "I wasn't talking about now, I was talking about long-term."

"I won't be here forever, although I have no idea where I'll go. It's not like I have somewhere to return to. College is over, and my friends are all going to different cities. At least here I have some purpose. I can take care of the things my father left behind. Alice and books."

"Do you like books?"

"I do, but not like my father did. But no one liked books as much as he did."

"You don't need to take over his business."

"I know."

"And I don't know why I'm about to tell you this, but I think that Alice is manipulating you. I don't know why. It might just be because she's scared of being alone, and that makes sense, but it might be for other reasons. You said you didn't really know her that well."

"She was my father's wife, but no, I don't."

"Was she married before? Does she have her own kids?"

"No. She was my father's real estate agent when he

decided to move to Maine. She doesn't have family, or if she does, she doesn't see them."

"Your father chose her. You didn't. I don't know if you owe her anything beyond what you've done already."

Harry didn't immediately say anything, and Caitlin felt bad about what she'd said. It had sounded callous, like she was the type of person who figured out who she owed and who she didn't. She was about to apologize when Harry said, "I don't know what to do or think."

"Tell me about this other person your father was having an affair with."

"Annie Callahan. I saw her at the police station. It was the day I found your sister. I was in the station all that morning, and I watched her being brought into one of the interview rooms to be questioned. She looked terrified, and when she was being led out of the station, she looked over at me where I was sitting and stared. I think it was because I look like my father."

"How did you know it was her?"

"I just knew, somehow. Later, I asked Detective Dixon about it and he said that it was, and that they'd be questioning her husband as well, but he was out of town."

"That sounds suspicious."

"I don't know. It doesn't make sense to me that either of them had anything to do with what's happened. It could be that Lou Callahan killed my father out of jealousy and anger, but why kill your sister?"

"I don't know," Caitlin said. They were both silent for a moment, Caitlin staring into the fireplace as though there was a fire in it. She found herself suddenly saying, "Do you know that the first time I ever saw the ocean was when I was fifteen years old?"

"Which ocean did you see?"

"The Atlantic. I'd gone to Washington, DC, for a school trip, then went to visit an aunt who lived in Ocean City, Maryland. She took me on a whale watch. And this is the first time I've been to Maine, even though I've been living in Boston since college."

"Sorry that you had to come up here for the reason you did," Harry said.

"Me too."

"There's a pretty walk right near here. Along the cliff. It's actually where my father was killed."

"Let's go," Caitlin said with mock enthusiasm. They both laughed.

"I've already been out there. Someone left a bouquet."

"Where your father died?"

"Yeah, I guess. Maybe it had nothing to do with

him, but . . . we can walk there if you like, I don't mind. Even though it's where my father died, it was still his favorite place."

"Okay," Caitlin said.

They left the bar and crossed the road to a bluff that overlooked a small half-moon beach, then cut north and picked up a path built into a cliff. Harry took Caitlin's hand to help her over a wide, slick slab of shale, and then held on to it as they continued to walk. It was a perfect day, the air crisp and the sun warm, and no one else was on the path. They ducked to go through a tunnel of stunted trees that had been twisted by the wind, and when they emerged on the other side, Harry bent and picked up a bouquet of berry-covered branches tied together by a strand of grass.

"See?" he said.

"Is this where your father—"

"I'm pretty sure. It's the highest point, and I know that he went over the edge and landed down below. Someone hit him first, though."

"That was how Grace was killed as well. Someone hit her on the head." Caitlin looked out toward the shimmery line where the ocean met the sky. "They didn't suffer, I guess," she said.

"I don't think so."

They walked a little farther, Caitlin taking Harry's

hand again. The path twisted inland around another copse of wind-gnarled trees, and Harry turned to Caitlin and they began to kiss, only stopping when Caitlin realized she had begun to cry.

"I'm so sorry," Harry said.

"No, don't be. It's just confusing, but the kiss was nice. It was intense."

"It was, but maybe we shouldn't be doing this."

"I've heard it's a reaction to grief. To feel—"

"To feel horny?"

"Yeah, I wasn't going to say it, but—"

They kissed more, their bodies pressing together, and Caitlin knew that if they'd been alone in a room their clothes would already be off. The feeling unnerved her, and she pulled away fractionally. He immediately did, as well.

"Should we keep walking?" he asked.

"Okay."

They continued to the end of the cliff walk, then turned and walked into the wind back to the Kennewick Inn. There, at her car, Harry kissed Caitlin again, but briefly. He put a hand on the side of her neck.

"What now?" she asked.

"Maybe I could come see you at your motel room later? I could say good-bye."

"Okay. I'm in 203."

"It might be late. Alice is making dinner, and like I said, she likes to have me in the house."

"Whatever. I'll be there."

Back in her room, Caitlin lay on the freshly made-up bed and stared at the ceiling, striped with the low sun coming in through the motel's cheap venetian blinds. She wanted to talk with Grace and found that she couldn't, that the words in her head weren't coming. The thought that she'd never talk with Grace again swept through her, and she cried again, then napped, waking in the dark. She was hungry and remembered that there was half a Monte Cristo in the minifridge from one of her meals at the diner. She ate two bites of the cold, congealed sandwich, then threw it out. Her stomach felt as small as a hard rubber ball.

She switched on the television, found a station that was playing a *Modern Family* rerun, and left it there, the volume turned low. She answered texts from friends, from work, and from her mom and brother. She saw that her father had called and not left a message. It pissed her off. Why wouldn't he leave a message after his daughter, her twin sister, had died? Why wouldn't he tell her to call him immediately? She could hear his voice—*I didn't want to upset you more, Caity. I know what you must be going through*—and decided to not call him back.

The *Modern Family* episode ended, and another one immediately began. She was tired again, and almost texted Harry to tell him not to come over. But no, she did want to see him one more time. But she wouldn't let him in. That thing that had happened on their walk now seemed like lunacy to her. Was she drunk from two beers? Yes, he was handsome, and sweet, but her sister had just been killed, and he was somehow involved. When and if he came by, she'd say she was exhausted (not a lie) and just say good-bye.

She dozed some more, the television on, and woke to the sound of knocking on her door. She sat up, and looked at the alarm clock on the bedside table. It was eleven o'clock. For a few seconds she was entirely disoriented. The room was dark, except for the illumination of the wall-mounted TV, now showing a weatherman in front of a map of New England. She remembered that Harry was going to come over. She went to the door, ready to tell him that he shouldn't come in. The kiss from earlier flashed through her mind. His hand on her neck.

She opened the door. In the exterior yellow lamplight he looked pale and young. He was wearing a hooded sweatshirt, and he was breathing hard, a hand pressed against the side of his head as though he had a headache.

"Hey, Harry," she said. "Sorry, I'm—"

"You should leave," he said.

"I should leave?" she repeated back, confused.

"You should leave right now. I think you're in danger." The words sounded clipped, like he didn't have enough breath to say them fully.

"What's going on? What happened?" She reached a hand toward him, and he flinched backward a little. He took his hand away from his head, and a trickle of dark blood ran down his cheek.

"You're bleeding," she said.

"Am I?" He looked at the palm of his hand, streaked in blood. "Oh," he said, then his knees buckled, and he fell into the motel room.

Caitlin reached out, trying to break his fall, but he hit the carpeted floor hard, his head bouncing. And then he was still.

Chapter 27

Now

D o you know where Kennewick Hospital is?"
"I don't," Caitlin said.

"You can follow us if you like."

"Okay, sure," Caitlin said to one of the very young,
very unconcerned EMTs after Harry had been strapped
onto a gurney and wheeled into the back of the ambulance outside her motel. Two preteens a few units down
had watched the whole ordeal from just outside their
door, their parents occasionally poking their heads out
to take a look.

After Harry had collapsed into her room, Caitlin
rolled him over, and he'd come to, his eyes wide with

surprise and confusion. She took a look at the side of his head. His hair was dark and sticky with blood; there was an inch-long gash just above his right ear, the area around it puffing up.

"I'm calling 911," she said.

"It's okay. I just fell and hit my head," Harry said, beginning to sit up.

"Yes, that's why I'm calling 911."

While they waited for the ambulance, Caitlin crouched and talked with Harry, now sitting against the wall.

"What happened?" she asked.

"There was a man. He was watching you."

"What do you mean?"

Harry's brow creased, and his eyes seemed to empty out, as though he'd forgotten what he was about to say. Then he lightly shook his head, and said, "I came here to see you. I walked, actually, because I didn't want Alice to hear me start the car, and when I got here there was a man standing"—he pointed straight up with the index finger of his left hand—"a man standing over near the woods."

"Where? On the other side of the parking lot, by the picnic tables?" Caitlin could picture what Harry was talking about. It was really just a cluster of pine trees that separated the parking lot from Route 1A.

"Yeah, he was by the picnic tables in the dark. But I could see him, and he was watching your window."

"Are you sure?"

"Yes, I watched him for a while."

"Where were you?"

"I was hiding behind a truck that was parked near the office." His brow creased again like he wasn't trusting his own words.

"Could you see who it was?"

"No, it was too dark and he definitely didn't want to be seen. A car went by and he'd crouch so the headlights wouldn't reach him through the trees."

Caitlin looked up at the cheap blinds in the window. They were pulled closed, but not tightly closed. There were some gaps between the plastic strips. Whoever had been watching might have been able to see her, and at the very least could see movement in the room.

"Who do you think—"

"It was whoever killed your sister, and probably my father. I don't know who it is, but you need to leave. I don't think you're safe."

"How did you get hurt?"

"Oh," he said, removing the towel from the side of his head, and looking at the dark stain. "I chased him. He must have seen me behind the truck because he was suddenly leaving, heading around to the back of the motel, and I shouted 'Hey' and was running between parked cars, and came down funny on my ankle, and then I was on the pavement. And my head . . ."

"What did you hit?"

"A car, I guess. I don't remember. Then I came to you."

"You were very brave."

Harry laughed, then grimaced. "I tripped and fell."

"What were you going to do if you caught him?"

"I don't know. See who he was."

"Did you get a better look at him when he took off?"

"Not really, but he looked funny when he was running. He was flapping, like he was trying to take off or something."

"Flapping?"

The window suddenly filled with intermittent red light. "The ambulance is here," Caitlin said, and opened up the door. She stood as the two EMTs entered the room, one dropping to his knees to take a look at Harry.

"I think he has a concussion," she said. "He fell and hit himself on the head."

The crouching EMT was already asking questions. She heard him ask Harry if he knew what year it was, but couldn't hear Harry's answer.

"What did he hit?" The slightly doughy EMT who was talking with Caitlin smelled like Bazooka chewing gum.

"I don't know. He thinks it was a car. He came here to see me, and he said there was someone lurking in the woods, or over by the trees, and he started to chase him and that's when he fell."

"Uh-huh. Did you see this person?"

"I didn't. He did."

After they'd placed him on the gurney and wheeled him into the ambulance, Caitlin followed them—no sirens, just lights—as they drove what had to be less than two miles to a modern, rectangular block of a building that looked more like a building in an office park than a hospital. She parked in the visitors' lot, then walked to the emergency room, where she was pointed toward a seat in the small, overly lit waiting area, a TV bolted into the wall playing CNN. She sat still for a moment, listening to the woman at the check-in desk talking quietly on her cell phone. One week ago, she was living in Boston, worried about how to tell her mother that her relationship with Dan was over, and wondering if her sister was going to spend the rest of her life chasing older men. And now she was here in Maine, waiting to fly with her sister's body back to Michigan and accompanying a stranger to a hospital. And someone had been watching her room.

She was so relieved when she saw Detective Dixon walk through the double doors that she almost began to cry. She stood up and waited for him as he talked briefly and quietly with the receptionist, then he came into the waiting area. "What happened?" he asked. He was wearing jeans and a flannel shirt with the sleeves rolled up.

Caitlin sat back down and told the detective everything that had happened that night.

"Why was he coming to your room in the first place?" the detective asked.

"He was just coming to say good-bye."

"And he sounded sure that there was someone watching your room?"

"That's what he told me."

"Have you felt watched at all, since being here in Kennewick? Any sense of being followed?"

Caitlin thought for a moment. "No, not really."

Detective Dixon was scrolling through his phone for something, then showed Caitlin the screen. There was a photograph—a mug shot, actually—of a scruffy-looking man somewhere in his thirties. "Does he look familiar to you at all?"

He didn't, and Caitlin said so to the detective.

"How about her?" He showed her another picture, more pixelated than the previous one, of a blond woman with a round face. The picture looked like it had been cropped from a larger shot.

"No," Caitlin said, shaking her head. "Who are they?"

Detective Dixon didn't answer, because two more people had entered the waiting room: a curvy, middle-aged blonde that Caitlin instantly knew was Alice, Harry's stepmother; and a much older man, maybe her father, with a bald head and a white mustache. Alice had her arm through his, as though she was unable to stand on her own. *Definitely father,* Caitlin thought, then remembered that Harry had mentioned an older man who worked at the bookstore, and she wondered if that was who it was, instead.

Alice and the old man both looked across the room at Detective Dixon and then briefly at Caitlin. Alice, her mouth slightly open, her eyes blank, showed no reaction, but the old man seemed to look at Caitlin for a fraction longer than he should have. Maybe he'd met Grace, and he was confused by how much Caitlin looked like her. If it was the man from the bookstore, then he probably *had* met Grace. It was where she'd gone to meet Harry.

The detective went to them, and the three talked

quietly for a moment, then slid through the swinging doors into the emergency room, Dixon glancing back at Caitlin, mouthing the words *Stay a moment* and holding up a finger.

Caitlin stayed, although the adrenaline from earlier had worn off, and she was now exhausted. Part of her just wanted to get up, go back to her car, and drive back to the motel. She had a big day tomorrow, flying back to Michigan, preparing for Grace's funeral. But the detective had asked her to wait, and besides, she wasn't exactly sure she wanted to go back to the motel alone.

Thirty minutes later, the detective returned and crouched in front of her.

"He's going to be fine, but he has a bad concussion," he said.

"That seemed pretty clear."

"He wants to talk with you, but his doctor wants him to rest."

"That's fine."

"He's very insistent that you are in danger, though, so I'd like to have one of my officers escort you back to your motel room, if that's okay?"

"Okay," she said. "That sounds good."

"Great. Five minutes, okay, Caitlin?"

The uniformed officer that arrived at the hospital was about fifty years old. He had jowls, and a sparse, blond mustache. He followed Caitlin back to the Sea Mist Motel, parking the cruiser next to her car, then together they entered her motel room. There was a quarter-sized bloodstain on the patterned wall-to-wall carpet where Harry had sat. She rubbed at it with the toe of her clog, but it had dried.

"You okay here by yourself?" the officer said.

"I'll be fine."

"Lock the door after I leave, and don't open it for anyone who's not a police officer, okay? And call immediately if you think something's strange, okay? We'll be swinging by all night for periodic checks. You're going to be fine."

She thanked him, and he left. She showered, then got into bed, thinking there would be no way she could fall asleep. But after texting her mother and brother about her arrival time for the next day, she curled into the fetal position, tucking one hand under her head, and the other, wrist turned, between her breasts—the only way she could fall asleep—and within five minutes she was out.

She was awakened at just past five by a soft, tentative rapping on the door. She opened her eyes, emerging from a dream in which she was swatting at a bee's nest with a tennis racket, and, for a moment, had no idea where she was. Then she was up, and moving toward the door, worried suddenly that something else—something bad—had happened.

She cracked the venetian blind and peered out into the hazy light of morning. She thought there'd be a police officer there, but instead, it was the old man from the hospital, the one who'd arrived with Harry's stepmother. He saw her through the window, grinned, and waved, but with a little too much eagerness. Her stomach buckled. Something must have happened to Harry. She cracked the door, aware that she was wearing nothing but an oversized T-shirt.

"Hello?" she said.

"Caitlin McGowan?"

"Uh-huh."

"Sorry to show up like this . . . Harry sent me. He's, uh . . ."

"Is he okay?"

"Fine, fine, we think, but he very much wants to see you, and so, I came. I'm John, by the way. I work with Harry at the bookstore."

"Oh, right," Caitlin said, and opened the door a little bit more as the man inched forward. Did he want to come into the room? "I'll go straight there as soon as I get dressed," she said.

"Oh, right," he said, moving back a little. "I'll let you do your thing. You don't need a ride?"

"No, I know where it is. I'll be right there."

Caitlin almost shut the door, but not wanting to be rude, she opened it a little bit wider, and said, "Thank you, John, for coming to get me. I appreciate it."

He was still smiling, but his eyes were darting quickly from Caitlin's face to the frame of the door and back, almost as though he were measuring something. "Okay, then," she said, all her instincts telling her to slam the door. Instead, she began to push it gently shut, but before it closed, the man shoved against the door and caused her to stagger back, surprised, as he swung something at her and hit her in the throat. She took a ragged, painful breath, and he stepped inside and swung again. She reared back, and something hard clipped her nose. Next thing she knew she was on her back, the world swimming before her eyes.

She heard the door of the motel room shut, and then he was crouching above her. He touched her face, and she flinched. He said, "Did he see me?"

"I don't . . . Who?"

Like a slightly exasperated teacher, he said, slowly, "Did Harry see me last night? Did he tell you who it was he saw?"

Blood was flowing from Caitlin's nose and pooling into her mouth. She tried to scream and began to choke.

The old man was looking over his shoulder, then he turned back, and said, "We'll talk later."

For one moment she actually, blissfully, thought he was going to leave her, but he lifted his arm. She tried to scream again, and then it was blackness.

Chapter 28

Then

Killing Bill had been easy.

Jake Richter, going by John Richards now, had asked him where he'd been walking recently, and Bill, ever the explainer, told him how most days he walked down to Kennewick Beach then followed the cliff path along to Kennewick Harbor, then back home.

"You see the same people every day?"

"No, I hardly see anyone. Except in July and August, but then I usually do a different walk."

A few days later, on a Wednesday, Bill asked Jake if he minded staying a little longer and doing the closing up. He was going to try to get a walk in before it got too dark. Jake had told him it wasn't a problem, then followed Bill outside into the cool evening and watched as he made his way down toward Kennewick Beach. Jake locked the front door and left out the back—in case anyone was looking, even though it was highly doubtful—and took Captain Martin Lane down toward Kennewick Harbor. He walked casually—just out for some fresh air, he kept telling himself—then passed by the Kennewick Inn, its east wing covered by scaffolding while it got a fresh coat of paint before tourist season began.

He found the southern starting point of the cliff walk, realized he was breathing heavily, and slowed his pace. If he timed this right, he'd meet Bill coming from the opposite direction. While walking he fiddled with the homemade cosh in the pocket of his suit pants. He had made it a few days ago by putting a handful of quarters into one of his nylon socks. He hadn't learned much from his father, but he'd learned how to make a cosh, something his father insisted on carrying in his jacket pocket at all times. His father's had been filled with ball bearings, but quarters worked almost as well.

The path ascended, views opening up, so that all of York Harbor and even some of Buxton Point to the north were visible in the grey, dusky light. He stumbled slightly on a slick rock and looked down, noticing that the laces were loose on one of his walking shoes. He was about to bend down (never an easy thing to do these days) and rectify the situation when he realized that he could use the untied laces to his benefit.

He walked another quarter mile—the path had reached its highest point, and decided to wait for Bill to arrive.

He'd killed before, of course.

Edith Moss died so he could be with Alice. That moment marked the beginning of the best period of Jake Richter's life, but it was also the beginning of the end. He realized that later. Watching her mother die had obviously awakened something in Alice, because only a few years later she let her friend Gina die in the ocean, then got away with telling the police that she'd had nothing to do with it. Jake had known the truth, though, and he'd revealed that to Alice, thinking it would make them closer. It hadn't.

Over the following few months after Gina died, Alice had grown distant and cold. She'd moved back into her old bedroom and started work as an office manager at a real estate company. Then, one day, she informed Jake that she had signed a lease on her own apartment.

"You can always move back here if you need to," Jake said.

"I won't need to," she said, then added: "But thanks for letting me stay as long as I did."

Jake lived for a few years alone in the condo, occasionally allowing himself a fantasy in which Alice, tired of living by herself, asked to return. But he knew, down deep, that their relationship was over, had been over before she ever moved out. Nearing sixty, he decided to retire early from the bank. His mortgage was paid off, and he bought a used, forty-six-foot cabin cruiser. He sublet his condo and took the boat down to Florida, where he decided that he didn't like boating as much as he thought he would. He docked the boat in the Bahia Mar Marina in Fort Lauderdale, and got a job renting beach chairs and umbrellas at the Atlantic Club. His hair had been thinning for a few years, and he'd been keeping it long to conceal the loss, but down in Florida he got a buzz cut and grew a mustache. It transformed him, and he told himself he was a new person, a retiree who deserved some enjoyment in the remainder of his life. From his concrete bunker where the chairs and umbrellas were kept, he could see out onto a strip of packed beach. There was the occasional teenage girl, but most of the clients of the Atlantic Club were middle-aged or older, and none of them, not even the occasional enthusiastic widow, could begin to erase the memory of Alice Moss.

He'd been in Florida three years when the Atlantic Club let him go. They told him that they thought he should enjoy more leisure time in his retirement years, but he pressed them for the real reason, and was told that one of the guests had complained that he'd been staring at her thirteen-year-old daughter. He left without a fuss, finally sold the cruiser, and rented a cheap one-bedroom apartment in North Lauderdale. He bought a personal computer and, through various message boards, made contact with a slew of other men all interested in younger women, teenage girls mostly. He even messaged with some older women who were interested in younger boys. At least he thought he was chatting to women. You never really knew on the Internet. He spent an enormous amount of time on the computer, but in the end it turned out to be an empty enterprise. He'd been looking for someone more like him, someone who felt that being with someone younger, teaching them all you knew, was the way to a better, larger life. It wasn't all about sex, it was about generosity, about the sharing of one's life force. No one really understood him. The other men just wanted to share pictures, and talk about the beauty of teen girls. No one understood what Jake understood—that what he'd briefly found with Alice was akin to the fountain of youth, and that you could pass it along. Emma Codd had gifted it to him, and he had gifted it to Alice.

He still had the pictures of Alice. They were his prized possession, and he'd handled them so many times throughout the years that they'd gone thin and ragged on the edges. He kept them flat and protected in the pages of a hardcover copy of *Moby-Dick* on his bedside table. Sometimes he wondered if the pictures were a way back into Alice's life. She'd probably forgotten all about them. Maybe he could get in touch, remind her of their existence, maybe ask if she'd like to come down and visit him sometime in Florida. It would be blackmail, he realized, but it would be worth losing the pictures if he could just spend a little more time with her. He thought about it a lot, but it was only a fantasy. When he did finally get in touch with her, via her work e-mail, he just asked her questions about her life. She was getting married, she told him. Another older man, and one with a young son. She still lived in Kennewick. They e-mailed back and forth, Alice's responses so rote and formal, it was as though they had never meant anything to each other.

Years passed, and Jake began to feel old. He became sexually involved with a teenage girl, a runaway from Miami named Valeria who spent a week with him in his apartment until one day a man showed up at the door, claiming to be the girl's brother (they looked nothing alike) and demanding a thousand dollars or he'd go to the police. He claimed Valeria was fifteen years old, even though she'd told Jake she was seventeen. He'd paid up, reluctantly and shamefully. The incident haunted him for several months—Jake deciding to leave Florida altogether—until he spotted the "brother" entering a nearby apartment complex. Jake began to watch him regularly, discovered his name was Edgar Leon, and determined that he lived alone. One night, after staking out the Jacaranda Estates for several hours, Jake followed Edgar up to his second-floor apartment, knocking on the door one minute after Edgar entered. It was two in the morning. He worried that Edgar, because of the time of night, would be armed when he came to the door, but he wasn't. He was shirtless and yawning and opened the door wide. Jake's first strike with his cosh put Edgar on the floor. Jake straddled him and repeatedly hit Edgar in the head until it was clear he was dead.

Jake felt better about himself after killing that cut-rate pimp. And he felt better about staying in Florida. He heard from his real estate agent in Maine that a long-term renter had just moved out of the Kennewick Beach condo he still owned, and Jake decided to sell. He was about to let the agent know when he got an e-mail from Alice, now going by Alice Ackerson, and with a new e-mail address.

The e-mail was short, just two perfect sentences: *Jake, you ever think about returning to Kennewick? It would be nice to have an old friend here. Alice*

The e-mail was a thrilling surprise; he'd assumed that he never would hear from her again. So he'd returned to Maine—an easy decision to make—and moved back into his old condo. He was shocked to discover that the carpeting was dirty, two windowpanes were cracked, and the wood of the balcony had rotted. Still, he was near Alice again. They met in a diner the day after he'd arrived. She was older, a little softer, but otherwise unchanged. He couldn't help seeing himself through her eyes, though. The completely bald head, the skin damage, the white mustache. He didn't mind so much; he knew that he hadn't been summoned by Alice to resume their love affair. It was enough that, for whatever reason, he was needed.

"I was wondering if you could do me a favor, Jake," Alice asked, as soon as they were settled in a booth.

"Of course, anything."

She asked him if he'd volunteer to help out in her husband's used bookstore. She said it was because he needed help—he worked nonstop—but the more they talked the more it became clear to Jake that Alice wanted someone to keep an eye on her husband.

"He's found someone younger, in New York," she said, her voice flat.

"How do you know?"

"I saw the messages on his phone, and then suddenly they stopped appearing. He must have another way of getting in touch with her now, probably something in the store. You could help me find out if it's still going on."

"Okay," Jake had said. "But are we pretending we don't know each other?"

"That would be for the best. Give him a different name, he'll never know."

"What if people around here recognize me?"

"They won't, Jake. You look totally different."

She'd been right. He hadn't been recognized by anyone, nor had he seen anyone he recognized. The bank had been two towns over, and the patrons from there didn't seem to frequent Ackerson's Rare Books. He went by John Richards now, and he liked the new identity. He liked Bill, too, for what it was worth, even though he did eventually find proof that he was involved with someone in New York. It turned out they'd been sending private messages through the store's rarely used Twitter account.

Jake had stumbled upon it by accident after going onto the store's computer to look up a health condition. He'd been experiencing a strange twitching in his left arm recently, and he'd put in the letters *T* and *W* when Twitter popped up, landing him on the bookstore's page. He'd never seen much of Twitter—Bill was the one who maintained it—and he noticed that there was a message icon on the top menu bar. He clicked on it, and there it was, several back-and-forth messages between Bill and a Grace McGowan in New York. They weren't overtly sexual, but they were intimate. Most messages ended with *miss you* from Bill, and *xoxo* from Grace. There was very little information on Grace McGowan's actual Twitter page—it seemed that maybe it existed only so that she could private-message with Bill—but there was one picture of her, and she was very young. Early twenties, maybe.

Around this time, Annie Callahan came to work at the store, a temporary arrangement because of a huge lot of books that Bill had recently bought. She was a local girl, somewhere in her thirties, and married to an out-of-work cod fisherman. She wasn't much to look at, Annie, one of those girls who had probably been pretty for about one year of her life, back when she was seventeen. But the years of marriage to a perpetually unemployed alcoholic had taken their toll. Her face was pinched, her hair colorless and dull. She wore a carpal tunnel brace on her left arm—"years of data entry," she said—but even with that bad wrist, she'd been an incredibly hard worker, managing to bring a semblance of order to the store that it had never had before, at least since Jake had started working there. Jake noticed that every time Bill thanked her for her work, or looked directly at her, she'd turn bright red, all the way from the dark roots of her hair down to her scrawny neck. She was in love with Bill. That much was obvious.

Jake also noticed how gingerly she'd move around the store, especially after weekends, and Jake assumed that whatever damage her husband did to her was visible under her long sleeves and high-necked sweaters. Bill, with his Gregory Peck good looks and calming voice, was clearly her idea of a knight in shining armor. He barely noticed her, of course.

Jake reported all his findings to Alice during one of her visits to the store when Jake was all alone. He told her about the full-fledged affair in New York, plus the smitten employee. Alice's face remained blank as she took in the information. She wanted to see the picture of Grace, so Jake found the one on Twitter and showed that to her. "What do you think?" he finally asked.

"I'm done with him," Alice said.

"Are you going to ask for a divorce?"

Her brow furrowed, and she said, "I would never get divorced, but I'm done with him."

That night Jake lay in bed and thought of the different ways he could kill Bill, how easy it would be to make it look like an accident, especially if he could kill Bill during one of his walks along the cliff. He even thought that if the death looked suspicious, it would be incredibly easy to suggest to the police that Lou Callahan, Annie's violent husband, might have been involved. But mostly what Jake thought about was that he would be doing this for Alice. He didn't think he'd be back in her life any more than he was now, but it would be one last thing he could do for her. It would give him purpose.

Annie stopped working at the store; one morning she just didn't show up and didn't answer her phone. She came by in the afternoon with Lou, her husband, and said that she could no longer work there because Lou had picked up some work. She did all the talking while Lou, a goateed cretin, watched silently, glowering at Bill, who was oblivious. Jake put the bizarre scene in his back pocket. If Bill was gone, then Jake could twist the encounter to fit any narrative. It was something to consider.

In the next few months, Jake slept less and less. He found he could survive on as little as four hours, but

he still spent about ten hours each night in bed, thinking about Bill, wondering whether he should tell Alice
his plans (he finally decided not to), and building up
a case against his boss. Bill was one of those careless
men who was perceived as sensitive because he was
bookish and reticent. But he had been hugely fortunate
to marry Alice, and now he had replaced her with a
much younger woman. He deserved what was coming
to him.

Waiting for Bill, cosh hidden in his hand, was the lon-
gest minute of Jake's life. He heard him before he saw
him, his boots scraping along the rocky path. Jake began
to walk as well, and rounded a twist, nearly bumping
into Bill, who smiled and laughed.

"John? What are you doing here?"

"Thought I'd take a walk myself, and was hoping to
run into you."

"Everything okay? You look pale."

"Yeah, yeah. I'm fine. Look, this is embarrassing but
my shoelace is untied, and I could get it myself, but . . ."

Bill looked down, then bent at the knee, saying,
"Not a problem at all. I got it."

As he was knotting the laces, Jake quickly looked
back down along the path to make sure they were alone,
then lifted the cosh and brought it down with all his

strength on the crown of Bill's head. It made a thunking sound, and Bill, groaning, fell to his side. Jake went down on one knee himself, and hit him two more times. He heard the skull crack.

Jake stood up. There was no sound except for wind coming in off the ocean. Bill lay right on the edge of a steep drop to the rocky shore below. Jake tried to push him off with his foot but couldn't quite manage it. He bent and, gripping Bill by his windbreaker, rolled him off the edge with both hands.

His heart was pumping as if he'd just run a mile, but Jake's mind was clear. He decided to keep walking north along the path, and exit along Micmac Road. There was less chance that someone would see him. If they did, they did. He'd say he'd been looking for his friend to go on a walk but hadn't spotted him. They could never prove otherwise.

But luck was on his side that day. There was no one else on the path, and Jake was back in the store before it had even gotten dark.

Chapter 29

Then

Sleep had never been easy for Jake, not even when he'd been young. It came reluctantly, if at all, and departed easily, scared away by the first appearance of dawn light through the cracks in the curtains. For a long while, he found he could drink himself into a good night's sleep, but in his fifties, he'd developed acid reflux, at its worst after a night of drinking. He'd prop himself on pillows, and after several hours of a revved-up mind and the rising taste of bile at the back of his throat, he would sometimes manage a few pre-dawn hours. He quit drinking and found that Ambien helped for a period of time, till something in him began to resist the drug, and he'd lie in bed half awake and half spooked by visual hallucinations. He returned to moderate drinking and over-the-counter acid-reducing pills that sometimes worked and sometimes didn't.

But after what he'd done to Bill on the cliff path, Jake wasn't sure he'd slept at all. He must have, a little bit, if you wanted to call those thin excursions into semiconscious states a form of sleep.

The worst part of his recent nights was picturing Bill, who'd offered him both a job and some semblance of friendship, groaning at his feet. And he kept hearing the sound the cosh made when he brought it down on Bill's skull, like an icy puddle cracking.

Jake reminded himself that Bill had been a selfish man, so caught up in his books that he barely paid attention to the people around him. Besides, he'd done this all for Alice. He'd done what *she* wanted. And now Harry was back, and Jake wondered if Harry had factored into all of this, if Alice wanted to start a new life with Harry. Lying awake, he'd try to remember that time with Alice immediately after Edith had died. It was comforting, but Jake found his mind wandering further back, thinking of Mrs. Codd, his neighbor, all those years ago. She'd been dead now for over fifty years, and Jake often wondered if anyone else ever thought of her. Her sons, maybe, if they were still alive.

Sometimes he thought of his parents, both long dead as well, his father from drinking at the age of fifty-five, and his mother from congestive heart failure ten years later. He'd kept to his promise and never gone to see either of them after that first year of college, although he'd sent his mother updates whenever he moved addresses, and she'd sometimes write back. She'd written him when his father died, describing the circumstances, but never mentioning that she'd like for him to visit. He wouldn't have, even if she'd asked. After she died, he'd received a letter from a lawyer, saying that there was some furniture and other possessions that he might like to have. Jake never responded. A second letter arrived, but that was it. He'd felt nothing at the time, but as he'd gotten older, his anger at his parents had increased. Why had they brought him into the world if they had no interest in loving him? It had made him what he was, of course: successful, able to find his own love and happiness, unburdened by guilt. But why had they done it? If he could go back in time, he would ask his mother that question, just to see her squirm.

Jake wasn't sure he'd be able to go to Bill's funeral, but knew it would look strange if he didn't. He went but avoided talking with Alice, who surely knew that he had done her bidding, and was shocked to see Grace

McGowan—it had to be her—sitting quietly by herself at the back of the church. The sight of her scared him, somehow, as though she knew what had happened. But that wasn't possible, was it? She was here because she'd loved Bill, and she was hiding in the back of the church, not wanting to be seen.

But then she'd actually come into the store. Jake watched from the back room as she talked with Harry, and then they exchanged numbers. After she left, Harry told him that she was looking for a job. He was alarmed, wondering if she knew anything, even though he thought that was impossible. But it gnawed at him.

On the Wednesday evening after the funeral, Jake closed up shop and went and sat on the bench across from the Village Inn to read that day's paper. It was something he sometimes did when the weather was decent. No one noticed an old man on a bench. But that night, he'd done it hoping to see Grace, maybe find out where she was living. Many cars drove by, plus a few pedestrians. He was about to give up when a couple came out of the Village Inn; he recognized Harry right away, and then he recognized Grace. Had she gotten a room at the Village Inn, and had Harry been in there with her? It was a definite possibility, but maybe they'd just had a drink at the bar. They turned left, up the hill, and Jake followed them at a distance, up to Barb Whitcomb's place, where they stopped and talked some more. Jake, not willing to risk being seen, turned back.

That next afternoon Jake talked with Barb, sidling up next to her as she was coming back from the Cumberland Farms with her Megabucks ticket. He found out that she'd been advertising one of her spare rooms on the Internet, and that the girl, Grace McGowan, had come up from New York City the previous Friday. "She cries in her room, that much I can tell you. I don't ask what's going on because it's none of my business."

"You think she's here because she knew Bill?"

"You'd know more than me," Barb said. She told him that she was leaving the next day to visit her adult daughter, who lived on the Cape. "She's back in rehab, telling me she's cured, of course, and don't I want to come down and see it for myself."

"Maybe it will take this time."

"That's what she says, John. I'll believe it when I see it."

That night he didn't sleep at all; he kept thinking of Grace, wondering why she was still in town, why she was clearly after Harry. He wanted to call Alice, but knew that would be a mistake. They talked frequently, but always at the store when no one else was around. She didn't want anyone to know about their connection. He paced the condo, then at dawn he got dressed and made a new cosh using a sock and quarters from his change bowl. He showered, then dressed for the day, pushing the coin-filled sock down deep into his suit pants pocket.

That night, after the sun had set, Jake went up the hill to Barb's house. There was no good place to sit and watch, so he stood quietly in the stand of birches across the street, his eyes on the bowed-out second-floor windows. He thought he caught movement a few times, maybe a shadow passing across a curtain, but he couldn't be sure. But if he stayed here long enough, he knew he'd eventually see Grace either arrive or depart. Either way, he could get to her. He shifted from leg to leg and shook his arms to keep his circulation going. He'd slept a little bit in the back office of the store that day, nodding off in the wooden swivel chair. He dreamt he heard Bill's voice, slicing through the wind, telling him to wake up, but his eyes were glued shut, and he couldn't open them. He was worried he was going to fall off the cliff and into the cold water below, but he couldn't open his eyes, and he couldn't stop walking forward, feeling for branches that would keep him on the path. Bill's voice got closer, then farther away, and Jake jerked awake only when his elbow slipped off the arm of the chair.

He'd been standing and watching Barb's house for

less than an hour when the front door opened. He stood as still as possible. The slender figure, too tall for Grace, he thought, walked from the dark house into the light of a streetlamp on the sidewalk. It was Harry, which wasn't surprising. How long had he been inside? Had they been fucking, or had she been telling him about his father? Probably both. Jake waited a few minutes, then crossed the road to the house. He tried the door but it was locked. Looking back over his shoulder, he pressed the doorbell; two chiming notes sounded from within the house. He pulled the sock from his pocket, and waited, hoping she'd swing the door open freely, expecting to see Harry again.

Instead, she cracked the door open three inches and peered out. Jake pushed against the door with all his strength, catching her unaware, and she stumbled back.

"Hey," she said, right before he hit her in the jaw with the cosh, dislocating it. She crumpled instantly to the floor like a knocked-out boxer in the ring. Jake stayed standing, his heart tripping in his chest, wondering if the blow had killed her, but her chest was still lifting and falling under her striped shirt.

The door was open behind him, and Jake pushed it almost all the way closed with his foot, then he crouched over Grace McGowan and hit her several times on the side of her head.

Chapter 30

Now

H arry had no memory of being at Caitlin's motel room, but he did remember the ambulance ride, and he knew that he'd tripped and fallen, even though it was a fuzzy memory.

There was a persistent, low-frequency ringing in his ears, and the inside of his head felt swollen, almost like a balloon had been blown up inside his skull. Earlier, one of several doctors who'd come in to question him had asked him what town he was in, and he was totally surprised that he hadn't immediately known. She'd moved on to other questions, but before she left, he'd said, "Kennewick. I'm in Kennewick, Maine."

She'd smiled and told him that was correct.

Detective Dixon came by, and Harry told him that Caitlin was being watched. It was all he really remembered.

Later, he opened his eyes, and saw Alice staring at him so intently and with so much love that he closed his eyes again, pretending to fall back asleep. He could smell her perfume in the room, and he heard a soft, deep voice in the background that sounded like John Richards. He kept his eyes closed. He'd been awkward around Alice ever since they'd had sex, the night before that terrible morning when he had discovered the dead body of Grace McGowan. After that long, surreal day, after being questioned repeatedly by the police, both local and state police detectives, Harry said to Alice, "About what happened . . . last night."

She'd looked at him with a tired, blank stare. He noticed, not for the first time, that the surfaces of her eyes, from some angles, appeared almost flat. It gave her a distant gaze even when she was looking right at him.

"You want to pretend it didn't happen," she said.

A little bit startled by the accuracy of her statement, Harry said, "No, yes. I just think it shouldn't happen again is all."

"Sure, it never happened." She half smiled.

That was all they had talked about it, and Alice had

not returned to Harry's bed, even though Harry, in the moments between sleep and wakefulness, found himself replaying the memories of Alice's naked body, the way she had controlled him, her voice in his ear. Those images fought with the constant image of Grace, dead on the hallway floor, one side of her face collapsed and ruined, the other looking just like she'd looked in real life. And he'd begun to obsess over every moment they had spent together, every word they had said during the short time they had known one another. What he kept coming back to was that Grace had come to Maine for one reason; she had come because she believed that Alice was responsible for his father's death. She'd been convinced of it. And now she was dead, and Harry couldn't help but think that it meant she'd been right.

The days and nights following Grace's death seemed interminable as Harry waited to hear about an arrest. He tried to talk more to Alice about Annie and Lou Callahan, but all she would say was that she was sure they were involved, and that she didn't want to talk about it. He also badgered Detective Dixon into repeated meetings; he felt better talking, again and again, about the events that had transpired over the last few days. And it was after one of those fruitless conversations that he'd met Grace's sister at the police station. Caitlin looked so much like Grace that when he first saw her he thought he'd seen a ghost. Her hair was a little different, as was the way she held her body, but her mouth, her eyes, they were Grace's eyes, and Harry, knowing it was insane, felt as though she was in Maine just so he could have a second chance, that she was there for him.

Harry, in his hospital bed, the lights now dim and the room empty, tried to focus on the man he'd seen outside of Caitlin's motel, but the focus kept slipping away from him, like two magnets that repel one another. Every time he felt like he could see the man hiding in the dark, the image would push itself away. All that remained was the terrible fear he'd felt. Someone was watching Caitlin. She needed to leave Maine.

The pressure in his head increased, and he opened his eyes. He knew Alice was close, probably out in the waiting room. He'd seen her earlier, hadn't he? Then he remembered that he'd also heard John's voice in the background. Why was John there, at the hospital? It wasn't totally surprising, but it was a little odd. It was so late at night. Had she gone to get him after she'd heard word that Harry was in the hospital? Why hadn't she called Chrissie Herrick instead?

He closed his eyes and listened to the sounds of the hospital, the undercurrent of humming machines, the distant chatter from the nurses' station. Then he heard rushed footsteps along the linoleum floor, a progressive clack-clack-clack, some nurse in clogs hurrying toward a patient in need.

His eyes suddenly opened on their own, the sound of the footsteps bringing back the woolly memory of the man running away the night before. Something had been strange about it. *What had it been?* Then Harry remembered. The man he'd chased had looked like he'd been flapping his wings, and there was something else . . . Yes, it was the flat slaps of dress shoes hitting the asphalt. The man must have been in a suit, unbuttoned, and it was the suit jacket that was flapping as he ran. A too-big suit jacket. And he'd been wearing dress shoes, as well.

And Harry suddenly was sure that the man watching Caitlin's motel had been John. He knew it. And it wasn't just the suit, John's constant uniform, it was also the size of him, the slope of one shoulder in the dim light. There was no doubt.

But why? If John was the one watching Caitlin, then he was the one who'd killed Grace, and also maybe his own father. It didn't make sense. John was an old man. Would he have been strong enough to overcome Bill, and also Grace, a young woman? If he'd had a weapon, sure. Harry, in and out of fuzzy consciousness, kept imagining John's strong hands and wiry frame, his body concealed by the loose-fitting suits.

A nurse came in to check on him. "Awake, I see?" he said.

"On and off."

"How's the head?"

"A little fuzzy, but getting better."

"You'll be glad to know your mother's still here. We told her to go home, but she insisted."

"My stepmother," Harry said.

"Oh, right. She's very concerned."

"She's awake?"

"No, she's sleeping now. There's a couch in the waiting room."

When the nurse left, Harry dozed for a few minutes then woke again, still thinking of John. What did he know about him? Not much, except that he was local, having spent many years in southern Maine. He lived on Kennewick Beach, in one of the dated condos up near Buxton Point. Bill had pointed it out to Harry once during a walk; this was right after his father had brought John in full-time at the store. "What's his deal?" Harry had asked Bill.

"He's just one of those guys who needs to be working, I guess. But I like having him around. He's harmless."

Harry's temples throbbed, and he closed his eyes. Bright splotches of color spread and contracted under his eyelids. He was exhausted again, despite the rising anxiety, and he fell into a thin, disturbed sleep.

When he woke, Alice was over him, her face registering the same overly concerned look from before. "Hi, Alice," he said, the words clicking a little because his mouth was so dry. How long had he slept?

"Hi, sleepyhead," she said. "How do you feel?"

"Okay. Thirsty."

Alice brought him a cup of lukewarm water.

"Dr. Roy's coming soon. She said she thinks you can leave this morning."

"Oh, good," Harry said. He remembered being convinced that it had been John outside of Caitlin's motel, and said, "Is Detective Dixon here?"

"I don't think so. Why?"

"What about John? Was he here last night? I remember hearing him."

"He was here, but he's back home now. Want me to call him for you, have him come back?" Alice pushed a lock of Harry's hair off his forehead, and the touch of her fingertips on his skin caused a ripple to race down his spine.

"No, I just . . . How long have you known John, Alice?"

Alice blinked. "Years, I guess. Since I was a teenager."

356 · PETER SWANSON

"You knew him when you were a teenager?" Harry asked.

Alice sat back on her chair. "He was married briefly to my mother. You knew that, didn't you, Harry?"

Harry didn't say anything right away. Was he still confused from the concussion? Had he somehow forgotten that Alice and John had been related?

"I didn't know that, did I?" he said. "He was your stepfather?"

Alice laughed. "I never thought of him that way. No, he was just someone who married my mother. I didn't know him well at all."

"And my father knew this, too?"

"Knew what? That John had been married to my mother? Sure, I suppose it came up when he first volunteered at the store, but I don't even remember talking about it."

"What was he like back then?" Harry asked. "Did you live with him?"

"Just for a little while. He was the same. He loved to work, was friendly to everyone. Why are you asking all these questions?"

Harry rubbed at one of his eyes where a nerve had been fluttering. A few hours ago he'd known for a fact that it had been John standing out in front of the motel room, keeping an eye on Caitlin. Now he wasn't so sure. He opened his mouth to ask another question, then stopped. Suddenly, he didn't want Alice to know about his suspicions. Why had he even had them? The flapping suit jacket? It wasn't enough.

"No reason," Harry said.

"You don't think he—" Alice began, just as Dr. Roy entered the room.

"Good morning," the doctor said, as Alice stood. "How are you feeling this morning, Harry? Better?"

"I'm fine," he said.

"I'll just step outside," Alice said, and moved quickly to the door.

Dr. Roy perched on one of the plastic chairs next to Harry's bed and asked him how he had slept.

"Except for being woken up every hour, fine."

"Are you sleepy now?"

"No. I'm just ready to get out of here."

"Yes, I totally understand." She pushed a dark strand of hair back behind an ear, and looked down at the clipboard in her lap. "I need to ask you some questions first, okay? Then you're free to go."

Harry nodded.

"I'm going to give you four words and I want you to repeat them back to me in the same order as I say them, okay?"

"Sure."

"Car, telephone, apple, and shoe."

Harry repeated the words.

"Good. Now, can you tell me the months of the year, but backward?"

He did that as well, as Dr. Roy scribbled onto a sheet.

"Very good," she said. "Now tell me about how your head feels. Last night you complained of a headache—do you remember that?—and said that the pain was a six out of ten. Do you still have a headache this morning?"

"No, not really," Harry said, even though his temples still felt pinched by a dull, throbbing pain.

"Not at all?"

"Maybe a slight headache."

"And how would you characterize the pain of that headache, on a scale of one to ten?"

"A one," Harry said.

She asked him a few more questions about how he was feeling, then used an instrument with a light to track the movement of his eyes.

"You seem good, Harry," she said, her fingers gently touching the area around his scalp where he'd received the blow. "I have one more question. Can you tell me the four words I said to you when I first came in here?"

For a brief moment, Harry blanked, but then it came

back to him, and he quickly said: "Car, telephone, apple, shoe."

"Good." She smiled, then looked at her watch. "I'll send the nurse 'round with your discharge papers. Who's taking you home, do you know?"

"My stepmother, I guess."

"Okay. Sounds good."

After the doctor left, Harry kept his eyes on the door, waiting either for his discharge or for Alice to return. He was eager to leave, frantic almost, anxious to check in with Caitlin, make sure she was okay. He'd tell her that he felt sure he knew who the man watching her had been. He hadn't decided yet whether to tell Detective Dixon. What if he was wrong? What would John think then?

He must have dozed off, because he woke to the sound of the nurse's voice as he came into the room holding a clipboard.

After being discharged by the nurse, Harry dressed in the clothes he'd been wearing the night before, and went to look for Alice. She wasn't in the waiting room, and a nurse told him she'd gone home to change, and that she'd be back soon. He walked outside to the emergency room entrance and stood under the awning. He tried both Alice's cell phone and the landline at the house, but she didn't pick up. He tried Caitlin, as well, and got no answer. He tried to figure out what to do next. It was too far to walk. He could call a cab, he told himself, have it take him back to the house, or he could call Detective Dixon, tell him he needed a ride. Before he decided, a rust-pocked yellow cab pulled up to the curb, and a wiry driver in a jean jacket leapt out to open the door for an obese passenger, a woman carrying her own oxygen tank who needed help getting through the hospital's sliding doors. When the driver returned, Harry asked him for a ride.

"I have another fare in ten minutes. How far you need to go?"

Harry gave him the address of Grey Lady and the driver agreed.

The car was stuffy, smelling of permanent body odor and the distant memory of cigarette smoke. Harry cracked the window as the driver barreled through the quiet backstreets of Kennewick. The day was overcast but warm. The driver dropped Harry off at the top of the driveway, speeding off as soon as Harry paid. Harry squinted toward the house, wishing he had sunglasses. It was the type of overcast sky that was still bright, a harsh whiteness suffusing everything. He pressed his fingers to his closed eyelids, and bright red spots swam in his vision.

When he felt better, he walked to the front door, checking his jacket pocket, happy to find his keys there. Alice's car wasn't in the driveway. It was strange; if she'd been heading back to the hospital, he would've passed her in the taxi. Where else could she be? Maybe she'd gone to see John? Clearly, they were much closer than he'd ever realized. He was still shocked by the revelation that John had been Alice's stepfather.

He entered the house, shouted "Hello" into its interior just to make sure he was alone, then walked to the kitchen, hoping to find coffee. He was desperate for caffeine. There was a quarter of a pot left, and he poured it over ice and took a long, bitter swallow. He thought some more about Alice and John. What if they were still close? What if John had killed Bill and Grace as a favor for Alice, as revenge for their affair? It was ludicrous, but possible. Both Bill and Grace were dead, and the only one with a solid motive to kill them was Alice, the spurned wife. Alice had acted as though John and she weren't close at all, but what if they were?

Harry remembered a few days earlier when he'd been looking through Alice's desk and found the old photograph in her passport, a photograph of her and an older man. He put down his coffee and walked to Alice's office. He found the photograph again in Alice's desk drawer. A young Alice with an older man, his arm around her. Harry studied the man. It definitely *could* have been John, even though the man in the photograph had a full head of hair and was clean shaven. But he had the same strong, slim build, the same slope of the shoulders. It was impossible to tell for sure. Harry riffled through the papers in the desk drawer, looking for another photograph. He didn't find anything, but he did find a Post-it note stuck to the wooden bottom of the drawer. Handwritten on the note was the phrase *missmossypants*. No caps, words all strung together. It had to be Alice's password. Harry flipped open the laptop on the desk, and hit the power button, then, while it was booting up, he had another idea. He opened the Phone Finder app on his phone. It allowed you to find out where someone was based on the GPS location of their cell phone, but you needed their password to do it. He punched Alice's phone number into the app, then entered her password. A map appeared, and an icon of a phone. She was near Kennewick Beach, just off Micmac Road on Scituate Avenue. Harry could picture the address, a three-story condo development, the same one his father had pointed out to him.

Chapter 31

Now

Alice hadn't been to Jake's condo on Kennewick Beach for over a decade. She'd passed it many times, of course, in the car, or while walking along Kennewick Beach, but since she'd been married to Bill she barely even noticed it anymore. It was a relic from the past, in the way her mother was long gone, and in the way that Jake, as she used to know him, was also gone.

But while she'd been waiting at the hospital she'd gotten a text from Jake asking her to come right away. She had a bad feeling, especially since Harry had been asking all those questions. Had it been Jake that Harry had seen in front of the motel? Nothing would shock her right now.

And now he wanted her to come to his condo, something he'd never asked. It could only be bad news.

Alice had thought it possible, after hearing that her husband had died, that Jake had been responsible. They'd had that conversation about Bill and the girl down in New York, and she'd seen something in Jake's eyes, that loyalty he'd always had, that told her he might do something about it. If he had done it, he'd done a good job of making it look like an accident. But then, Jake had probably gone and killed Bill's girlfriend who'd come up from New York for the funeral. That was a stupid move, drawing more attention to Bill's death, and probably drawing attention away from Annie and Lou Callahan. And then she'd gotten the call late last night about Harry, and she'd wondered if Jake had something to do with that as well. He was spinning out of control. She'd immediately called him, left him a message telling him to meet her at the hospital, and he had, though she'd yet to be able to truly talk with him. But she'd seen him. He looked terrible when she spotted him in the entranceway, like he hadn't slept in days. His eyes were bloodshot, and he even smelled bad, like something had gone rotten inside of him.

She pulled in front of his unit in the condo parking

lot and stared up at the faded grey wood of the four-unit development, and the flat, white sky above it. *This is where my mother died*, she thought, surprising herself. Usually, when she thought of the condo, she thought of the beautiful years she had lived here with Jake. It had been one of the happiest times of her life, even though a part of her now knew that it had all been lies, like so much else in her life.

She stepped out onto the parking lot, smoothed her skirt down along her thighs, and locked the car behind her.

She walked across the asphalt, gritty with sand, then up the exterior stairway to Jake's door. She rang the bell, and listened to the familiar bong from inside the condo.

The door opened. Jake was standing there, his suit jacket rumpled, his eyes puffy. His mouth looked slack, hanging open slightly, and the white hairs of his mustache had grown over his upper lip.

"Jake?" she said.

"I screwed up," he said. "I screwed up everything."

She stepped inside the condo, and Jake shut the door behind her. She walked into the living room, dark because the curtains were closed, but what she could see looked grimy and unkempt. And it was too warm, the windows yet to be opened since winter.

"What did you do?" she asked.

Jake scratched at his scalp. The sides of his lips were crusted in white, like he needed to drink a glass of water. "Did he see me?"

"Did who see you?" Alice asked. She decided if Jake was suddenly going to confess everything to her, she wasn't going to make it easy for him.

"Did Harry see me last night, outside of the motel?"

"I think he did, Jake. What were you doing there?"

"I went to her motel room to keep an eye on her. I still thought—"

"Who, Jake?"

"Grace's sister. She'd come to identify the body."

"So what?"

"Because she must have known about Bill and his affair with her sister."

"So what?" Alice said again.

"I just wanted to keep an eye on her, Alice. I haven't been able to sleep for days."

"You killed Bill's girlfriend?"

"She was talking with Harry, Alice. She knew something. I know she did." He sat down on the recliner. Alice's eyes had adjusted to the dark living room, and she saw dust particles rising in the light from the kitchen as Jake settled his weight onto the chair. "I'm tired, Alice."

"Were you going to kill her, too?"

Jake sighed through his nose. "Who, Caitlin? She was after Harry, as well, as it turned out. I was watching her motel, and he showed up there. I took off running, but, Jesus, I don't know . . ."

"Relax, Jake. Maybe you need to tell me everything you've done."

"If he saw me, then he's probably already told the police. They could be on their way here right now."

"He didn't tell the police anything."

"He told Caitlin about me. He'll tell the police."

"What do you mean? Did you go see Caitlin?"

"She was scared of me, Alice. She knew. And if she knew, then the police know."

"What did you do to her?" Alice asked.

"I took care of it. She's in the trunk of my car in the garage."

"Jesus. Jake, you need—"

"Don't worry about it. It's all taken care of."

"It's not all taken care of. You're right, the police are going to come after you. You need to either leave town, or—"

"Shhh, I know what needs to be done. That's why I asked you here. For your help. I know it's a lot to ask, but I need you to do this. I don't think I can do it myself."

"I don't know what—"

"Yes, you do. I'm old and I don't want to go to prison. All you need to tell them is that I invited you here, and when I attacked you, you defended yourself. You can tell them I'd stopped being able to sleep, and that I did it all for you. Or just tell them you have no idea what went wrong with me, and they'll come up with their own ideas."

"It's too warm in here, Jake," Alice said, standing and going to look at the thermostat on the wall.

"Do you remember when we first met? Right down there on the beach. You were in a green bathing suit and I'd never seen anyone so beautiful."

"You were with my mother."

"No, I don't think so. It was just the two of us."

Alice turned from the thermostat to look at Jake. He was wrong about how they'd met, but she did remember meeting him, how strong he looked, how sure of himself he was. He'd lost all that now.

"Okay, I'll do it," Alice said.

"Yes?"

"How . . . exactly?" Alice walked to the nearest window, the one that looked out over the parking lot. She twisted the lock, noticing the grime that had accumulated on the sill, and cracked the window. The smell of salt air came into the condo almost immediately.

"There's a knife in the kitchen," Jake said. "I'd get it for you but I think you should be the one who pulls it from its block. I'll hit you once, very lightly, with the cosh, and then you stab me. There won't be any suspicion, and even if there is, they'll never prove you weren't protecting yourself."

Alice watched as a familiar car—it looked like Harry's green Honda—turned from Scituate into the condo's parking lot, pulling into an empty spot next to Alice's Volvo.

"Harry's here," she said, still watching the car.

"What?"

"I'm pretty sure Harry's here," she said, then watched as the driver's side door opened, and it was Harry who stepped out, turning and looking up at the condo building. Alice moved back from the window. "It's him. He's here."

"Then it has to be done right now."

"Okay, I'll do it," Alice said. "Where?" And suddenly she did want to kill Jake, not as a favor to him, but because she was angry.

"In the kitchen." Jake picked up the sock filled with quarters from the coffee table, and Alice followed him into the alcove. "Tell them we were talking in here. I wasn't making any sense, and I threatened you. You pulled out the knife and protected yourself."

"You have to hit me."

"I'll hit you lightly. It won't matter." Jake pointed at the knife block. "Take that one there, top right, it's the sharpest."

The kitchen swam in her vision as Alice walked and gripped the knife's wooden handle, pulling it free from its block. She turned to Jake.

There was the loud, echoey bong of the doorbell ringing.

"Just do it," Jake said. "There's no time now."

"Hit me first."

Jake nodded, and feebly swung the sock with the quarters, glancing them off of Alice's shoulders.

"It's got to be harder," she said.

He swung again, clipping her left ear. It hurt more than she thought it would. She blinked rapidly.

The doorbell rang a second time.

She punched the knife into his chest, where she thought his heart was, but the knife only went about an inch in, and Jake staggered backward a step, dropping the cosh on the floor. She looked into his eyes, trying to remember the man who had once lifted her into his arms and carried her like a bride into this very home. Now all she saw in his eyes was confusion, and a little bit of panic. He lifted a hand up, his fingers spread, and Alice took hold of his wrist, pressed his hand up against the side of her face, bringing him in closer to her. His fingers gripped her neck, his nails ripping at her skin. They were both breathing heavily, Jake's lips apart but his stained teeth clenched together. He squeezed harder at Alice's neck, and she felt a trickle of blood run down into her collarbone. She stabbed him again harder, and this time, when she pulled the knife out, blood began to soak his shirt. He dropped to his knees and then to the ground. Jake put his hand on his chest, and the blood pumped out between his fingers, pooling in the folds of his shirt.

The doorbell rang again. Alice watched Jake, just to make sure he'd stopped breathing. She dropped the knife to the floor, where it skittered away, leaving a trail of blood. She touched her fingers to her neck, puffy where the welts were already rising up.

He nearly killed me, she thought. Then: *I had to do it. I had to do it,* the words running through her head as she moved, trancelike, to the front door.

Chapter 32

Now

Alice's car was outside in the parking lot, so Harry knew she was in the condo. He pressed the doorbell, telling himself that if no one answered maybe he should just inform the police of what he thought he'd seen. Still, it would be better if he could get one more look at John, just so he could know for sure if he was the one he'd seen in front of the motel. And with Alice here, he had an excuse—he was concerned, looking for his stepmother.

He rang the bell again, hoping he had the correct door; he'd picked the unit closest to where Alice's car was parked. An exterior stairway led up to the entryway, above a garage. It was low tide, and the air was filled with the smell of rot. Harry pulled his phone out just as the door swung inward.

"Harry," Alice said. Her neck was smeared with blood. "Harry," she said again. "Call the police."

He stared at the phone in his hand. How had it gotten there? Then he dialed 911 for the second time in a week. He gave the dispatcher the address, but wasn't able to tell her what had happened. She kept insisting he find out, but he hung up, and stepped into the dim condo. Alice had retreated, and was now sitting on a white leather sofa, holding her hands out to either side. She looked like she was meditating.

"Where's John?" Harry asked.

"He's in the kitchen, Harry."

Harry took another tentative step into the living room. His eyes began to adjust; to his left was a lit alcove kitchen. Harry took another step and looked toward it. He could see the upturned feet of a body lying on the linoleum.

"What happened?"

"He was crazy, Harry. He asked me to come here, and I came, and he wasn't making any sense. He kept telling me how he had to kill all the people who were threatening him, and then he tried to . . . I had to protect myself. Is he dead, do you think?"

Harry forced himself to take two more steps toward the alcove. Recessed fluorescents in the ceiling lit the scene. John was on his back, one hand sprawled in the spreading pool of blood, the other resting gently on his chest. The smell of the blood—like tidal mud—reached Harry's nostrils, and he took three quick steps back out the condo's door and vomited over the railing. In the distance he heard the sound of sirens.

"Is he dead, Harry?" Alice's voice was closer, and Harry's body jerked, involuntarily, the way it sometimes did when he was falling asleep and thought he was actually falling.

He turned back, wiping at his mouth. Alice was in the doorway, her hands still held out from her body, her palms up.

"He looks dead."

"He killed Bill, you know. He killed your father. He just told me."

"Why did he do it?" Harry asked.

"He didn't make a whole lot of sense, but it was about me. He was protecting me, I think, and that's why he killed the two girls as well."

"What two girls?"

"He said their names. Grace, the girl who was murdered, and then he mentioned another girl. Her sister."

"Caitlin's her sister. Where is she? What did he say?"

"I can't—"

"What did he say about Caitlin?"

"Don't yell at me, Harry. He said she was in the trunk of his car."

The sirens were louder.

"Where's his car?" Harry asked.

"Harry, let the police—"

"Where is it?"

"Downstairs, I think, in the garage. Harry, don't leave me."

But he was going down the steps. He reached the garage, and pulled up the unlocked door just as the first police cruiser slanted into the parking lot and came to a halt. John's red Audi, nose in, was parked in the dark garage. It looked far too ordinary to contain a body, to contain Caitlin's body. It wasn't possible, Harry thought.

"Did you call 911?" an officer was asking him.

Harry turned. "There's a body up the stairs from here. In the kitchen. He's dead."

Another uniformed officer was already making her way up the wooden steps.

"Is this your car?" The officer again. He was young, with sleepy-looking slanted eyes.

"It's . . . it's not. I think there might be someone in the trunk." Then Harry turned and said, in a slightly louder tone than his usual talking voice, "Caitlin? You in there?"

If I don't open it, he thought, *then it's not happening.*

"Sir," the officer said, but didn't add anything. His radio squawked, then Harry heard a few muffled words, the policewoman asking him to come upstairs.

"Stay right here, sir, okay? I'll be right back." The policeman looked frozen for a moment, unsure of what to do.

Harry nodded and said, "I won't leave."

The policeman made a decision and moved toward the stairs. There was another siren in the distance.

Harry pulled the driver's side door, and it swung open. He fumbled along the floor near the bucket seat, finding a lever and pulling it. The trunk made a popping sound, but the lid stayed down. There was no other sound as Harry went back to the rear of the car, grasped the lid in his hand, and lifted it, praying silently to himself.

The body was on its side, in the fetal position, facing in. The sharp smell of urine stung at Harry's nose, and he was hit by a wave of dizziness, dark nothingness pinching at his vision. Then he thought he saw the body twitch, shoulders contracting in as though she was cold.

"Caitlin," he said, and shook her shoulder, rolling her onto her back. The bottom half of her face was coated in dried blood.

She stared up at him with what looked like lifeless eyes, and then she blinked.

Chapter 33

Now

They'd driven through the night, and the sun was now coming up behind them as they glided through flat Canadian farmlands in Paul Roman's Prius. The sky, streaked in pink and orange, was like an enormous bowl. They'd crossed into Canada at Buffalo, skirting north of Lake Erie, the fastest route to get to Ann Arbor, Michigan.

"You okay to keep driving?" Harry asked Paul, who was lighting up another cigarette.

"You're awake?"

"I've been awake. I haven't slept."

Paul turned up the music—an Alanis Morissette

album ("just while we're in Canada")—and told Harry that he'd be able to drive the rest of the way.

They reached the outskirts of Ann Arbor by mid-morning, the sky a deep metallic blue, and picked the first motel that didn't look like it was owned by Norman Bates. They each stood by the car for a few moments after getting out, Paul doing jumping jacks while Harry stretched out his legs. The air was cool and smelled of nothing.

They rented a room with two double beds. The woman at the front desk, her sparse white hair combed over a bald pate, suggested they go to the Nichols Arboretum if they wanted a nice activity for later in the day. Paul told her they were attending a funeral Mass, and Harry watched as her eyes flicked from Paul's face to his, then quickly back down to the computer. The murders in Kennewick, Maine, were national news, and Harry was sure that they were much bigger news in Ann Arbor, where Grace McGowan's memorial was being held at three that afternoon.

They each ate an enormous breakfast at a Shoney's, then went back to the motel room to sleep.

Paul crawled under his covers fully dressed, and said, "I don't have to go to the service, if you don't want me there. I'll be happy to tour Ann Arbor's bar scene instead."

"Oh no, you're coming," Harry said.

Paul didn't answer. He was asleep already.

Harry tried to sleep, but found himself alternately staring at the ceiling and then his phone, hoping to get a text from Caitlin, who knew he was arriving that morning. He hadn't planned on texting her himself— it was the day of her sister's funeral, after all—but he was secretly hoping she might reach out to him, just to acknowledge his arrival, to tell him it was okay he was there, although she'd already given him that blessing.

It was five days since he'd opened the trunk of Jake Richter's car and thought he was looking at her dead body. The returning policeman had helped Harry lift her from the trunk as an ambulance arrived. She'd started to shiver once his arms touched her, and called his name, her voice barely audible. When she was on the gurney and about to be rolled into the ambulance, she lifted her hand and beckoned to Harry. He came close to her, placing his ear down by her mouth.

"It was John Richards," she whispered.

"I know," Harry said. "He's dead now."

Caitlin was initially brought to Kennewick Hospital, but was moved that evening to Portland and kept under observation for two days. Detective Dixon told Harry that her physical issues were comparatively mild—a broken nose, a contused neck—but that she was now under psychiatric care. Harry didn't get a chance to see her before she returned to Michigan; he'd asked, several times, if he could see her, but was always told that she wasn't seeing any visitors.

And then he was informed she was back in Michigan with her family.

During those bizarre days after Jake Richter's death, Alice, hounded by the throng of journalists that had arrived in Kennewick Village, had moved into a spare bedroom at her friend Chrissie Herrick's house. Paul Roman had immediately arrived in Kennewick, found an Airbnb near the harbor, and Harry had moved in with him, bringing Lew the cat from the store. He got far more information from Chrissie than he did from Alice, who'd barely spoken since being attacked by Jake in his condominium. Harry tried to elicit more information from Detective Dixon, but he was tight-lipped because of the ongoing investigation. Harry also wondered if Dixon was somehow ashamed at not having arrested Jake earlier. According to the articles that Harry read online, Jake *had* been a person of interest in the investigation into the murders of Bill Ackerson and Grace McGowan, but the police were convinced that the perpetrators were Lou and Annie Callahan, neither of whom had solid alibis for either murder.

Since the events that led to his death, more had come

out about Jake Richter's past, including from a school-teacher from Albany named Joan Johnson who claimed that Jake Richter, back when he'd been a coworker of her mother's, had seduced her when she was just a teen-ager. It also turned out that Jake Richter had lived for a number of years in the Fort Lauderdale area in Florida, where he'd been fired from a job at a beach resort be-cause of "inappropriate behavior." A picture emerged of a lifelong sexual predator.

There was much speculation that when he'd been married to Alice Moss's mother, he'd been sexually as-saulting Alice, and that he'd most likely killed Bill Ack-erson out of some form of jealousy. Alice hadn't spoken publicly yet to dismiss any of these rumors, but Vivi-enne Bergeron, a longtime resident of Kennewick, sold a story to one of the tabloids in which she said she knew for a fact that Jake and Alice had been lovers. But she also said that Alice had murdered her daughter, an erro-neous claim she had apparently been making for years.

Harry had seen Alice just once since they'd been together in Jake's condo. Chrissie had texted him to ask if he could get some more clothes from Grey Lady, plus Alice's straightening iron, and deliver them to her (*a ginormous favor, I know*), and Harry had done it, going late at night back to the house to avoid news reporters, although one enterprising journalist had raced from his car when Paul and he emerged from the house with two suitcases filled with Alice's things. They'd refused to answer the reporter's shouted questions, and the next morning Harry went to the Herricks' house. Alice had given him a short hug after he'd brought the suitcases into her bedroom. "I'll leave you two alone for a while," Chrissie said and disappeared.

"How are you holding up?" Harry asked. Alice still held on to one of his hands, then let go and sat on the edge of the bed. Harry sat on a wicker chair that had been painted white.

"I'm in shock, Harry. I'd known Jake my whole life."

"Why was he calling himself John Richards?"

"I asked him, once, and he said he just wanted a fresh start. But now I think he was trying to escape something from his past, maybe something he did in Florida."

"And you're sure that my father knew he was your stepfather?" Harry asked.

"Oh, I'm sure he did," Alice said quickly. "Still, it wasn't a big thing. He and my mother were married barely any time at all. I just can't believe . . . I had no idea he was capable . . ."

"You must have thought it strange that he changed his name?"

"It should have concerned me more, I know, but—"

"I just wondered," Harry said. It was bothering him, not so much that Jake was calling himself by a different name, but that Alice had gone along with it. He wondered if his father really knew who his employee was, but there was no way to find that out now.

They spoke for just a little bit longer, Harry trying to read Alice's emotions, her thoughts, but it was something he'd never been able to do. And he still couldn't.

"I should go," he said.

"Where are you going next?" Alice asked.

"Paul rented a place near here, and I'm staying with him."

"No, I mean, after this is all over. Will you stay here in Maine?"

"I don't think so, Alice."

"No, I know. I understand."

"How about you?"

"I'll stay here. I don't know where else I'd go."

They hugged good-bye, and Alice held on to Harry a little too long, her face buried in his neck, as though she was smelling him.

"Jake probably killed my mother," she said, as soon as they'd broken the embrace.

"What do you mean?" Harry asked.

"He probably killed my mother. She died of an overdose when I was in high school."

"Did you tell the police?"

"I told them everything, but there's nothing they can do about it now."

He walked back to his car, feeling as though he might never see her again.

Harry spotted Caitlin at the funeral Mass before she saw him. He and Paul had arrived very early to St. Julia's, a pretty stone church with a circular stained glass window, and taken a seat far at the back. The church was quiet, a few guests filtering in, whispering among themselves. The music began—Harry recognized it as Schubert's "Ave Maria"—and a few minutes later, there was Caitlin, dressed in black, walking down the aisle on one side of a woman who was clearly her mother. On the other side was a tall, gangly boy, probably a brother. They walked toward the front of the church. A minute or so later a lone middle-aged man came down the aisle. Tears streaked his face, and Harry thought that was probably the estranged father. He sat in the second row, alone. Music continued to play as the church filled. Paul and Harry had to slide down their pew to allow room for late arrivals. When the Mass began, several people were standing toward the rear of the church.

Harry had never been to a Catholic funeral before, and he found it disconcertingly formal but comforting, as though the rote prayers and the familiar hymns connected Grace's death to all the other deaths within her faith. Paul went up to receive Communion, but Harry stayed put, suddenly wishing he hadn't come. He felt a little like an impostor; he'd barely known Grace, and he barely knew Caitlin. Why was he here?

After the service, Grace's body was carried out of the church, accompanied by a modern-sounding hymn about being raised up on eagle's wings. Something about the corny song, and the slow procession of mourners, and Harry was crying, Paul's arm around him. They were among the last to leave the church. The family had already departed, and several groups of young people lingered outside. Cigarette smoke wafted through the air.

"Bar?" Harry said to Paul.

"You don't want to go to the reception?"

"Not really."

"Bar it is."

They walked into downtown Ann Arbor, a wide street flanked by square brick buildings, and numerous college bars, and picked a place called the Library that turned out to be much more of a sports bar than its name implied. They each got a shot of Jameson and a Guinness, Paul saying there was no other drink choice after a Catholic funeral, then loaded the jukebox with as much 1980s music as they could find, and claimed a booth next to a *Big Buck Hunter* video game. Harry checked his phone.

"I'm not complaining," Paul said, "but we came a long way for this. Are you not planning on trying to see her?"

"I don't know. I didn't just come for her. I came to go to the funeral, and we've done that."

"Okay, then. It's your call."

They stayed a couple of hours as the place filled up. Paul got a lesson from a group of fraternity brothers on how to play *Big Buck Hunter* and ended up, as usual, with a bunch of new best friends. Three rounds in, Harry was drunk enough to text Caitlin, saying how he'd been to the funeral, and wished he'd had a chance to say hello. To his surprise, she texted back right away.

I thought I saw you at the back. Come to Kildare's
Pub tonight if you're up for it. It's a gathering of
all our high school friends. I'll be there at nine but
can't promise I'll stay more than one drink.

Harry wrote that he'd be there, and he told Paul to make him go, no matter what. They left the Library at dusk and went back to the motel and changed. Then they walked back toward downtown, getting dinner at a

family-run Italian restaurant. They made it to Kildare's
at just around nine thirty. It was a typical faux Irish pub:
dark red walls, unvarnished wood floor, the Dropkick
Murphys playing on the speakers. There was a separate alcove on the opposite side of the bar, and it was
crammed with young people, some still in funeral wear,
suits and black dresses. Harry's stomach hurt at the
thought of navigating his way into the crowd to try to
find Caitlin, but he knew he should do it. He went with
Paul to the bar for a beer and, just before he was about to
order, saw Caitlin, in jeans and a black sweater, come out
from the crowd, scanning the room. She spotted Harry
and came right over.

"You came," she said, and something about the way
she was standing stopped Harry from trying to hug her.

"I did. This is my friend Paul Roman."

Paul turned from the bar, and took Caitlin's hand
in his, leaning in and saying something Harry couldn't
hear over the music. Caitlin smiled, showing a lot
of gum.

"I'm leaving, actually," Caitlin said. "Harry, can
you walk me home?"

Chapter 34

Now

They walked past a succession of crowded bars and restaurants, then hooked left onto a residential side street.

"It's about two miles. You sure you don't mind?"

"Not at all."

"I couldn't stand being there. Everyone's saying all the right things, but it still just feels like life is going on without her. Which it is."

"The funeral Mass was nice. I'd never been to one."

Caitlin's phone was buzzing, and she stopped, apologized, then rapidly texted to someone on her phone. "My friend who brought me to the bar is freaking out that I left." She texted some more, then put the phone away. They kept walking.

"Tell me what happened between your stepmother and Jake Richter," she said. "I know what the police told me, but that's it. She stabbed him before you got there?"

Harry told her everything that had happened after he'd been admitted to the hospital. He told her about waking up and thinking that the man he'd seen outside of the motel was John Richards, and how Alice told him that John had once been her stepfather. He told her about going home and using Phone Finder on his phone to learn that Alice was at John's house, and deciding that he needed to see him one more time just to be sure. He told her in detail what Alice had looked like, the blood on her neck, that he'd seen Jake dead in the kitchen, and that before the police came, Alice told him Jake had said Caitlin was in the trunk of the car.

"You must have thought I was dead," she said.

"I did. And then when I opened the trunk you were just laying there, not moving at all."

"I told myself to pretend I was dead, to just be still. For some reason, even though I knew it was you in the garage, I couldn't make myself move."

"Why didn't he kill you, do you think?" Harry asked.

"He came to the motel to find out if you knew it was

him, I think. That's what he was asking me, anyway, and when I didn't tell him anything, he hit me again and put me in the trunk of his car. I remember that he was gentle, and some part of me was thankful."

"I think he was insane," Harry said.

"Ya think?"

Harry laughed. "He didn't say anything?"

"He did. He said something about being tired after he put me in the trunk, and then he took a tie from his jacket pocket and he rolled me onto my side and bound my hands together. And I let him do it."

"You'd been knocked out, right?"

"Not really. A little. He'd hit me twice, and my nose was broken. I could have fought back, but I didn't."

"Maybe that was the smart move. Maybe if you'd fought back, then he would have killed you."

"I know. That's what everyone tells me, but I still can't stop thinking about it. I just gave up. I think I was telling myself that it was my best chance, that he had somehow changed his mind about killing me, and I didn't want to do anything that would make him change his mind again."

"It was a good instinct."

"After he shut the trunk he drove back to his house, I guess. I could tell he parked in a garage by the way the engine sounded in there, and then I heard him pulling down the garage door. I thought he was just going to let me die in there. I didn't move. I didn't even try to see if there was a way out of the trunk, a release lever or something."

"There probably wasn't," Harry said. "His car was pretty old."

"It's not that . . . Sorry, I know. You're right. I still wish I'd tried. I just lay there, praying that the next person who came along wasn't him, and then my prayer came true. It was you."

"Do you remember telling me his name, that it was John Richards who did that to you? You could barely talk."

"I do remember that. Of course, it wasn't his real name."

She shivered a little, even though it was still pretty warm out, the sky purple hued and filled with stars.

"It was the name he was going by. And it was a smart thing to do," Harry said. "Remembering his name. Telling me right away."

"Do you keep thinking about it?" she asked.

"Oh, yeah," Harry said. "Every minute of every day. It's a loop in my head. What he did to my father and to your sister, and then to you."

"What he *almost* did to me."

"Yeah, I think about that, as well. He could have killed you, then killed my stepmother."

"He could have killed *you*."

"He could have, yes."

They were quiet for a few steps. They'd taken several turns, and the houses were now larger and spread farther apart. "It's not far, now," Caitlin said. "This was good. I needed to talk about what happened with someone who was there. Everyone keeps tiptoeing around me."

"They're just worried."

"I know they are."

They turned again, down a street lined with tall trees, their leaves bristling in the light breeze. "I'm right down here," Caitlin said, and pointed toward a white Colonial, lights on in all the windows. "Want to walk around the block? I don't want to stop talking."

"Okay."

As they walked, Caitlin asked Harry about his plans, and he told her he didn't have any, except that he wasn't going to stay in Maine.

"Will your stepmother be upset?"

"I'm sure, but I can't go back to living with her. I feel for her, because of what she went through, but there's still a part of me . . . It's hard to explain, but I don't entirely trust her. I feel like there's more to the story between her and Jake than I'll ever know."

"You think she was in on it?"

"No, not really. I don't know."

When they reached the front of Caitlin's house again, Caitlin said, "Can I ask a favor?"

"Sure, anything."

"Will you come in and spend the night? Not *with* me, but there's a guest room you can sleep in."

Harry hesitated, but Caitlin's eyes, dark in the moonlight, were large with fear and anticipation, and he said, "Of course."

Inside, she introduced him to her mother, who was standing in the kitchen, wearing a robe, and drinking a cup of tea. "Oh, Harry," she said. "I'm so sorry about your father." She looked like both of her daughters, but more like Grace, Harry thought, with her firm jawline and upturned nose. She had kind eyes. Harry told her how sorry he was about Grace, about how much he'd liked her in the short time he had known her.

"She was troubled, but she'd have turned it around. I know it."

"She would have, Mom," Caitlin said, and rolled her eyes slightly so that only Harry could see.

The guest room was on the second floor. Caitlin, suddenly hostess-like, showed him where the spare blankets were in the closet, and brought him a pair of pajamas that belonged to her brother, plus an unused toothbrush. "Pajamas are clean, I promise," she said. "This is weird, me wanting you to stay here, isn't it?"

"No, it really isn't."

"When do you think we'll feel normal again?"

"I don't know," Harry said. "I don't know if we'll ever feel normal, but I think we'll feel better."

Caitlin shut the door of the guest room almost all the way closed, and kissed him. Her sweater was thin cashmere, and he could feel her ribs through the fabric, her heartbeat, the ridge of a bra strap. They kept kissing until there were footsteps on the stairs, and Caitlin opened the door wider, stepped out into the hall, and said to Harry, "Breakfast will be at the crack of dawn, unfortunately."

"I heard that," Mrs. McGowan said from the hall.

"Perfect," Harry said.

After she left, he changed into the pajamas, texted Paul to let him know where he was, and slid into the unfamiliar bed. After turning the lamp off, he thought, *There's no way I'll ever fall asleep here,* but then the next thing he knew there was faint light coming through the curtains on the window, and he could smell bacon being cooked. He sat up a little in bed, and listened to the sounds of the house coming alive. He had slept through the entire night—a dreamless abyss of sleep. It was definitely strange that he was suddenly here, in Caitlin's childhood home, but it was no stranger than anywhere else he might be right now. He had no real home.

He was about to get out of bed when his phone on the bedside table began to vibrate. He checked the screen. It was a Kennewick number.

"Harry, it's Detective Dixon. Sorry to bother you so early."

"It's okay. What's happened?"

"I was wondering if you knew where your step-mother was."

"Is she missing?"

"She is, actually."

"I don't know where she is. I'm actually not in Maine right now. What do you mean, she's missing?"

"Well, she never came home to her friend's house last night, and no one can find her. Her car's at Jake Richter's condo, but she's not there."

"I'm sorry. I have no idea where she might be."

"We'll keep looking. I'm sure she's fine, but call me if you hear from her, okay, Harry?"

Harry promised he would, and ended the call. The mention of Alice jarred loose a dream he'd had the night before last. Alice, naked, in the window of Grey Lady,

Harry watching from the driveway. She was tapping on the glass, but it wasn't making any sound. His father was there as well, changing a tire on his old Volvo, not paying a whole lot of attention to anyone. The house was stirring, and the dream disappeared. Harry sat for a moment longer in the bed, knowing, somehow instinctively, and with complete certainty, that Alice, despite what Detective Dixon had just said, was not going to be fine.

Chapter 35

Then and Now

Once Alice went back to her bedroom—after Jake had told her he'd seen her return from the beach the night Gina drowned—she knew she'd never sleep with Jake again. That part of her life, the part with Jake, was over. Life was restarts, one after another, and some were good and some weren't. Her life had first restarted when her mother got the settlement money and they moved to Kennewick. It started again when Jake arrived, standing over her on the beach, and she could feel the way he was looking at her. It even restarted after Scott Morgan told everyone at school she was a slut, and she decided it didn't matter, that whatever they said couldn't touch her. And now she would have to start again, because Jake thought she'd had something to do with killing her own mother, or letting Gina drown, when both those things had happened accidentally. They'd happened *to* her, not because of her.

Jake, in the days following, tried only once to get Alice back. She was in her room, the door closed, rereading *Tender Rebel,* a dumb romance novel she'd read many, many times. Jake knocked, then half entered, standing in the door frame.

"What're you doing?" he asked.

She held the book up. "Reading."

"Thought you might like to read a little in bed with me. It's lonely in there."

"I'm fine here, Jake."

"Okay," he said. "Just checking." She remembered what he'd been like immediately after her mother's funeral, the way he'd taken control of her. He'd become a different man now that she didn't love him, or trust him, anymore. Her indifference gave her the upper hand, a fact she decided to file away.

"Jake," she said, as he was departing.

"Yeah?" he said, a hopeful look on his face.

"I'm going to look for a new job. And a new apartment."

"Oh."

"I thought I'd let you know. In advance."

She gave her notice at Blethen's Apothecary and got a job as an office assistant at a real estate company. She stopped taking classes, since she was working full-time, and rented a one-bedroom apartment in a stucco building not far from the real estate office. It was quiet in the apartment, and she liked it. She made simple meals, and watched television, and on the weekends she'd go swimming at the Y.

Coast Home Realty grew, relocating to a new, larger office in a strip mall off Route 1A. Alice coordinated the move, even working with Caroline, the big boss, to design the new office, and when the company was firmly established in their new plush surroundings, Caroline asked Alice if she ever thought about getting her real estate license. "I hate to lose you as our office manager, but you'd be a good agent, I just know it."

Alice had never really considered this, partly because the real estate agents, at least the ones who made the most sales, all seemed to have big, vibrant personalities. Alice told Caroline that she didn't think so, but Caroline insisted. "You're the hardest worker I've ever had in here. It just seems a shame that we can't get you making some fat commissions."

So Alice got her license, and two months later sold her first property, a starter home for a young couple, both schoolteachers, who had moved down from Orono. She celebrated by getting a larger apartment and a new car. She began to spend more time with Chrissie Herrick, another Realtor at the agency, who'd gotten her license when her second kid began grade school. Chrissie, a talker, reminded Alice of Gina, but a Gina that had life all figured out. She was happily married to a dull and faithful man, and was basically content with her lot. Chrissie's favorite activity was telling Alice how pretty she was, and how she wanted to set her up with some nice man.

Alice let her have her way just once, more out of curiosity than anything else, and Chrissie and her husband plus Alice and a local divorcé who worked in Portland in insurance all went out to dinner. At the end of the interminable night, the divorcé walked Alice to her car, one hand on the small of her back, his thumb making circular motions. She imagined sinking her teeth into that thumb, the surprised look on his piggy face when the blood began to flow. But she didn't do it, just quickly slid into her car, shutting the door and cracking the window enough to thank him for the evening. That night she lay in bed, ignored the ringing phone in her house that could only be Chrissie hoping for an update, and slid gradually into sleep, wondering if her life would ever start again.

Then she met Bill Ackerson, a suave New Yorker looking to relocate to Maine and open a bookstore. She knew he was attracted to her, and she thought he seemed to be a nice man but decided she wasn't interested. When he next contacted her, he asked if she'd mind if he brought his son along to revisit some of the places she'd shown him before. He brought Harry, who looked just like his father but was almost beautiful, if a boy could be beautiful, with high cheekbones and wavy hair. He was so perfect that it almost hurt Alice to look at him. Something clicked in her. She didn't know exactly what it was, but she knew that a new part of her life was just beginning.

Alice returned to Jake's condo, pulled off the police tape, and tried the door. It was locked. She'd thought that would be the case, and removed a credit card from her purse, picking the lock the way she'd done as a teenager whenever she'd forgotten her key.

It was dusk outside, and the interior of the condo was dark. Her phone had a light on it, and she used that to look around. She went straight up the stairs and into the bedroom, so unchanged since she'd last been in there that she could almost feel time falling away. She turned off her phone's light and let her eyes adjust. The bed was made, loosely pulled together, and she ran her hand along the chenille bedspread. She remembered that her mother used to sleep in this room before she did, and then was suddenly alarmed to realize that she was nearly the same age as her mother was when she died. She shook the thought of her mother out of her head, and reminded herself of the reason she was here. Jake had taken pictures of her, many years ago, back when she hadn't known any better, and she wanted to make sure they weren't around for just anyone to find. When she'd lived here, he kept the photographs in a copy of James Michener's *Hawaii* that was always on his bedside table. She should have taken them back then, but she had decided to leave that small memento to Jake. But now he was on the national news, and so was she. She needed to get those pictures back.

It took a while, but she found them in one of the hardcover books stacked on Jake's dresser. She quickly riffled through them, marveling at the beauty of her young body. She stared into her own eyes in the photographs, wondering what that different person had been thinking. She put the pictures in her purse.

Walking back to her car, she noticed that there was a station wagon with a boat trailer next to her Volvo that hadn't been there before. The vehicle gave her a bad but familiar feeling, as though she should have known whose car it was. But the feeling passed, and then she was annoyed by how far the trailer jutted out, and how hard it would be for her to navigate her own car out of the lot. Rounding the boat on its trailer, she could see two people still in the car, and decided she would ask them to move out of her way. But as she got closer, the light in the station wagon went on, the driver's side door opened, and a familiar man got out.

"Alice," Mr. Bergeron said, and stepped toward her, hand extended.

Then Alice heard a sound like a fuse being lit and her entire body stiffened. She felt herself trying to speak but no words came out, and she fell, the side of her head smacking the pavement. Her whole body hurt. Then her face was covered with a damp, sweet-smelling cloth, and the world went dark.

She jerked awake, her nostrils burning, her head throbbing, and something sharp pressing painfully into her back. There was the sound of water, and the world was rocking back and forth, and she thought: *I'm on a boat.* And then she remembered the parking lot, and Mr. Bergeron. She was nauseous, spit pooling under her tongue, and she shut her eyes. The darkness closed in, then her nostrils were burning again, and she shook her head, her body tensing.

"Hi, Alice. You awake?"

She tried to say something but all that came out was a groan. She opened her eyes again—the nausea had begun to pass—and found she was able to keep them open. She could see a sky filled with stars, the dim figure of Mrs. Bergeron crouched over her, her face ravaged by cancer, wearing a woolen hat on her head. Sitting up, Alice looked around, the twisting motion of her neck making her head hurt worse. They were far out in the ocean, the outboard motor silent, with no sign of land in any direction. Mrs. Bergeron slid back and seated herself across from Alice. Water sloshed in the bottom of the boat.

"Where am I?" Alice asked.

"This is right around where Gina drowned, more or less," Mrs. Bergeron said. "I thought you'd remember it."

"You know I don't," Alice said.

Mrs. Bergeron sighed, then coughed, four sharp, dry hacks that didn't sound healthy. Alice knew she was dying from bronchial cancer, because Mrs. Bergeron had come by and visited her shortly after Bill had died. She'd confronted her about Bill's death, telling Alice she knew she had something to do with it, just as she'd had something to do with her daughter Gina's death twenty years earlier. It was disconcerting, the visit, but not surprising. Over the years, Vivienne Bergeron had accused

Alice of being with Gina the night she had drowned many times. But for the previous ten years Alice had barely heard from her, and she had almost begun to believe that she'd never hear from her again. But Mrs. Bergeron had come to Grey Lady, wrapped in a too-big raincoat, the yellow skin of her face barely concealing the skull underneath. Alice had invited her in, listened to her rant, and, as she always did, attempted to be civil. She'd asked after her health, and Mrs. Bergeron said she had bronchial cancer, and was happy to leave a world where people like Alice Moss got away with murder. Alice wondered if the old woman's mind was going, as well as her body.

"You can tell the truth now, Alice," Mrs. Bergeron said from the other side of the boat. "It's just you and me." The wind off the ocean snatched at the faint words, but Alice could still hear them.

"Your husband," Alice said, remembering him from the condo parking lot. "Where . . . ?"

"He's a good and loyal man, my husband," she said, her voice cracking. "I needed him to do one last thing for me, and he did it."

"You're crazy."

"I am a little crazy, you know, I think. That's on you, too, Alice. I was fine before you took my Gina away. I never beat it."

"What are you going to do?" Alice said. Her mind was beginning to clear, and she realized that something was cutting into her left wrist. It was a pair of handcuffs, attached to a linked chain. She tugged at it. The chain was snaked through one of those large bodybuilding weights, a disc that looked like it was probably a hundred pounds, sitting on the middle seat of the old boat. The chain passed through the weight, stretching across to Mrs. Bergeron, attached to a handcuff around her wrist.

"I've already done it," she said, holding up her arm, showing it to Alice, rattling the chain. "There's no getting out of these. The keys to the handcuffs are already on the bottom of the ocean. It's over, Alice. It's just you and me." With her free hand, Mrs. Bergeron raised what looked like half a cigarette to her nose and inhaled deeply. Alice thought: *smelling salts.* It was what she had used to wake Alice up, and what she was using to keep herself going.

Alice's body went cold. She shook her head, trying to concentrate on what was happening. The sloshing at the bottom of the boat was getting louder, and water was now licking at her ankles. "The boat's sinking," she said.

"It is. You don't have much time. We have the same time now, the two of us."

Alice tugged harder at the cuff around her wrist. "You can't do this."

Mrs. Bergeron smiled and she looked like a skull, her teeth too big for her face. "I *am* doing this," she said. "You took my baby away from me, and this is my last wish." She laughed weakly at this, then said, "It's my 'Make-A-Wish.'"

Alice stood, and took a step toward Mrs. Bergeron. The boat lurched, and her foot crunched through the hull. Water began to rush in.

"It's no good," Mrs. Bergeron said. "I couldn't stop it if I wanted to. We are going to die together. The only thing you can do now is confess. I can't make you do it, but it might make you feel better. It's for you, not me. I already know what you did. I just want you to have the opportunity to know it as well."

"Gina was a drug addict. She was nuts."

The boat tipped hard to one side, and Alice gripped the edge as the bodybuilding weight slid off the middle seat and into the water. Her mind was rapidly flipping between shock at what was happening and a calculation of her odds. She wrenched at the cuff around her left hand, but it wouldn't come off. She scanned the boat for anything that would help her float.

"Maybe she was, but that's not why she died," Mrs. Bergeron said.

"She was lucky to die when she did," Alice said.

"That's it, honey, tell the truth." Mrs. Bergeron gripped the side of the boat as well. Her eyes were huge in her head. "There's no way out."

"I couldn't have saved her. That's the truth."

"You were swimming with her, though, right?"

"There was nothing I could do. This isn't fair." The boat tipped, and Alice leaned hard the other way. "How did you . . ." she began. "How am I here?"

Mrs. Bergeron laughed. "I have less than a month to live, and I could have died in a hospital bed in pain, or I could take you with me. It was an easy choice, and I have a husband who was willing to help me."

Alice started to lunge toward Mrs. Bergeron, but the boat turned over, and the two women went into the cold, salty water, the splintered boat drifting out of reach. Alice felt the pull of the weight on her left wrist. She desperately pawed at the water with her free right hand, then grabbed out at Mrs. Bergeron as though she could help her stay afloat. Together, they went under the surface, holding on to each other, almost hugging, as they sank.

I'm dying, Alice thought, and the thought was scary, but it was also so unfair. She had never hurt anyone in her life. Her mother's face flashed through her mind, not as she was toward the end, but the way she once looked, back when she'd been pretty. She was on a beach, sun and the scratchy sand and a swarm of scary gulls. Alice held on to the air in her lungs as long as she could, the black water roaring in her ears.

And when she could hold out no longer, she opened her mouth and tried to breathe. It was seawater, cold and final, that filled her lungs.

About the Author

PETER SWANSON is the author of *The Girl with a Clock for a Heart,* a Los Angeles Times Book Prize finalist; *The Kind Worth Killing,* winner of the New England Society Book Award and finalist for the CWA Ian Fleming Steel Dagger; *Her Every Fear;* and his most recent, *All the Beautiful Lies.* His books have been translated into thirty languages, and his stories, poetry, and features have appeared in *Asimov's Science Fiction, The Atlantic, Measure, The Guardian, The Strand Magazine,* and *Yankee.* A graduate of Trinity College, the University of Massachusetts at Amherst, and Emerson College, he lives in Somerville, Massachusetts, with his wife.